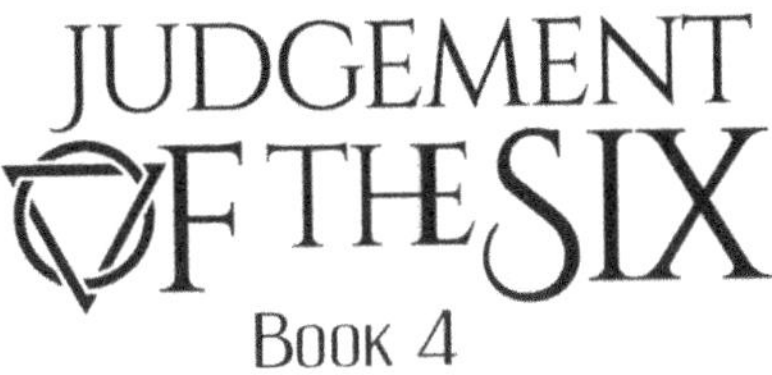

UNBIDDEN

JUDGEMENT OF THE SIX

Book 4

Melissa Haag

ISBN 978-0-9888523-5-8 (eBook Edition)
ISBN 978-1-502952-14-1 (CreateSpace Paperback Edition)
ISBN 978-1-943051-83-0 (Paperback Edition)

Editing by Ulva Elderidge
Cover design by © Cover Art by Cora Graphics

(UN)BIDDEN

I left home because I didn't want to end up in a cage like a lab rat. Hitching rides, begging for cash, and sleeping on the ground got old fast. That was the only reason I braved an overgrown path to a group of buildings. I'd hoped to find a bed and a decent night's sleep. However, what I found was a place overrun by werewolves.

While on the run, Charlene finds herself surrounded by werewolves, creatures she can't control with her mind like she can humans. Their existence has her believing she's found a safe place to stay, a place where secrets are okay. However, she soon discovers she's anything but safe. Charlene must learn how to use her abilities to influence the strange new species because if she can't, the next bite she suffers might just kill her.

Read how the cycle begins, and have no doubt. Charlene's past will shape the future of the Judgements.

NOTE TO THE READER

(Un)bidden is Charlene's story. Not Isabelle's. Don't worry, though. Isabelle's story is next. :) You needed Charlene's story first so events in Isabelle's story would make more sense.

CHAPTER ONE

In the soundproofed room of the Compound, I listened to Bethi tell us about the three races and the purpose of the Judgements. Her story sounded surreal. How could I possibly be part of something like that? Yet, I didn't doubt what she said. My abilities were proof of her words.

I studied Bethi for a moment and knew she felt it, too—the separation from the three races we needed to balance.

Charlene. Thomas' thought nudged mine back to the conversation.

"...to buy us some time to plan," Bethi said.

It took a moment to recall what she'd just said. *I Claimed him to stay alive...to buy us some time to plan.* She was talking about Elder Joshua, one of the Urbat.

"To plan what, dear?" Winifred asked.

"An evacuation, to start," Bethi said.

Evacuation? My heart stopped and panic surged. An immediate sense of calm washed over me, and I knew it was Thomas.

He understood my panic. This was the only home I knew.

My sanctuary for the last—how many years had it been? I couldn't leave. It wasn't safe out there. Even after all these years, I had a sense of foreboding. If I left this place, things wouldn't end well.

"What do you mean?" Thomas asked.

"When the Urbat come, they will use the people we love to try to sway us. First, they use our families, torturing them until we do what they want. If that doesn't work, they start torturing us."

Torment filled her gaze. What had the poor girl already endured? I could only imagine how the weight of our past lives burdened her.

"What do the Urbat want?" Grey asked.

"For each of us to Claim one of them." Bethi's eyes darted to Michelle, Gabby, then me.

"We've already Claimed someone," Gabby said. Clay rested a hand on her shoulder.

I was glad to see the two of them had found an understanding. The first time I'd met Gabby, so alone in the world just as I'd been, I felt the need to protect her. Looking at the girls at the table, I realized I felt the same for each of them. I needed to protect them. They were unique, like me; and the Pennys of the world were still out there, waiting.

"It won't matter," Bethi said, pulling my thoughts back. "A Claim can be broken by death or simply by Claiming another."

Shocked silence invaded the room. I felt Thomas' reassurance once more.

"That's why I was willing to Claim Joshua."

Luke looked angry at the mention of the Claiming.

"The next step is for life," Bethi said. "Once Mated, we don't Mate again. I mean, they *could* force us to Claim another and mate, but it doesn't do any good. Our hearts stay with the first lost Mate. The new Mate holds no influence."

"Influence for what?" Sam asked.

"For balance," Bethi said. "They have been after power since they figured out what we were. The Judgements. In the beginning, we always judged in favor of the humans. At least, that's my guess. I haven't dreamed what really happened yet. Since then, as far as I've seen, we haven't made another Judgement. I'm guessing that's why, despite the inferiority of humans in comparison to your races, they have thrived."

Her words troubled me. Power was a dangerous thing. My thoughts turned toward my first days here.

"The Urbat are tired of living in the shadows," Bethi said, unaware of my partial attention, "and want to be the dominant race for a while. The last cycle they almost had it, but one of us died. Without us, things will stay the way they are, with humans maintaining control. The cycle doesn't last forever—only fifty years—so they try not to risk our lives. But they will, if they must. After all, we can still be reborn into the same cycle."

"So you're saying we need to clear the Compound because they will come for the four of you and use the people here to force you into surrendering?" Thomas asked.

"Don't doubt it. They will come. They always come. And death always follows."

I considered her ominous words and studied the fear on her face. I knew I needed to speak up, yet after all these years, I still worried what would happen when everyone discovered what I'd done, what I could do.

"What then? Where do we go?" he asked.

"That's the tricky part. I don't know where the pack should

go, but I know where *we* need to go. We are missing two of our group. We need to find them."

"About this evacuation...," I said. How could I explain it was unnecessary?

I glanced at Thomas, feeling the fear from the past grab me. Once again, he soothed me. If I revealed my secrets, what would he do? What would he think? Would he still want to soothe me?

"Out of all of us, you and Michelle are the most vulnerable. Michelle's brothers need to be sent away and protected. Emmitt, if he's taken, will be a risk to both of you. They will want to break the Claim Michelle has, as much as they will want to hurt Emmitt to sway you."

I glanced at Emmitt. Though he was a man, I still saw my baby boy; and no one would hurt either of my boys.

He gave me a reassuring smile. "Don't worry. We know now, so we can make sure it doesn't happen."

I nodded. I would stay near both my boys and make sure nothing happened. I would do whatever it took, even if it meant revealing the past and the secrets I still held.

CHAPTER TWO

The past...

"Ms. Farech. Is there a problem?" Mr. Melski asked from the front of the room.

"Yes." I struggled to keep all the emotion from my voice. "Someone just threw gum in my hair." I stood and picked up my books. "I'll see if someone in the office can help."

His eyes flicked to Penny. The faculty knew. So why in the heck did they let her sit behind me? It was a small school. Because we were in the same grade, we had most of our classes together. Not all, though, because I'd managed to squeak into a few of the advanced ones. Hard classes, but I loved them because she wasn't there.

I kept my pace even, as I walked out the door.

The secretary, an older woman who yelled at most kids, made a sympathetic noise when I walked in and showed her the gum. I hadn't touched it much and had walked carefully so it wasn't too embedded.

"Charlene, why on earth does Penny dislike you so much?" she asked as she worked.

"Because when we were kids, I told her not to hit her mom." The truth, yet not all of it. Penny was the only one who knew my secret. Never once did I give the rumors she had started any credence. But she and I both knew, I could do what she claimed. I could control people with a thought. I just didn't let her goad me into doing it openly.

The secretary extracted the gum wad within minutes, only taking a few strands with it.

"Make sure you don't sit near her at the assembly," she warned just before I left.

As if I would purposely do so.

I went to the bathroom to check my hair before heading back to class. Hopefully Penny wasn't chewing more gum in anticipation of my return.

The door opened behind me. Penny's gaze met mine in the mirror. She wasn't done with me yet.

"Why?" I asked, turning. "What do you get from doing this? You were never mean when we were little." She continued to eye me hatefully. I tried again. "We were friends once."

"Ha!" she barked bitterly. "You were never my friend. You never listened to me."

I knew exactly what she meant. She'd wanted me to use my ability to make her mom look away, so we could sneak candy when we went to her house. She didn't understand, as I did, that my ability wasn't meant for that. Somehow, I'd always known I shouldn't misuse my power.

"You always asked too much," I said sadly. "Just let this go."

"No. At some point, you'll make a mistake, and I want to be there so everyone knows I was right about you." She reached out and slapped the books from my arms. They tumbled to the floor.

"All you're going to prove is how mean you can be," I said, glancing down at the books. She didn't answer.

When I bent to pick them up, she pushed me over. I snapped and grabbed hold of her will.

"Stop." She froze, poised in a half-crouch ready to come after me. I held her still with my will, but I forced nothing else on her. I felt bad enough for holding her as I did.

"I'm really sorry, Penny, but this has gone on long enough. Forget your hate. Remember the friendship we once had." I picked up my books and stood. "Don't try to hurt me again."

I walked out the door, intending to get a good head start before I released her. From behind, I heard her yell through the door.

"I still can't move!"

Before I rounded the corner, I let go. For the rest of the day, I managed to avoid her. When the teachers released their classes for assembly, I followed the flow of students to the gym. The crowd moved slowly, with the upper classmen claiming the top bleachers. Sophomores, like me, spread out in the middle.

Sitting on the bleachers, surrounded by the entire student body, I looked around warily for Penny. She would hate me even more, now, after our confrontation in the bathroom. I should have made her forget. I just couldn't bring myself to mess with someone's head like that. It wasn't like anyone really believed her anyway. Other than the bullying, she wasn't a threat to me. I had no justification for taking the extreme measure of robbing her of her memories.

"As some of you know, there have been cases of bullying. This is a serious matter that this school will not take lightly. We have a short film to help educate you on what steps should be taken if you are bullied, or witness bullying."

The overhead lights dimmed, and a beam of light from the AV room near the top of the gym pierced the gloom. The AV room, a recent addition accessed by a set of stairs outside of the gym, was prized by the faculty as a means to broadcast school news.

A shot of the girl's bathroom burst onto the white gym wall we used for projection. My mouth popped open as I saw myself walk into the bathroom and go to the mirror. Some students near me started laughing quietly. The faculty, standing on the gym floor, started conferring in whispers as on screen, Penny walked in, and we started talking.

One of the teachers left the gym, presumably to reach the AV room and stop the movie. The lights in the gym turned on as Penny knocked the books out of my hand. No one moved. Everyone stayed focused on the projection. My stomach filled with piercing shards of ice.

"The assembly is over. Return to your last hour class. Those with Physical Education should go to the locker rooms and wait there," the principal shouted, unable to use his microphone as the PA system had been taken over by my voice. "All you're going to prove is how mean you can be."

No one moved. All eyes remained riveted on Penny as she stared at me, and I moved to retrieve the books. I could taste my panic, the flavor disgustingly reminiscent of vomit. Penny had finally succeeded. Everyone would believe her about me.

I closed my eyes as the recording of my voice rang out. "Stop." A murmuring rose in the gym, loud enough that others started shushing their neighbors as I gave Penny my little speech and then left the bathroom.

Opening my eyes, I caught the angle of the video change as the cameraman climbed off the toilet and opened the stall door to zoom in on Penny's outraged face. Penny's words, "I still can't move," echoed through the eerily quiet gym. The last image on the wall was of Penny suddenly falling to the floor. The projection shut off.

My face heated unnaturally. Someone next to me whispered to their neighbor, "Holy crap! Penny wasn't lying."

I sat up in the bleachers, surrounded by my peers. All eyes turned to me. A side door opened, and a teacher escorted a beaming Penny into the gym. As I stood, I grabbed everyone's will but hers and planted a seed.

"You just witnessed proof of Penny's dogged determination to expose something extraordinary. Instead, all she did was paint herself as a bully and show she has an amazing ability to act."

Releasing their wills, I nudged my way through my stunned classmates. As I moved, I heard things like, "I can't believe she was so mean," and, "I would have slapped her face instead of walking out."

Penny's smug expression faltered as she noticed the change in everyone. Her mouth dropped open as she stared at me. I walked up to Penny while holding the faculty back with simple wait-and-see thoughts. I stopped just in front of her.

"Whoever you had filming did a wonderful job," I said. "If you're this good over a no-name nothing like me, I can only imagine how good you'll be when you're reporting on something real. Good luck."

I walked from the gym with my head high. The sound of whispers faded as I went to my locker and emptied it of everything except the textbooks. It was more than I could jam in my backpack. I stared at the loose papers and various work that still needed to be completed. Then, I threw everything into the trash. I wouldn't be back.

I picked up my bag, closed the locker, and made my way to the main entrance. Any remaining faculty who moved to question me, I turned away with a thought.

Outside, the air smelled of warm blacktop. Spring was making way for summer.

I stopped on the steps and turned to look back. Despite releasing the wills of everyone in the gym, I continued to sense their threads. They still watched Penny. My throat tightened as I pictured her red, angry face. I'd made a serious enemy of her as a child, one I'd underestimated all these years. Her determination to expose me consumed her, and I considered going back to make her forget everything.

Instead, I walked away.

The trek home didn't take long. Neither Mom nor Dad was there, yet. I went to my room, set my backpack on the bed, and looked around. Memories of a happy childhood decorated my space. Shells collected from a beach sat next to the barrettes Mom had given me for my last birthday. I touched the little clips. I rarely wore them. I was too old. But she didn't see me that way. My hand dropped to the first dresser drawer, and I pulled it open. Slowly, I started to remove the essentials I'd need and placed them in the backpack.

Thirty minutes later, Mom came home. I waited for her in the kitchen.

"Hi, sweetheart. How was your day?"

"It didn't go well, Mom," I said, grabbing her will. An ache grew in my chest for what I knew I needed to do.

"Oh? Tell me what happened." She set down the groceries she'd been carrying and looked at me.

"What happened doesn't matter. I need to leave. And I need you to be okay with that. Don't look for me. Don't report me missing."

She nodded and bent to give me a hug.

"Call me when you can, so I know you're all right," she said softly and gave me one last squeeze.

"I'll try. Tell Dad I love him. I love you both." I stood and shrugged into my backpack. "And if Penny comes around, let her know I left, and I'm not coming back. Ever."

The thread of her will changed suddenly. It grew soft and slippery. I fought to maintain my hold.

"Ever?" she said.

The thread seemed to melt away further, and I struggled to ignore how badly I knew I was hurting her.

"Mom, listen to me. Penny knows I'm different, and she'll do everything she can to get someone to believe her. If I stay, I won't be safe. I have to leave." My voice broke on the last word. Regardless, I firmed my hold on her will.

The thread stopped softening as she nodded.

"We love you, too," she said. Then, she left the kitchen. I could hear her crying.

I released her will, and with nothing more than my backpack, I walked out the door.

As the sun set, I realized my mistake. I hadn't packed a sleeping bag or blanket. To be fair, neither would have fit in my backpack. Miles separated me from home, and I wasn't about to go back. Instead, I found a quiet tree in a park, leaned against the trunk, and dozed in the dark.

A few hours later, I woke, shivering. Silence surrounded me. I wrapped my arms around myself and stared up at the stars. I'd stopped asking the universe "why?" a long time ago. The only question I ever asked anymore was "what next?"

When I'd left home, I'd planned to hitch rides and see where they took me. Older kids talked about hitching all the time. It seemed the best way to disappear. But I had no money to feed myself.

As if the universe listened, a man walked past my spot. I quickly stood.

"Excuse me, sir. Would you be able to spare any money?"

When he kept walking, I grabbed his will and repeated my question. I didn't demand that he help me, only that he consider it.

He stopped moving and turned toward me. He frowned slightly and rubbed his jaw.

"I don't have much, but I could spare a dollar. Will that help?"

"It would. Thank you," I said, trying to ignore my guilt. Using my ability for personal gain made me sick. Yet, what other choice did I have? The faster I left town, the safer I would be. If I thought of what I did as self-preservation, it made what I was doing tolerable.

He reached into his wallet and pulled out a dollar. I felt better when I saw it wasn't his only bill. After thanking him again, I left the park.

Walking kept me warm, so I stayed on the move as the sky lightened. The rising sun heated my back. I continued to speak with people I ran into and forced them to consider helping me.

I managed to collect ten dollars before one man offered something other than money; he offered me a ride to the next town. I gratefully accepted, and we drove west, away from Penny and my parents.

Bud was a mellow fellow who didn't ask many questions. He still liked to talk, though. He'd woken up that morning and decided he wanted to visit his brother in Canada. So he'd quit his job and gotten in his car. He wasn't sure if he had enough money to get there, but it didn't seem to concern him.

The prospect of leaving the States intrigued me, and I asked if I could tag along. He smiled, told me I was good company, and agreed to take me with him. Over the next few days, we made our way north.

At our first stop, just on the other side of the Canadian border, I told him I was ready to travel on my own and thanked him for the ride. I couldn't take any more of the rank smell from his hand-rolled cigarettes.

With a wave, I walked away from Bud. I'd put enough distance between Penny and me. Yet, every time someone glanced my way, nervousness would grip me. A little voice told me I needed to keep moving and find somewhere to hide until Penny forgot.

Recalling her furious expression, I wondered how long that might take.

I ROAMED FOR WEEKS, begging for food or money and sleeping in the open. The full bloom of summer made my nights more comfortable as did the knit poncho someone had given me. Yet, each sunrise brought less light to my life. How could I keep going like this? I wanted a bed, a shower, and a real meal. More than that, I didn't want to be alone anymore. I wanted a friend.

A kind soul to shelter me from the reality of the scary world I lived in.

Distracted by self-pity, I took a drink from my canteen, stood, and started walking again, paying little attention to the road. I didn't need to. It was the same with every town. I drifted in, stayed a day—any more than that drew attention to my begging—and drifted out after buying some food. Then, I walked until I came to the next town. Sometimes, it was the same day. Sometimes, it took more than a day. I figured it didn't really matter as long as I kept moving.

Hours later, the pavement ended and turned into a narrow dirt road. I kept walking. It wasn't until the sun kissed the treetops that I really looked around. There was nothing but trees and the dirt road on which I stood. No, not true.

A sign stood sentinel in the overgrown ditch. I stared at it, not reading the words but focusing on the numbers. Over one hundred miles separated me from the next town. I turned around and looked back the way I'd come. Nothing but the narrow road and trees. How long had I been walking? How many nights had I slept against a tree?

The leaves rustled in the light breeze as I stood there trying to decide what to do. I didn't have much food left. The container of water I'd refilled yesterday at a creek beside the road was still fine, though.

With a tired sigh, I kept walking.

Just before dark, I spotted a trail that led away from the road. Waist-high grass covered the breadth of the path. No trees obstructed it, however, and I wondered if it was an old logging trail. Nothing about it seemed welcoming. In fact, dusk had already sent most of the track into shadow. Yet, for some reason, I felt compelled to walk the lane as if the universe were again answering my "what next?" question.

I started forward, parting the grass. The trail seemed never ending, and as I walked, night claimed the sky. Only the soft glow of the moon kept me from wandering around lost.

The trees ended abruptly and revealed a large clearing with several buildings. Excitement and relief filled me. Finally, a bed. Then, as I studied the dark and quiet structures, a sense of abandonment touched me. Moonlight glinted off the broken glass in a few of the windows. Weeds crowded against the walls and surrounded the stubby porch.

The buildings were alone and forgotten, but it didn't matter. The largest of them appeared to have a solid roof, and that was more than I'd had in weeks.

I waded through the grass and stepped up onto the sagging porch. Thankfully, the boards held my weight. I reached out and pulled the latch on the large door. The panel quietly swung open, and the scents of must and dust drifted out. An abyss waited just inside.

I eased the backpack from my shoulders, and from an outside compartment, I withdrew a lighter. It sparked to life on the first strike and created a pocket of light. It was bright enough to see my way as I stepped over the threshold into a large, empty room.

Weathered boards lined the floor and made up the walls. In a straight horizontal line, a few rusty nails poked from the boards near the door. An obvious place to hang coats. I slowly made my way into the interior, swinging the lighter back and forth to see.

On the far side of the room, I found a hallway. I wandered

down its length and watched the spiderwebs that clogged the ceiling disappear as my flame neared.

When I came to a partially closed door, I paused to nudge it open with my foot. It was just an empty room with a broken window. I moved on until I found another door. Each room I found equally disappointed me. There was never a bed, just broken glass and leaves that mingled with the dust on the floors. Yet, the number of rooms amazed me.

When I found a set of stairs, I carefully ascended and continued to check doors until I found a room that still had a whole window. The window afforded a view of the moonlit clearing. The weak light through the window was enough to see by, so I extinguished the lighter and closed the door.

Exhausted from a day of walking, I was ready to sleep, even without the bed I'd hoped for. Using my bag as a pillow, I made myself comfortable on the floor. As I lay in the moonlight, I wondered what I'd found here. Based on what I'd seen outside, the buildings were definitely not new. Yet, they weren't falling apart either. There were so many rooms, all of varying sizes. I wondered if perhaps this was an old commune or something.

I exhaled slowly and shut my eyes, listening to the night sounds. It didn't take me long to drift off, but I woke often since the hard floor was more uncomfortable than the ground.

By morning light, I stood with a slow stretch. My spine cracked in several spots, and I felt sore.

Shouldering my pack, I began exploring the rest of the building. The empty rooms seemed never ending. Then, I came to a set of heavy double doors.

I pushed them open and stared at the enormous space I'd discovered. Two old stone fireplaces, blackened by soot and age, were the room's source of heat. I frowned, thinking back to the rooms I'd checked, and couldn't recall one outlet or heating vent. How had the people who lived here kept warm in winter?

Along the interior wall to the left of the main doors, a rough counter set with a small stone trough and an old hand pump gave me a good indication of the lifestyle of those who'd once lived here. I stepped into the room and pushed the doors closed behind me. There weren't as many cobwebs in this room, but just as many leaves littered the floor near the room's broken window.

I walked over to the pump and started pumping. A loud, metallic groan filled the air; and though I cringed at the noise, I didn't stop. My arm grew tired by the time any water came out. It ran brown at first, then clear. I scooped a handful and sniffed it. It smelled fine and was cold in my palm. I tried a bit and smiled at the fresh, crisp taste.

As I pulled the water container from my backpack, I heard a distant howl. The sound didn't scare me. I rather liked it. It meant I wasn't alone.

I set the container in the sunken trough and started pumping again. Water splashed the top of it, almost knocking it over. I kept the handle moving with one hand and held the container steady with the other. It took a few minutes, but I filled it.

After the handle fell for the last time and the water stopped splashing, I thought I heard something. As I quietly capped the container and slid it into my pack, I listened. Slight noises reached me. Nothing definite. It could have been the building settling; or because of the racket of the pump, I might have drawn the curious attention of whatever had howled.

It didn't overly concern me. Animals were generally

cautious around humans. I slipped my arms through the straps of the backpack.

A noise came from the other side of the double doors. I froze. Perhaps it was a wild critter looking for a nice place to stay, just as I had.

I crossed the large area and pulled the latch of another door I had yet to explore. Sunlight poured through the opening. I stepped outside, gladly leaving whatever it was to roam as it might. The latch fell into place; and a moment later, a loud thud echoed in the empty room. My eyes widened, and I started to back away.

For a moment, there was silence. Then, the faint sound of snuffling carried through the broken window. Something bumped against the other side of the door. I jumped. What was in there? It didn't sound like a little critter. It sounded big.

A howl filled the air.

Dear God. A coyote or wolf.

I turned and ran.

Glass shattered behind me. I didn't glance back but pushed myself hard. It didn't matter. I'd only made it halfway to the path when something struck me from behind. It was solid and heavy and brought me to the ground.

Dry grass and dirt abraded my cheek, and my breath left me at the sudden impact. I tried to get to my hands and knees, but something weighted me down. A growl filled my ear, stopping my attempt. I brought my arms up to cover my head.

The weight on me shifted as another growl, not far away, joined the first. Two of them? I'd been so worried about people discovering me that I'd never thought to worry about animals. They weren't supposed to act like this. I'd been sleeping under the stars undisturbed for weeks.

The sound of their snarls escalated. Taking a risk, I lifted my head for a peek while I remained cowered on the ground. I saw a furred leg. I shifted a little further, and a large furry head came into view.

One of the creatures stood above me, long legs boxing me in, as another one stalked it, just ten feet away. I lifted my head further, catching the attention of the one circling. Its gaze met mine briefly, and I trembled. Of all the ways I imagined my life ending when I left home, I'd never considered death by wolf attack.

I moved slightly, trying to position myself so I could spring to my feet and run if the opportunity presented itself. My backpack bumped against the beast above me and distracted it. The newcomer lunged forward. The two clashed together, forelegs locked and mouths open. One of them stepped on my lower back, its claws digging through my shirt. As soon as the paw moved, I scrambled away.

Neither noticed me as I struggled to my knees and then my feet. I darted toward the trees, thinking to climb one.

A high-pitched yip sounded behind me followed by silence then the sound of paws thrumming against the dirt. Once again, I was brought down from behind. Only this time, the thing dove for my neck. I grunted as its teeth pierced my skin. I thought of my mom and dad as tears stung my eyes.

The teeth released me, and a tongue swiped the bite. It took me a moment to realize I could move. Why had the creature stopped? With a shaking hand, I touched my neck. It felt tender and bruised. There were four small holes. My fingers came away bloody. My hand shook.

Numbly, I lifted my head and found a wolf sitting on its

haunches, watching me. Beyond it, the defeated wolf watched me as well. Their focus and complete stillness terrified me.

Slowly, I lifted myself off the ground into a sitting position. Neither moved. Blood tickled my skin as it trailed down my neck. I ignored the sensation and warily got to my feet. They both studied me.

"It's okay," I whispered in a soothing voice. I wasn't sure if I was talking to them or myself. Tears continued to trickle from my eyes. My heart raced.

"Please don't attack me again." My voice caught on the last word.

The second wolf tilted its head. The first one stood, and I choked on air as I jumped back in fear. It stalked forward, crowding close to me. Without a thought, I kicked out. My foot connected solidly with its face. Its teeth clacked together, and the second wolf started to make a chuffing noise as the first one shook its head.

I spun, intending to run. However, I landed face first in the dirt as something hit me from behind again. This time, desperation made me angry. Using my elbow, I hit it in the danglies. The wolf yipped, yowled, and struggled to stay on its feet as it backed off. I sprang up, breathing hard.

The second wolf stood and ran toward me. In a flash, I was on the ground again with another set of teeth piercing my skin.

"Damn it, Jack. She's mine. I already Claimed her," a male voice said.

The teeth left my skin, and I twisted in time to see the wolf beside me stand on its hind legs. Its fur retracted into its pale skin, and its legs lengthened. Hands replaced paws, and long ears shortened.

"She didn't smell Claimed."

I watched the abnormal mouth form the words yet didn't believe what I witnessed. I wheezed as I struggled to my feet. Both men watched me.

The world tilted. I stumbled and pressed a hand against my neck. Everything seemed fuzzy. I didn't think it was due to blood loss, though. It was the two very naked men standing in front of me. Moments ago, they'd been wolves. I was sure of it...wasn't I?

"She still doesn't smell Claimed," the first one said.

"Why is she bleeding so much?" Jack asked, tilting his head at me.

I couldn't believe he actually asked. "Because you bit me," I said. "Twice."

"Roy...I don't think she's one of us." Worry clouded Jack's features.

One of us. The phrase pinged around in my mind.

Roy lifted his head. His nostrils flared as he inhaled deeply.

"But she smells so—"

"I know," Jack said.

I blinked slowly. "This isn't real."

"Call an Elder," Jack said, stepping toward me.

"Don't touch her," Roy snarled at Jack.

Jack stopped moving, turned toward Roy, and growled. "She is not yours."

"I Claimed her first."

Jack snorted. "There's no first or second. Either you Claim her or you don't. And you, my friend, didn't."

"Neither did you."

"I know that!"

Their arguing was making my head hurt as badly as my neck. Before I could tell them to stop, a long howl filled the air.

On the far side of the clearing, six wolves stepped through the trees.

More? I couldn't take more.

"If one more of you tries to bite me..." My words came out slurred.

The lead wolf looked back at his followers then at me. He trotted forward, gave the two men a cursory growl, and stopped in front of me.

My vision tunneled, and I caught a glimpse of the sky before nothing obliterated everything.

I WOKE to the sound of my own breathing and something squeezing my neck. When I opened my eyes, darkness surrounded me. I coughed and reached to pull away whatever was at my throat. My fingers touched cloth, and I remembered everything. I sat up, beginning to panic.

My world, which I'd already thought insane, was crazier than I realized. Wolves were actually men, and they argued over who had a right to bite me.

Nearby, I heard the rasp of the lighter. An instant later, I squinted against the radiance of the tiny flame and looked away for a moment. I was once again in the room with the whole window.

Glancing back, I saw the glow illuminating a girl's face. She didn't look scary; yet, despite her open expression, my heart beat harder once I saw her. Within the tangled mass of her brown hair, her large brown eyes reflected green light back at me. She was one of them.

"My name's Mary. What's yours?"

I stared at her, waiting for her to make some kind of move toward me. But she didn't. She just studied me with open curiosity. I studied her in return. She didn't look dangerous, just dirty. And she wore one of my shirts. I frowned, remembering how the two men had been naked after they'd changed from wolves. How could any of this be real?

I licked my dry lips and answered her question. "Charlene."

A storm of growling and snarling broke out in the hall just beyond the door. I shrank away from it. How many were out there?

"Don't worry. My dad will protect us until the Elder gets here. She is on her way."

I stared at her as what she said penetrated my stunned mind. Her father was out there. Guarding the door? And someone was coming to help. What was an Elder?

Mary's eyes continued to reflect at me. It wasn't the bright reflection of an animal. It was rather dull, and I might have easily overlooked it if not for the flame she held so close to her face.

"What are you?" I finally asked.

She smiled, showing perfectly normal looking teeth, to my relief, lifted her thumb from the lighter, and plunged us back into the black.

"A friend, I hope. Sleep, Charlene. The rest can wait for tomorrow."

The rest? Of what? And how did she think I could sleep with the racket still going on in the hall? Anger laced the already intimidating growls, punctuated by thumps against the wall. It sounded as if a pack of them were trying to fight their way to the door. Were they really still trying to get to me? I trembled in the dark.

"Why did they attack me?" I asked.

The noise quieted.

"They attacked you?"

"Yes. Didn't you see my throat?" Perhaps she had arrived after they'd bandaged me.

"Oh. That wasn't an attack. They were just trying to Claim you."

"I don't know what Claiming is, but it sure felt like an attack. Why did they do it?"

"Well..." Her tone conveyed her sudden and extreme discomfort. "It would be better if we waited for the Elder to explain."

In the dark, I heard her shift her position, but she didn't say anything more. Her silence annoyed me.

"Fine. They're going to try again, aren't they."

"Yeah. Sorry."

The fighting in the hall started back up.

I closed my eyes and sighed. "I have to go to the bathroom," I said, mostly to myself.

"I brought a bucket. Dad doesn't want us to leave the room."

A very heavy something hit against the door just then, and I agreed with her father. I didn't want to leave the room, either.

CHAPTER THREE

EVEN THOUGH MOST OF THE NOISE OUTSIDE REMAINED MINIMAL once I lay back down, fear and frustration kept me awake the rest of the night. At some point, Mary's breathing slowed, and I knew she slept. The harmless sound helped ease some of my fear of her. However, the creatures that waited outside the door were a different story. I stayed on the floor, moved as little as possible, and thought about what might come next.

A gentle tap on my door at first light gave me the answer.

"If you want to bite me again, go away," I said, staring at the panel.

Mary immediately sat up and glanced at the door. A smile lit her face.

"She won't bite you," she said, standing. As she moved to open the door, I saw Mary wasn't wearing any pants, just my shirt. I looked away. Who were these people?

The door swung open, and an adult strode in. She wore normal clothes. I couldn't have been more relieved. Mary closed the door behind the woman, and I noted the complete silence in the hallway.

"Can you sit up, dear?" the woman asked me.

"Are they gone?" I said, sitting up.

"No. But they will behave." She squatted beside me.

She had very light blonde hair, so light it almost appeared white. She smiled at me and smoothed back my hair with a gentle touch.

"Can I take a look at your neck?"

"I'd rather leave it well-protected." There was a good two inches of material covering my skin at the moment, and I didn't want it taken away.

"I understand. However, I would like to check for infection. It wouldn't do to have you become sick."

The image of me even more helpless around these people had me nodding. She carefully began to unwind the bandage.

"You were lucky Mary's pack was near and knew where the first aid supplies were hidden. Let's see what they did for you."

The end of the material stuck to my skin. She moved closer and began to work it away with small, slow movements. Most of the cloth was clean, but pink and red stained a few places. When she had the mass of material on the floor next to her, she tilted her head to study what she saw. I wished I had a mirror.

"Who Claimed you?" she asked.

"No," I said, shaking my head the tiniest bit. I'd stumbled into a world I didn't understand, and she wanted to start questioning me? "That's not how our conversation is going to start. First, you'll tell me who you are, then what you are. After that, I'll leave."

The woman chuckled. "You'll need that inner strength to deal with us. I'm Winifred Lewis. According to Mary, you saw one of us change yesterday. So, I think you know what we are. We're having trouble figuring out what you are, though."

My eyebrows shot up before I could stop the reaction. My heart did a quick double tap against my ribs.

Hearing her say that I already knew what they were definitely troubled me. I'd seen them change from wolf to man. I'd watched movies, and I knew the Hollywood legends. Never once had I thought any of it real. Yet, believing in werewolves bothered me a lot less than having her question what I might be.

I relaxed my face before I warily asked, "What do you mean?"

"Our kind doesn't mingle with humans," she said. "You, however, seem to be causing a stir. There are two males out there who both insist they have Claimed you."

She'd circled back to the Claiming stuff again. I sighed.

"Since I don't understand what you're talking about, I can't say what they did other than bite me." I gestured to my neck. "It hurt, and I didn't like it."

She studied me for another moment. "Did you find either of them...attractive?"

Two men had bitten me on the neck and she wanted to know if they were attractive? I blinked at her, got to my knees, grabbed my backpack, and stood. This place was crazy, and I wanted nothing to do with it. Neither Ms. Lewis nor Mary moved to stop me as I walked toward the door.

"There's something special about you, Charlene. Don't you want to find out what that might be?"

I stopped with my hand on the latch.

"How do you know my name?"

"Mary told me. I can communicate with her silently. It's a bit hard to explain."

Still facing the door, I considered what she said. She could do things with her head? Things that most people couldn't? She had my attention. She knew it, too.

"If you're willing to stay for a bit, I'm willing to try explaining how it works though," she said.

"I'd be foolish to stay."

I couldn't ignore the fact that these beings had the ability to change from a dog to a person at will and that they liked to bite. Did I want to find out more about them? Yes. They were unique, like me. But they'd already hurt me twice.

"What if I promised no one else would bite you without your permission?" she said.

I snorted. "Permission?" Turning, I shook my head at her. "In what universe would I ever give someone permission to bite me?"

"There's a lot you don't know, Charlene. You might find yourself willing at some point. Consider staying. Let me introduce you to the people here."

"People? No disrespect, but I don't think that's the right term." Not for what I'd witnessed.

She didn't say anything. I kept my hand on the latch. If I left, where would I go? If I stayed, how long until I died? I closed my eyes, tilted my head back, and silently asked "what next?"

As I stood there waiting, something tickled my senses. Then, I felt the threads of their wills drifting in the stillness around me. Animals didn't have those threads. Only people. And I could control people.

I opened my eyes and found both Ms. Lewis and Mary watching me closely. Ms. Lewis was right; I was special. So special I needed to hide from the world.

"I won't allow anymore biting."

"Neither will I. I promise you are safe."

"No one is ever safe, Ms. Lewis," I said. I pictured Penny and the gym of people I'd controlled. "I'd like to leave this room now."

She stood with a smile. "Certainly. Mary, your father has everyone in the yard."

Mary, who'd quietly watched our exchange, glanced at the window with worry. "How many?" she asked as she stood.

I walked to the window and looked out. A pack of wolves, at least twenty, waited. And they all watched the window. My stomach churned. I automatically searched out the threads of their wills. The thin strands hovered around them. It gave me comfort. I would be safe, but not because Ms. Lewis said so.

"Twenty," I said, moving back to the door. I pulled the latch and let myself out. Ms. Lewis and Mary followed behind me.

The halls were clear of most the cobwebs. I doubted it was due to any cleaning effort but rather their fighting and general presence in the halls.

Recalling the layout, I descended the stairs and kept to the hall to the right. At the main entry door, I hesitated a second before pushing it open.

They remained as they were, waiting in a group. As soon as I stepped onto the porch, a collective, angry growl rumbled from the gathering. I stopped moving forward. Before I could do anything, Ms. Lewis spoke.

"No one will bite you again without my permission," she said. Complete certainty echoed in her words.

I didn't turn to look at her. I couldn't take my eyes from the hackle-raised pack of wolves before me. They certainly looked ready to bite.

"How can you be sure?"

She stepped around me so I could see her.

"I've told them they couldn't," she said, setting a hand on my shoulder.

Her kind smile did little to reassure me as the growling increased in volume. She looked out at the group.

"Protect her. Make her welcome for as long as she wants to stay here. I will return Friday evening to listen to your requests."

The crowd before us quieted, and she stepped off the porch, obviously intending to leave me. I panicked. My mouth opened, but before I could ask her to wait, the woman disappeared and a white wolf stood in her place. My heart beat hard against my ribs. I struggled to breathe as she turned. Was I a fool to stand in a yard full of wolves? I swallowed hard against the remembered sensation of teeth breaking through my skin. The white wolf nudged my hand with her nose.

"We can smell your fear and hear your heartbeat," Mary said gently from beside me. "We can sense lies and taste freedom. She says she sees so much potential in you and wonders, if we can do all that, what can you do, Charlene?"

I met the white wolf's steady gaze and struggled with my choices. These creatures attacked me, bit me, then bandaged me up and protected me. They could do things regular people couldn't. How long had they existed yet remained hidden from the real world? I was foolish to stay, but was I more foolish to consider leaving?

"I can keep secrets," I said. Theirs and my own.

The wolf bobbed its head, turned, and I barely caught the streak of white as she left. The other wolves in the yard hardly gave her a glance; they watched me.

"Are you hungry?" Mary asked after a moment.

"Very." I looked over at her. The shirt just managed to cover her. Still, I blushed seeing her standing there, close to naked, in front of a group of twenty wolves. Wolves that were also men. Given her complete ease with it, I wondered how much time she spent as a girl versus a wolf. Then, I cringed as I considered what her idea of food might be.

"Um, what do you eat?"

She smiled at me. "Rabbit's good. Let's go back inside. Someone will bring in wood and a rabbit or two for us, and we'll have roasted meat."

I glanced at the group and blushed further as I imagined them strolling in, wearing nothing. I leaned toward Mary.

"If they change into men, can they wear pants, please?" I whispered. A few of the wolves made a coughing noise.

"We have very good hearing," she said with a laugh. She tugged me back through the door. "We'll see what we can do about clothes. Wini mentioned you might find it embarrassing if we walked about without them."

"Do you usually? Walk around without clothes, I mean," I said as I followed her down the hall.

She smiled and touched the shirt she wore before answering.

"I usually walk around with fur."

We entered the main room, and I was surprised to see wood near an already lit fire. She walked toward the fireplace and sat near the flames. Though it was warm outside, it was cool enough inside that the fire wasn't too much.

"I'm glad you're staying, by the way," she said.

"I never said that." Yet, here I was. "Will everyone else stay outside?" I asked. The possibility of lying down for a nap drew me to her side. My throat was getting sore, and I was tired from so little sleep the night before. But I wanted to know how safe it would be to sleep.

"Yes. Not many of us like to stay in these buildings."

"Good. If it's all right with you, I think I'll lay down for a bit. You'll stay with me?"

She nodded, and I lay on the floor and closed my eyes.

THE SMELL of roasting meat invaded my dreams, and I woke with a growling stomach.

Mary knelt by the fire, watching a rabbit cook. She wore loose pants, now, though her feet were still bare. As if sensing my regard, she turned.

"It's just about done," she said.

I sat up and winced at the soreness in my neck.

"Wini suggested we clean your neck with alcohol a few times today." She tilted her head and watched me closely. When I didn't say anything, she grabbed the white bottle beside her and handed it to me. On top rested a clean cotton cloth. I stared at the cloth and frowned. Where were they getting all these supplies from? She caught my look.

"Dad sent others for more things. I have clothes, and you have a bed."

I wet the piece of cloth with alcohol as I turned my head and saw a narrow bed set up beside me. It looked very similar to the bed I'd left behind. The white, wood frame supported the metal spring on which the mattress lay. A clean comforter covered the mattress, and a fluffy pillow rested by the headboard. I reached out, tugged the comforter back, and saw white sheets. A complete bed. I touched the mattress with longing. How had they managed that?

Mary took the rabbit from the fire and set it on a ceramic plate, pulling my attention from the bed. I absently started to dab the alcohol on my neck and cringed from the sting of it. Trying to distract myself, I looked around and noted other additions.

A pitcher, two glasses, and two plates waited on the mantel. On the foot of the bed rested another blanket and a stack of clothes, including a towel. A bowl sat on the floor under the bed along with a large cooking pot. Further away was a familiar bucket. I didn't think I could use it in an open space like this.

The new items were as far as they'd gone to improve the living conditions. Wind swept through the room, rustling the leaves still on the dusty floor.

"Here you go," Mary said, drawing my attention to the plate she held out. Half the rabbit lay on it.

I accepted the plate and dug in. Between bites, I started asking questions.

"What happened to the two that bit me?"

She grinned. "The rest chased them off. They had their chance and failed."

"Chance for what?"

"To Claim you for their own. For whatever reason, their bite didn't take hold. Probably because they weren't meant for you. Either way, they won't get another chance. Word is spreading. There are many more who will want a first chance, and they won't allow those two a second one.

Many more? The idea of others wanting to...wait, what? "What do you mean Claim?" I knew it meant biting me, but they kept talking about it like it was something beyond just that.

She gave me a look. "To be a pair."

"Pair? You mean like boyfriend and girlfriend?"

She shook her head slowly then shrugged, obviously not understanding what I meant, either.

"It's where the male tells the rest that the female is his. Mating usually occurs shortly afterward."

I stopped chewing and stared at her. I totally understood what she meant by mating.

"I'm glad you're here with me," she said again. "This was supposed to be the start of my Introductions. That's why we were on our way here. Finding you distracted everyone a bit."

"What do you mean?"

"Instead of looking at me to see if I'm suitable to Claim, everyone's looking at you. I don't mind. The thought of Claiming..." She shrugged and glanced at my neck. "I was nervous. Still am."

She'd come here with the purpose of meeting a "nice" wolf who would bite her neck and then immediately...I shook my head. She seemed close to my age. Too young. I preferred my dreams of the ring-proposal method and the delays brought with it.

"So you'll stay here until someone Claims you?" I asked.

"Not usually. We tend to meet here every few days so the attention doesn't become overwhelming for me. Dad promised Wini he'd stay here, though, until she returns. That means I'll stay too."

"When's Friday?"

She shrugged. "I was going to ask you that."

I'd lost track of the days weeks ago. "Where did Ms. Lewis go?"

She giggled. "No one calls her Ms. Lewis. Wini or Winifred. She's different. She lives in the human world as a teacher. She had to go back to teach her kids."

The way she said that told me a lot. Most of their kind did, then, live in their fur. Winifred did not. It explained why she appeared with clothes on and how she knew I'd be uncomfortable with Mary walking around naked. A werewolf teacher. My mind had difficulty with that. I tried to picture my chemistry teacher as a werewolf and just couldn't.

"What happens next?" I asked.

"We wait for her to come back to talk to the males who want to Claim you."

I chewed in silence for a moment. My eyes drifted to the broken window. The bright light of midday made me squint. Throughout the entire conversation small sounds had drifted in from outside: a distant bark, general movement, and the chirping of birds.

"How many?" I said, using her words from earlier.

"I didn't go out. But there are more."

We finished eating, and she took the bones and threw them into the fire. Using the bowl under the bed, we worked together to pump water and wash the plates.

"If you get hungry, just say. They're all willing to do anything that might win them some favor."

"What kind of favor?" I wasn't about to offer up my neck.

"Wini probably won't give anyone permission to Claim you unless you agree to it. They're looking for ways to win your support."

"Ah." That was unlikely to happen. We set the plates on the

mantel and looked at each other at a loss. A light breeze stirred a leaf on the floor.

"Got a broom?" I asked finally.

"What's a broom?"

I shook my head. How did she know what a bed was but not a broom?

I eyed the door. If we opened it, we might be able to kick out most of the debris. I hesitated because of the men outside and mentally scolded myself. If they were going to come in, they would have already. Nothing was stopping them. I doubted Mary's presence was that much of a deterrent. But would they see an open door as an invitation? I didn't want to put myself into a position where I'd need to control them like I had with Penny and all the people at school.

"Is it safe to open the door?"

"Sure. They won't come in, but they'll watch us."

Just as I'd figured and hoped.

Once we kicked the leaves out, we could maybe use one of my shirts to screen the window and give us privacy. Standing there watching the fire burn low, I realized the direction of my thoughts. I wanted to clean the place up as if I intended to stay, not just until I learned more about them, but permanently. Did I really want that?

Despite what had happened, I did. This place had no electricity or plumbing; and, without the generosity of the people here, I had no source of food. Was I crazy? I didn't think so. I realized there was a high threat here. I allowed my fingers to drift up to my collarbone, but I caught myself before touching my wounds. I didn't want to contaminate the bites. Was the threat here any higher than in the real world? No, it was just different.

In the real world, I could picture myself caught and taken to a secret lab where cold-hearted scientists would poke and prod me. It would only take one person of importance to believe Penny. If they caught me by surprise and knocked me unconscious, my ability wouldn't save me. Here, I had a chance at freedom. These people didn't want to dissect me, they wanted to, what? Date me?

Decided, I walked to the door and opened it. All the wolves in the yard turned toward me. I didn't look at them and tried to pretend my heart hadn't just leapt in fear at their attention. Instead, I focused on the sun angling through the door. The light warmed me.

Sunlight and fresh air won over a cage.

I took a step back from the door, then turned to get my bag. From a pocket, I pulled the money I'd hoarded during my journey. Ms. Lewis—Winifred—had asked them to make me welcome, and Mary had said they would be willing to help me. Standing with the money, I nervously approached the door once more.

"Would any of you be willing to get a few things for me? I'm not sure how close the nearest grocery store is, and you'd need clothes to enter the store."

Immediately, several of them dashed from the yard into the trees.

"It'll take them a bit to find clothes," Mary said from behind me.

"They have them hidden somewhere?"

"No. Usually they take them off a laundry line. Some of the clever ones can get into houses without being noticed."

I glanced at my bed. "You mean these things are stolen?"

"How else would we get them? We have nothing to trade."

"Only Winifred has a job?" I asked.

Mary stared at me for several long moments.

"She says there are a few others. But not many. Mostly, the men only resort to jobs when they want something they can't steal."

"She says?" I asked. Then I realized she meant Winifred. "You're talking to her now? How?"

"In my head. Elders, like Winifred, connect us all. They help us communicate with each other. That's how the families know to meet here for an Introduction and how the unMated males know when to show up." Mary looked outside at the remaining wolves while I tried to wrap my head around what she'd said. Winifred's abilities were impressive.

I followed Mary's gaze and found the remaining wolves watching us. My pulse jumped a little; their scrutiny unnerving me.

I'd hoped to send one of them for supplies and to start cleaning. But to start cleaning, I'd need to leave this room. The idea of walking around out there...well, I was having a hard time picturing it without them running after me.

"Can I go out there?" I asked.

"Sure. Why?"

"I was thinking. If we took a bunch of that thick grass at the edge of the clearing and tied it into a tight bundle, we could use it as a broom and start cleaning this place out."

However, my feet stayed where they were, safely inside. My hand drifted up and hovered over the marks on my neck. I closed the door, walked back to the bed, and sat down. Logically, I knew I could stop them from biting me. I'd felt their wills; they weren't just wild animals I couldn't control. But that understanding didn't overcome my fear.

"Are you okay?" Mary asked.

"No," I said. The sound was more a hoarse rasp than a word. "I can still feel their teeth on me. Seeing all of them out there..."

She didn't say anything. I stared at the dying coals until someone knocked on the door. We both turned toward the sound, but neither of us moved. It wasn't fear that held me this time. It was surprise. They knew to knock? I looked at Mary. She looked at me and shrugged.

"Yes?" I called.

"We have the grass," a rough voice said.

Mary walked to the door and opened it. Men, wearing pants, stood outside. Each held a bundle of grass. When the ones in front saw Mary, they shifted their positions in an attempt to see around her. Those behind them craned their necks, too. They wanted to see me. However, they didn't try to enter. They just waited and watched, each holding a clump of long grass.

I forced myself to stand and went to the door. The first man held out his fistful of grass.

"For you." Red tinted his cheeks as he handed it over.

"Thank you," I said, feeling equally uncomfortable.

One by one, they handed me grass until I had a pile next to the door large enough for several brooms. After the last one left, Mary closed the door, gave me an undecipherable look, and motioned for me to follow her. We went to the room I'd first slept in. She shut the door and turned to me.

"I have never seen anything like that before," she said in a whisper.

"What do you mean?"

She motioned for me to keep my voice down and peeked

out the window. I followed her gaze. Men and wolves mingled in the yard.

"They don't do that," she said, moving away from the window. She caught my puzzled look and pointed at my neck. "They do that. They see a female and Claim her. If there's someone else interested, they fight for the right to her. They'll hunt for you, but they don't bring you things. They don't try to get on your good side first. I thought they might be nicer to you, but that was unbelievable."

Bringing grass to a girl was unbelievable? It hardly seemed worthy of her astonishment. Yet, it was their way. I sat on the floor and started winding together some of the grass I still held. Mary sat next to me.

"No flowers, nice dinners, or seeing a show. Just a life-threatening bite on the neck." It seemed a very harsh courtship. Nothing I wanted any part of.

"It's not life-threatening to us. We heal quickly. The ones who bit you didn't know you wouldn't heal."

I didn't think it made it any better, but tried to look at it from her point of view. Would I feel differently about the bites if they were already healed? I couldn't decide.

She watched as I wove the top of two clumps together. When I had a decent bunch, I stood and tried it. It worked all right.

"Here," I said, handing the sad little broom to Mary. "Can you start sweeping this room out? I'll get more of the grass."

She took the broom with an arched brow but nodded. I left her there, sweeping awkwardly, and made my way to the main room.

As soon as I entered, someone knocked on the door, and I regretted leaving Mary behind.

I'll be fine, I told myself as I squared my shoulders. I'd run from Penny. I wouldn't run from them, unless they started eyeing my neck again. My shoulders slumped, and my hand drifted upward in a protective gesture. I didn't want to experience that ever again.

Another knock on the door pulled me from my thoughts. What to do?

"You said you needed supplies." The hesitant voice beyond the door gave me my answer.

With a sigh, I cautiously opened the door. Men waited, and the rest of the wolves shuffled around behind them. They were so different. I was different, too. Different didn't necessarily mean bad. As Mary had pointed out, the first two hadn't known I wasn't one of them. I needed to give the rest a chance, didn't I?

"Have any of you ever been inside a grocery store?" I asked.

No one responded.

"Have any of you used money before?"

They remained quiet. It looked like I wouldn't get any of the things I'd wanted.

"Winifred is willing to help whoever you send," the one closest to me said. He had dark brown eyes and wore his light brown hair in shaggy waves back from his face. Sparse whiskers grew on his chin and upper lip. He watched me with interest but seemed relaxed.

Since he'd answered, I handed him the money from my pocket.

"Canned vegetables and a can opener, nails—as many as you can buy—and a hammer, toilet paper, and a handsaw. I don't know how much of that you can get. Just don't steal anything."

When he turned, the men parted and watched him leave.

I eased the door closed, collected my grass, and went to join Mary. If I worried each time I had to open the door, how would I ever be able to live here?

We had the bed moved into the newly cleaned room and another rabbit roasting on the fire by the time the man returned. When he handed me the bag, he gave me an expectant smile. I wasn't sure what he wanted.

"Thank you. What's your name?"

"Anton."

"Thank you, Anton."

He grinned wider, nodded, and walked away. With relief, I went to sit by Mary, who waited near the fire. Inspecting the bag, I pulled out each item and found we had the nails we needed but no hammer. There were also several canned goods, an opener, a handsaw, and my change.

"Why do you need all of that?" Mary asked.

"Because, if I'm going to stay here, we need to fix this place up. Winter will be cold, won't it?"

She started shaking her head then stopped. "Without fur, yes. So you know how to fix things?"

I shook my head. "But it'll be easier to learn that than it would to grow fur."

She nodded, and we ate the rabbit as the light faded.

CHAPTER FOUR

MARY SLEPT IN THE ROOM WITH ME. SHE DIDN'T MIND THE FLOOR, so I gave her the extra comforter and gladly took the bed. I slid under the covers, closed my eyes, and pretended I was back home. Despite everything that had happened, I slept well.

When I woke at first light, Mary continued to breathe softly from her place on the floor. I quietly used the bucket then went to the window. In the yard, several of the wolves slept on the ground while some already walked in and out of the trees. Those who wandered seemed bored, yet they didn't stop to talk to one another or interact in any other way. I watched them for a while and noticed some studied the area. It seemed as if they were new here, like me.

One stopped and stared at a shed directly across from the main building where I slept. The small structure leaned at a precarious angle. Many of the cedar shake shingles had disappeared into the black hole that pierced the roof. However, the boards covering the walls seemed solid enough. As I studied it, I thought a few of those boards might help cover the broken windows in the main building.

"I smell..." Mary said suddenly, startling me. I turned and watched her sit straight up and sniff the air. "Pheasant. Good. I was getting tired of rabbit." She stood and stretched. I heard her stomach growl and grinned at her.

We made our way down to the main room and found the pheasant roasting.

"Who brings the food?"

Mary shrugged. "They're either hunting on their own and the first one here provides it, or they're fighting for the right."

The idea that they would argue about who could bring us food had me shaking my head. Why was that okay to do, but helpfully collecting grass was not?

I opened a can of green beans to eat with the bird and scooped half onto Mary's plate. What I wouldn't give for a bowl of Sugar Crisps.

We ate in companionable silence for several minutes before she spoke again.

"So what do you want to do today?"

"Start boarding up some of the windows, I think."

"You know it's summer, right?"

Since I'd left home, I'd watched spring change to summer, and with each passing week, I knew summer's hold wouldn't last forever. Just another reason to find somewhere to burrow in.

"Summer and sunny. But it'll rain eventually and start getting cold. There are a lot of broken windows and no ladders. It'll take time to get it done."

She gave me a long look.

"Where's your family, Charlene?"

Hopefully, safe where I left them, I thought. I finished chewing before I answered.

"Where I'm not." I tossed the bones into the fire as she'd done the day before and went to wash my plate. Thankfully, she didn't push for more of an answer.

"Some of the broken windows still have unbroken panes," she said, coming up behind me. "Do you think we can take them apart and fix a few of the windows in some of the other rooms?"

"Sure."

Someone knocked on the door. She handed me her plate. I washed it as she moved across the room and opened the door.

"We'd like to help," a deep voice said.

I turned and glanced at the men who stood just outside. Their faces were familiar this time, and I recognized Anton from the day before. When his gaze met mine, he offered me a smile, which I automatically returned.

"Thank you for the offer," I said. I wiped my damp hands on my jeans and moved closer to the door. "We need some of the boards from that shed over there." I pointed in the general direction of the building since I couldn't actually see it through them.

"Will you show us what you mean?" one of them said.

He wanted me to step out the door? I glanced at Mary. She nodded.

My stomach churned as the men parted to make a narrow path between their bodies. They waited, watching me closely as I hesitated, swallowed hard, and tried to obliterate my fear with logic. If they made a move toward me, I'd grab their wills and force them to stop. However, the thought of using my power like that didn't reassure me. It disturbed me as much as the idea of going back outside. Yes, I'd used it like that before. But the situation at the gym had been different. I hadn't put myself in that situation on purpose. I'd only used my ability instinctually. And I hadn't hurt anyone.

If I wasn't willing to use it here, where did that leave me? I couldn't stay inside forever.

"Maybe you should give her a little more room," Mary said.

She watched me just as closely as they did. I felt weak and stupid. Clenching my teeth, I took a deep breath and stepped forward.

They moved around me like gnats before a storm. I tried to ignore them as I made my way across the yard in the early morning light. Those still on four legs watched me with interest.

When I reached the shed, I found it was bigger than I'd thought. I glanced back at the main building and noted all the broken windows in the daylight. It was a good thing the shed was big; we would need many of the boards.

I scanned the men around me and patted one of the shed's walls.

"These boards," I said. "If you pull them off carefully so they don't crack, I want to use them to board up some of the broken windows. Actually, if you can take apart the whole shed, I'm sure we can find a way to reuse all the wood."

The men nodded, and Anton went inside the building.

"Don't break the glass in the window," Mary said from somewhere behind the men. "We want to reuse the unbroken panes, too."

I was glad she'd followed. I stepped away from the building and heard the screech of nails pulled from dry wood. A board popped away from the wall, and I caught a glimpse of Anton before he moved out of sight again.

A younger man with light blonde hair stepped in front of me, stealing my attention.

"Is there anything else?"

"Um..." I tried to find Mary in the bodies crowded around me but couldn't. The urge to start backing away took hold. Yet, I remained where I was. I didn't have a choice. Another man stood behind me.

"Yeah," Mary said, her voice floating around us. "The rest of you can go to the junkyard and look for useful things."

The men shifted so I could see Mary. She reached through, wrapped a hand around my wrist, and pulled me out of their circle.

"Like what?" one asked.

"I don't know," she said. "Useful things. Like...a bathtub. She doesn't wash in a stream." She tugged me toward the main room's door as she spoke.

"A bathtub?" I asked under my breath.

"Ask Winifred," Mary said over her shoulder as she nudged me through the door. I wasn't sure if she was telling me to ask Winifred or the confused men behind us, but as she quickly closed the door, I didn't care.

I breathed a sigh of relief, turned, and threw my arms around her. "Thank you."

She awkwardly returned the hug. "Wini suggested the bathtub."

I pulled back, confused. "Is she listening to everything?"

"No. I've been talking to her, so she knows what they're doing," she said, nodding toward the closed door. "When they started crowding you, she suggested we send them to the junkyard since this place could use a few things, and you don't like stealing. They'll reach out to her, and she'll help them figure out what's needed."

"How exactly does that work? Her connection to everyone, I mean. Is it like little mental strings that connect her to everyone?"

Mary was quiet a moment. "She says it's like a two way radio. You just need to know the right frequency." She gave me a puzzled look. "What's a two way radio?"

I grinned. "Your head, apparently. It's far out you can talk to her like that. But doesn't it get a little noisy in her head?"

This time Mary laughed.

"No. It's usually pretty quiet for her. We keep to ourselves unless there's a problem our leaders can't resolve."

"Leaders?"

"Yeah. Men like my dad. Typically, heads of families. I don't know if there are any non-family packs. Wait. Wini says there aren't."

I had no idea what she meant but didn't ask any further questions. I didn't want to know about their hierarchy. Not yet anyway.

"Let's go start on the windows," she said after I remained quiet for a moment.

We went upstairs, split up, and started looking for windows that had one or more whole panes left in them. Sometimes, just one of the four panes had a thin crack; those windows we left alone as they would still keep out most of the wind and rain. Usually, though, the glass was missing from at least one of the window's four squares.

Any window missing glass, we removed altogether and brought the frames to the main room. There, we puzzled over how to remove the good glass without any tools. The cracked glaze that held each pane in place barely clung to the wood and was easy to pick away. But the little metal pieces stuck into the wood to pin in the glass were much trickier than the nails that had held the frames in. Mary had been able to pull the frame nails out with just her fingers.

"We'll have to ask for help," Mary said after trying to remove one. "I don't have enough control to just change my nails or I could do it." She glanced at the closed door. "You want to ask?"

I totally didn't want to but moved to the door anyway. It opened with a creak and drew everyone's attention.

A pile of neatly stacked boards lay on the ground to the right of the door. Anton was in the process of setting another on top and looked up at me. It relieved me that someone I knew was nearby.

"We need a hand for just a minute," I said to him and stepped back.

One of the wolves in the yard softly growled as Anton stepped through the door. The men who had been removing additional boards from the shed stared at me. Did I sound too demanding?

"Um, thank you for your help," I called. One of them nodded in acknowledgement, but they all appeared angry anyway.

I closed the door and nearly walked into Anton, who stood just behind me. I put my hands up to stop myself and almost touched his bare chest. He smiled at me, the glint in his eyes making me nervous.

"Uh...Mary can explain," I said, motioning to Mary who watched us with interest.

He reluctantly went to Mary's side and listened to her point out the tiny metal pieces he needed to remove without breaking the glass. He nodded; and as I watched, the nail on his first finger grew to a lethal point. He gently prodded the metal and worked it from the wood.

After he'd picked out all four, he scraped away the remaining chunks of glaze and removed the pane. He turned to hand it to me. His searching gaze and hesitant smile made me sad for him. Mary was right. They totally were trying to seek my favor.

"Thank you, Anton. Mary, if you want to work with him, I'll get some more windows." I left them and pretended not to notice his disappointed look.

He worked with us for the rest of the morning. By midday, we'd removed all of the windows from the second story and had salvaged enough whole glass for ten complete windows. Anton had replaced the glass and pressed the metal back into place while Mary and I reinstalled the frames. I made sure to fix the window in the main room first. When we finished, I thanked him again for his help and awkwardly walked with him to the door.

"Will you consider me?" he asked before leaving.

I met his hopeful gaze. He was good-looking and seemed nice. If we'd met in the real world and he'd stopped to talk to me, maybe my heart would have given a little kick. But we hadn't, and I knew what he was. When I answered, I didn't pretend to misunderstand him.

"I won't consider anyone. My neck isn't healed."

His eyes drifted to my neck, and he gave a slow nod. "I would be gentle," he said.

I didn't say anything. Anything I had to say would upset him. He wouldn't be gentle. No one could be when they intended to bite my neck. I bore eight puncture wounds already.

He gave me a last pleading look before he finally left.

Sighing, I went to help Mary sweep out the rooms with the restored windows.

"Do you mind if I keep sleeping in your room?" Mary asked when we finished the last one. Daylight was starting to fade and our makeshift brooms were wearing down.

"Not at all."

In fact, I preferred it. I'd only known her a few days, and two of her kind had bit me; yet, I felt safe with her in my room at night.

Sounds of fighting in the yard woke me. It wasn't yet light. When I sat up in bed, Mary flicked the lighter. She was sitting up, too. Our eyes met. Outside, the noises quieted.

"What was that?" I whispered.

After a moment, she shrugged and lay down again. The light went out. I stayed upright, listening. Nothing but silence remained outside.

Mary's breathing slowed once more. Obviously, whatever had happened wasn't important or worrisome to her. However, it took several minutes before I settled back on the bed.

I had no idea how long I lay there in the dark, but gradually the room began to lighten. Lying on my side, I watched Mary as she woke with a stretch on the floor.

"How can you sleep like that?"

"I've never slept any other way. We don't have beds out there." She glanced at the window.

Out there, where fights broke out in the middle of the night, where there was no protection. The warmth of my blankets wrapped around me, and I appreciated that I'd found this place. I'd slept outside often since leaving home, but I'd longed for something more permanent, somewhere I might belong. It was that longing, and the possibility of their understanding about my ability, that had me fixing windows when I wasn't even sure I wanted to stay.

"Maybe they can find you a mattress or bed, too," I said.

"That'd be nice, but I doubt they would be as willing to fetch me a bed as they were for you." She grinned at me.

I didn't want to think about their eagerness to please, so I changed the subject.

"What was that fight about last night?"

"This morning," she corrected. "I don't know. My dad wouldn't say when I asked him. He just told me to turn out the light and go back to sleep."

"You asked your dad? How?"

"The same way I talk to Wini. All leaders can talk to their pack members, just like Wini can talk to everyone." Mary moved to the window and looked out. "The yard's busier than it was yesterday. Come see. They've brought back a lot of stuff."

I tossed back the blankets and joined her. She was right. More wolves and men milled in the yard below. Amidst them, items lay scattered about. I spotted an old claw foot tub, several wooden chairs, a tipped over table, a dresser with no drawers, and several other objects I couldn't identify from the window.

"Want to go see?" she asked.

"I'll join you in a moment."

She nodded and left me. I pulled the bucket from under the bed and wrinkled my nose. I needed to figure out a better way to pretend this place had plumbing. It had been embarrassing emptying the bucket yesterday. Thankfully, Mary had shown me a back door.

Joining Mary in the main room, I asked her to help me pump some water. There, I washed my hands with the bar soap I'd set out from my bag and brushed my teeth.

"Winifred wants to know how your neck feels," Mary said as I dampened the cloth with alcohol to dab on the healing marks.

"Still hot and tight."

Mary nodded at my words and, after a worried glance at the door, frowned.

"What is it?"

"She said that a few of the males have contacted her asking when she means to return."

I didn't see why that would upset her. After all, Winifred had told them they couldn't bite me without her permission. Of course they wanted to know when she would come back. Maybe the frown was because my neck still hurt. But why the look at the door? Was Winifred thinking of sending someone my way?

"I'm definitely not up for another bite if that's what she's suggesting."

Mary shook her head. "She knows you're not ready."

A relieved sigh escaped me. Mary gave me a crooked grin.

"Come on. Let's go see what they brought back," she said, tugging me toward the door.

I reluctantly let her lead me.

As soon as the door opened, we gained everyone's attention just like the day before. Many of the men stood possessively by some item or a pile of items. They all watched me closely as I followed Mary across the yard. She went to the bathtub first and stared down at it with a scowl.

"You wash in this?" she asked me with heavy skepticism.

I tore my wary gaze from the tense men and looked at the claw foot tub. Its porcelain coating had chipped in many places showing the cast iron beneath. It had a drain hole in the bottom, but no holes for faucets. Mud coated the entire thing.

"Not as it is," I said to Mary. I looked up at the man. My disinterest in the man warred with my interest in how he'd managed to carry it here from the junkyard. "This is perfect. Thank you. Was it heavy to carry?"

"Not at all," he said.

I didn't fully believe him. Dirty sweat streaks lined his face. If they weren't from carrying the tub, then what? I gave him a small smile of thanks and turned to Mary.

"Where do you think we should put it?"

"You fill it with water, right?" she said. I nodded. "Then close to the water, I guess. There's that little room just inside the meeting room."

I had no idea which room she meant but turned back to the man.

"Would you be willing to bring it in for us?" I was very careful to include Mary in the request for further help. I didn't want to raise this man's hopes as I had Anton's. The man agreed with a smile, and Mary tugged me to the next pile.

As we meandered through the yard, we collected more dishes, some silverware, cooking items, furniture, and a hammer with a roughly hewn "new" handle. Yet, there were items I refused. A moth-eaten cushioned chair that had a huge, and very questionable, gnawed hole in the seat; and a mattress, likewise gnawed. The men with those items looked like I'd slapped them when I shook my head to decline what they'd brought. I quickly moved away from them to inspect the next man's items.

Near the woods, a wolf stepped out in front of me. My heart froze for a moment. Mary set her hand on my shoulder, stopping me from running as it stepped closer. It walked with a limp and one of its eyes didn't open all the way.

"It's Anton," Mary said softly. All of the small noises in the yard stopped, and the hostility of those around us grew palpable.

The wolf dipped his head to the ground and dropped something from his mouth. Half a thick candle lay in the dirt and dry grass.

"Thank you, Anton," I said as I cautiously retrieved it. "Why aren't you..." Was it rude to ask why he wasn't a man?

Mary seemed to understand my half-spoken question, though.

"I'll explain later." She pulled me away. Her tight hold on my hand worried me as much as the angry stares of the men around us.

Mary stopped when we reached the door. As if it were a sign, those who'd brought useful items began to carry everything inside. I thanked them once more as they left. When we had the room to ourselves again, we went in and closed the door.

I looked at her but she shook her head.

"Let's go upstairs."

In our room, she finally confided in me.

"The noise we heard this morning? They confronted Anton because you seemed to favor him."

I stared at the candle still in my hand, then quickly set it on the floor. Sane thoughts scattered as I numbly walked to the window. Most of the men either were no longer in the yard or had changed to their other form. But Anton still stood near the edge of the woods, looking at the main building.

How many of them had he fought? My hand moved to my throat. How many men had I thanked today? Had I looked at any of them too long?

"Winifred wants you to know it's in our nature and not due to anything you've done. Males will compete for females. The strong ones usually prevail. It means stronger young."

Young? I didn't want young. I didn't want males. I didn't want any of this. Except maybe a place to stay. I set my hand against the sill. My earlier thought rose again. Perhaps I could just stay inside. If I didn't mingle with them, they couldn't hurt me and they wouldn't hurt each other.

Anton happened to glance up and catch me at the window. His head bobbed in acknowledgement then turned and disappeared into the trees. Despite his beating, he'd found a candle and brought it to me, risking more retribution. And why? He knew I didn't want anyone to bite me. It didn't seem to matter to him. He still wanted to win my favor. He still hoped I'd agree to what he wanted. My throat grew tight, and I knew something had finally killed most of my fear: pity. I pitied not just Anton, but all the men for their desperate hope.

"Charlene?" Mary said, her voice heavy with concern.

"It's fine. I'm fine," I said turning to face her again. "Let's check out that tub."

It turned out there was a small, windowless space off the main room, very close to the hand pump and trough. The tub sat in the center of the area, but something didn't look right. The wood creaked under our feet as we walked in, and I saw what looked off. The boards bowed under the weight of the empty tub, flexing further with each step we took. I couldn't imagine the boards would hold the weight of the water too.

"It doesn't look very safe," Mary said.

"Yeah." And I didn't see how I'd be able to use it. Where would the water drain? Emptying it the same way I would fill it didn't sound like much fun.

"Maybe we could use some of the boards they pulled off the shed," Mary said. "If we laid them cross ways on top of the other boards, I mean."

"Maybe." I glanced at the door. I worried that going out to get the boards would draw attention and prompt offers of help. Unable to stand the thought of someone else being beaten for helping me, I stayed where I was.

"Want me to get them?" she asked.

I nodded.

While she did that, I moved the table between the sink and the fireplace. I'd just started to place the chairs around it when Mary walked past followed by two men. They carried boards over their shoulders, and both men nodded at me. I gave a small smile and a nod in return then ignored them. While they were in the tub room, someone tapped on the outer door she'd left open. Reluctantly, I went to answer it. This man looked older than the others. Grey hair covered his chest, and vines held up his loose pants.

"Hi," I said simply.

"Hello." His deep, rumbling voice sounded amused. "Mary said you needed food again."

I nodded hesitantly. We hadn't eaten yet, but I hadn't planned to ask anyone for anything. There was still another can of beans I could open and share with Mary. I preferred beans over asking someone to hunt for us and risking showing favoritism.

The man at the door pulled out a skewered rabbit from behind his back. "I hope you're not as picky about eating rabbit," he said with a slight grin.

I tilted my head and really looked at the man. I saw some familiar features and smiled wider.

"You're Mary's dad, then?"

"I am. You can call me Henry."

"It's nice to meet you, Henry," I said, moving aside for him.

"It's nice to meet you, too," he said. "Want me to put this on the fire for you?"

"That would be great. Thank you."

He moved into the room and squatted by the fire while I closed the door.

"Mary's glad you're here."

"I'm glad she's here, too."

He stood and turned toward me. "They mean well," he said with a deep sigh. "I remember how it was when I saw Mary's mother that first time." He shook his head, and a fond smile tugged at his mouth. "That beautiful, angry woman...she fought me, you know. When I tried to Claim her. She had big plans. She'd watched some people building a house and decided she wanted to live like them." He looked around the room. "This was our compromise. She loved this place, but we never lived here."

Mary walked out of the tub room and smiled at her dad.

The two men followed her. Henry nodded at both and watched as they left. Neither closed the door.

"You two stay inside for the rest of the day. They're getting restless waiting for Winifred."

Mary nodded, and I glanced at the door. Many of them unabashedly looked in as they walked past.

When Henry left, he closed the door behind him.

"Let's bring this up to our room," Mary said, patting the dresser with the missing drawers.

FRIDAY IT RAINED and tempers flared. Mary and I ate a quiet breakfast of rabbit and beans—I was growing to hate beans—while listening to faint snarls and muted growls. We'd moved all the items from the day before to their proper places, soaked the dishes in boiling hot water, and cleaned out the tub. The small additions made the place feel less run down and vacant.

We'd worked so much the day before that we had nothing with which to occupy ourselves. So Mary started the long process of heating water for a bath. We watched the floor carefully as we poured in each pot, but the extra boards held steady as the depth of the water increased. When there was enough water, I took a quick bath. Sitting there undressed with no lock on the door made me nervous. However, stepping away clean made it worthwhile. Emptying the tub by hand wasn't very fun; but with Mary's help, it went fast. We then worked to fill it for her. When she finished her bath, we sat together and dried our hair by the fire.

Twice someone knocked on the door, but we didn't answer it. After the second time, I noticed the men were starting to watch us through the window. I nudged Mary. We glanced at each other, stood, and went upstairs to our room. The fighting outside grew worse afterwards. It was a long day and a longer evening.

I restlessly lay on my bed, wondering if they would decide to ignore Winifred's command and come inside to bite me again. Mary's father had no chance of holding them all back if they decided to come for me. And I worried he'd just get hurt like Anton.

The scabs were beginning to itch on the very outside, and I knew I was starting to heal. It didn't mean I was ready for another bite, though.

Mary seemed to sense my anxious mood.

"Want me to sleep on the bed with you?" she asked.

I nodded and closed my eyes as she lay by me. I pretended the world and I were normal and that nothing could hurt me. I knew better, though.

CHAPTER FIVE

"GOOD MORNING," WINIFRED SAID AS SHE OPENED THE BEDROOM door.

Late morning sunlight glared through the window, blinding me, and I squinted at her. She gave me a wry smile.

"They kept you up late?"

I nodded. The motion nudged Mary, who lost her precarious perch on the edge of the bed. She fell to the floor with a thump and a grunt.

"Sorry, Mary," I mumbled as I sat up.

"It's all right," she said. She didn't bother moving, just closed her eyes again.

I grinned down at her. Her brown hair fanned around her head in a tangled web and partially hid her face. She hadn't slept much either as we'd lain in the dark, listening.

"How is your neck?" Winifred asked, pulling my attention from Mary. "May I look?"

She swept my hair aside after I nodded. The skin on my arms prickled at her light, cool touch. She studied the area for a moment then sighed.

"It doesn't look much different," she murmured. "Which, I guess, is to be expected for your kind." She moved my hair back in place.

"What do you mean?" I asked, looking up at her.

"You're a slow healer compared to us. Don't worry, though. There's still the other side of your neck."

"What?"

"I'm teasing," she said with a laugh as she sat on the end of the bed. She reassuringly patted the blanket over my leg when I continued to stare at her. Her comment wasn't very funny.

"I'm not ready to permit anyone within five feet of you. But I would like you to come out and speak with a few of them." I opened my mouth to decline. However, she kept talking. "I also brought a few things for you, which I think you'll like. Coke, chocolate chip cookies, squeeze cheese and crackers, and bread and jam."

I knew it was a bribe but didn't care; I was out of bed before she finished. My mouth watered for all of it.

"Mary, wake up. You're going to want to eat," I said as I moved toward the door. She grumbled but stood and followed.

"I saw you made your own bathroom," Winifred said as we descended the stairs.

"Not a very good one. It's not easy to empty the last three inches from the tub," I said. I didn't even mention the bucket, which we'd relocated.

"Don't worry. It will get better," she said.

I SAVORED the last bite of my chocolate chip cookie. It reminded me of home. Although I missed my family, I still believed in my choice to leave them despite the new, crazy world I'd discovered.

Winifred waited until I'd stuffed myself before she asked if I was ready. The food had mellowed me, and I sat back to study Winifred.

"I've been outside, several times since arriving and have spoken to just about everyone out there. Why do I need to do it again?"

"That was different. That was their chance to impress you. This is their chance to present themselves before you as a viable option. I know you're not ready for anything yet. They just want you to know they will be whenever you are."

I didn't want to go out there, but I'd watched enough over the last few days to know they wouldn't go away. Perhaps once they had their chance to say hello in an official way, they would leave. It was a fragile hope. Still, I sighed and nodded. If they'd been trying to impress me in a positive way, they'd failed. They were too intense and aggressive. I thought of Anton and frowned as I stood. Winifred stood, too, and started toward the door.

"You can talk to all of them in their heads, right?" I said.

"Yes. Individually, like I've been doing with Mary, or all at once like I did when I told them not to bite you."

"Could you tell Anton I'm sorry?"

She stopped walking and turned to study me.

"Do you care for him?" she asked. Her gaze searched mine, and I knew she didn't mean general caring for the welfare of another human being.

"I don't know him well enough to care for him the way you mean, but I do care about him as a person. I care that he was hurt just because he helped me. It was wrong, and I'm sorry it happened."

"It wasn't a random, vengeful attack," she said. "It was a challenge for dominance. The others saw your preference and challenged him to prove his worth. You want the strongest of them, the one who will keep you safe."

"I understand you have your own traditions, and I don't condemn them. Yet, I won't condone them either. Your beliefs are not mine, and I won't follow them. I do not want the strongest man. I don't want any man."

She considered me for a moment. "Letting him know you're sorry will only encourage him to pursue you. If you intend to stay, that is."

Apologizing would ease my conscience, but I understood what she was telling me. Staying here would mean making some hard choices. It would mean compromising my ideals about how people should be treated. At times, I might have to sacrifice what I wanted to appease those around me. And there were other definite pros and cons to consider.

Fighting would occur, and I wouldn't be able to do a thing about it unless I was willing to use my power. Could I enforce my will upon others to keep peace? The hypocrisy of the idea wasn't lost on me. I'd just told Winifred I wouldn't bend to their beliefs, but here I stood, considering bending theirs.

Not only did they fight often, but they thought nothing of stealing and tended not to wear clothes. Could I ignore all of that? I doubted I would. So, if I didn't want to bend their wills or ignore their less than appealing qualities, where did that leave me?

Although I knew they would keep fighting over me, I was willing to bet they would use that same instinct to fight to keep this place hidden. Living here would mean I, too, could remain hidden from the world. I looked at the ceiling, hoping the universe would give me an answer. However, I received silence.

I sighed and said what I felt was true.

"Despite the bites I received as a welcome, I think this is the safest place for me to live." Winifred smiled at my words. "But, I'll leave if that ever changes."

"If this isn't the safest place for you, I'll drive you to a better place," she promised.

Safest wasn't always the best place, but I didn't say more. When she turned and strode to the door, Mary and I followed her.

Due to the recent rain and the many people milling about, the yard had turned into mire. The ground squished up around my shoes as I stepped out behind Winifred. We didn't go far. She had backed a pickup truck to the door. Several piles of pants were stacked in the bed along with a few paper grocery bags.

Activity stopped when we appeared, and the men turned toward us. Winifred hopped into the bed of the truck. Elevated so everyone could see her, she addressed the men.

"Charlene is not like us. Though I'd like to consider her one of our own, we can't treat her the same. When you step forward to introduce yourself, you will keep a minimum distance of three feet."

The men moved restlessly, and several eyed Winifred angrily.

"This isn't to limit your contact or time with her but to ensure her safety. Look at her."

All eyes turned to me. No one looked angry any more. Impatient, yes. Eager, definitely. But not angry.

As they continued to stare, I began to feel like an exhibit at the zoo. I gave Mary a sidelong glance. She wasn't looking at me but at the men around us. I focused on them as well.

"Look at her neck," Winifred said. "She doesn't see those bites as attempted Claims but as hostile, aggressive attacks. These last few days, how has she been around you? Did she seem completely comfortable?"

Heat crept into my cheeks, and a few of them looked concerned.

"She hasn't healed yet. She doesn't know our ways. Would you blame her if she feared you? Is keeping your distance too much for her to ask?"

I hadn't said anything about them keeping their distance. Yes, they made me uncomfortable, but I didn't care for how Winifred painted me. I wasn't a weak coward.

"It's not the distance that worries me," I said, looking at Winifred. "It's the teeth."

A man stepped forward from the rest.

"I am—"

The man behind him reached out and grabbed his arm. The first man growled, turned, and morphed in one fluid motion. Shredded pants flapped around his furred loins as he launched himself at the man who'd grabbed him.

After that, I lost my patience. Didn't they just hear me? I searched for the threads of their wills and grabbed them. The strands slipped away from me. I tried again.

The male bodies piled on one another as they continued to fight.

On my second attempt, I held tighter. The unyielding firmness of their thin wills surprised me as each one slid from my grasp as if oiled. Panic set in. I'd counted on being able to control them. If I couldn't... My breathing grew harsh, and my throat tightened.

A hand clapped over my shoulder and pulled me backward just as a male body flew past me.

"Come on, Charlene," Mary said as she continued to guide me back toward the door. My hands shook as terror set in. They were human enough to have wills, to reason with, but not to control. And they were animal enough to hurt me. Badly.

"Enough," Winifred shouted.

Her will caught my attention, and I stopped moving. Wills weren't something I could actually see as much as I could sense and visualize. But what she did amazed me. She split her will.

The single fiber of her resolve divided into twenty, like a tree with branches. Each branch whipped out toward a fighting man. The threads flew so fast I thought they would pierce the men. Instead, at the last moment, they slowed; and the glowing end of her determination touched the center of each man's forehead. It happened in less than a second. All of the men stopped fighting as if listening to her command. Yet, it wasn't just that. She'd implanted the need to listen.

The branches of her resolve shrank as she pinned the men with her narrowed gaze.

"It's not enough," one of them said. "You've already taken away our right to Claim her. You cannot take away our right to speak with her."

Chills swept through me as several of the men glanced my way. Mary's hand tightened on my shoulders, but neither of us moved closer to the door.

"Of course not," Winifred said. She didn't soothe or try to persuade them with words. Again, her will whipped out and tapped their foreheads, fast and brief.

She wasn't trying to grab their will as I had. She was doing something else. Hope and excitement filled me, and I tried to puzzle out what exactly she had done.

"Have you determined an order?" she asked.

The men started shuffling and shoving. The air filled with growls again. While they moved about, Winifred glanced at me.

"Charlene, you look pale. How many do you think you can meet before you need a break?"

Zero. I wanted to finish backing up so I could slam the door shut. Instead, I studied her. Her promise to protect me hadn't been idle. She really could control them, and I wanted to know how. Learning meant staying right where I was. So, I scanned the yard. There had to be around forty men now.

"All of them, I suppose."

Winifred's brows rose, but she didn't contradict me. The first man in line stepped forward, keeping the required three feet away.

"I'm Stephen," he said.

"Hello."

He didn't look familiar but stood there watching me as if expecting some type of reaction.

"It's nice to meet you," I said when he still didn't move away.

He looked disheartened by my words, gave me a last look, and walked away. The next man stepped forward.

MARY SAT across from me at the table. We were supposed to be eating a late lunch. I could feel her gaze but didn't look up. The half-eaten cookie on my plate and the flat Coke by my elbow no longer interested me.

"If you choose one, it will stop," she whispered.

I snorted and rubbed a hand over my face. Sounds of fighting drifted in through the closed door. They fought for a place in their imaginary line up. It was as if they hadn't heard me say I would meet them all. Their persistent fighting was turning an already long morning of awkward introductions into a longer afternoon.

Winifred seemed to have the same hesitation as I did about using her abilities to control others. She didn't take away freedom of will, either; she only calmed the worst of the aggression when it looked like it might be dangerous to me. And, now that I was inside, there was little Winifred seemed to do about the fighting. Yet, she remained out there, probably trying to prevent outright killing.

"I doubt choosing will make it stop," I said, keeping my voice low. "Winifred seemed surprised that two had bitten me. You made it sound like one bite should have been enough. I doubt another bite will change anything other than my willingness to stay."

Mary sighed and agreed with me. "What are you going to do?"

"I don't know." And I didn't. I'd already asked the universe "what next?" and so far, I'd received no obvious answer. My choices, as I saw them, were limited. Out in the real world, I truly felt I'd end up as a lab rat. Here...I sighed and rubbed my face.

"Can you ask Winifred how many more are left? I don't understand why it matters in what order I meet them."

"Ultimately, it doesn't. Well, it wouldn't for me. If it's right, it's right. But for you, they're worried you'll pick someone before they can all meet you."

I doubted that telling the men I wouldn't pick any of them would help.

"Back when Wini was our age, she said their Introduction practices were less refined. In a few cases, females would ignore instinct and go with a stronger male that had a weaker pull on them."

"Why?"

"Protection. We're a dying race, Charlene. Women need to choose their best option in order to survive. Our people—like my mom—leave for hunts and never come back. Between hunters who try to shoot us, human population growth, shrinking woodlands in which we can roam, and reduced birth rates, we're not going to last very long. Winifred gave up her chance for a Mate to protect our interests. Girls like me are few. Girls like you...well, there have never been any before. You represent a chance for all of us."

"If you see what's causing your race problems, why aren't you changing your ways?"

"What do you mean?"

My mouth was open to say more, but I noticed an unusual silence outside. Mary tilted her head, and I watched her closely. Her expression remained curious as she tried to listen.

"Let's go upstairs," she finally whispered.

I followed her from the room and struggled to keep up as she raced down the hallway and up the stairs. The door to our room was open, and she went straight to the window where we had a clear view of the yard below. Winded, I moved close beside her and tried to quiet my breathing so we could both hear.

All the men in the yard faced the woods. I looked at the distant edge and saw three wolves. The wolves stared at the group of tense men surrounding the truck. Everyone in the yard, even Winifred, who once again stood in the bed of the truck, watched the wolves. No one moved. No one talked. The wolf that stood a half a step in front of the other two looked straight at Winifred.

My stomach dipped as I stared at the lead wolf. He had dark fur, not quite black because of the grey that scattered over his muzzle and underbelly. There was something about him that hypnotically called my attention, and I didn't like it. Who was he? Why did he face down Winifred like that? He felt dangerous to me, most likely due to the snarl pulling back his lip.

I glanced at Mary. With a serious expression, she studied the scene before us.

"What's going on?"

"They're arguing," Mary said after a moment.

I looked back at the yard. No, they were still just standing there.

"Who's arguing?"

"Winifred and those others."

"About what?" My voice had slipped from its whisper—I was feeling a little left out and a little frustrated after the long morning I'd suffered. One of the wolves glanced our way. I quickly moved away from the window. I didn't need any more attention than what I'd already received.

I watched Mary's eyes widen, and a blush crept into her cheeks.

"They're moving," she whispered. "They're getting pants

from the truck." Her eyes tracked their progress, and her expression grew soft and wistful.

"He's gorgeous," she breathed after a moment, and I knew that they'd changed from wolves to men. I fought not to blush and lost the battle. Mary didn't notice, though. Her eyes remained riveted on an unknown person. I totally wanted to look.

"Are they dressed yet?"

She grinned at me and nodded. I peeked around the edge of the window. The mood in the yard had changed. Those who'd previously crowded around the truck now stood well back, giving the newcomers plenty of room.

The three stood near the end of the truck. The angle of the view the window afforded wasn't good for seeing much more than the top backs of their heads. But from what I could see, if not for their obvious exclusion, the new men fit in with the rest. Their hair was slightly longer and unkempt, they wore no shirts or shoes, and their pants were ill fitting.

Two of them were young, though. I guessed just a few years older than Mary and me.

One of them stood out. Perhaps it was because Winifred was glowering at him as he stood before her with his arms crossed. Or maybe it was the way the muscles of his shoulders bunched in agitation. Or better yet, the smooth skin of his corded back. My blush reignited as I stared.

My stomach spun and dipped again at the sight of him shirtless.

His muffled voice reached us through the glass.

"Winifred," he said with a stiff nod. "We've heard some rumors that there's a human here and that you're exposing our kind to her." His angry tone carried his dislike of the idea.

My instinct to be wary of him had been right. I narrowed my eyes at his back.

"That's correct," she said.

"How is allowing a human here in the best interest of the packs? Of our people? The last humans who were here shot four females and a cub. She needs to leave. Now."

"I disagree," Winifred said calmly. "You know nothing of her. She's not like other humans."

"I don't care," he said. "For the safety of our kind, there can be no exceptions."

"For the safety of our kind, we need to adapt. You need to listen to reason."

She looked away from him and addressed the listening men.

"There can be no life without purpose and no purpose without reason. We struggle to survive because, as a species, we've lost our purpose. The world is changing, and we need to change with it. We need to find our reason. It is the only way to continue our existence. Even nature is telling us it's time to change. Charlene is human and a potential Mate. Turn her away, and you might be turning away your future. Think about it."

She turned to the young man in front again.

"Some leaders are born. Some rise out of necessity and are refined by circumstance. The best leader is one who listens openly and considers all possibilities."

Winifred looked up at the window, and I ducked away again. Not Mary, though. She stayed centered within the frame. A slow smile curled her lips.

"He's looking at me. I have to go meet him."

She turned away from the window and started toward the door. I quickly moved to follow.

"He was pretty handsome," I agreed, trying to keep up with her. "But enough to let him bite me? No thanks."

Her steps slowed, and she gave me a troubled look.

"I guess I wasn't thinking of that."

How could she not?

"What were you thinking about?"

She sighed and gave a slight smile. "I don't know...just him."

"You don't even know his name."

"No, but that doesn't matter."

"Maybe it should. I think that's what Winifred was trying to say. You need to think more. All of you. Don't just let instinct rule you. You're intelligent people capable of reasoning. What if he's grumpy most mornings or snores at night? What if he wants twenty kids, but you only want two? You need to think about what comes after the bite. Plan ahead."

Her frown grew, and her steps slowed further. We reached the main room while doing a slow shuffle.

"You're right. But I still need to meet him, to talk to him. If he tries..." She glanced at the door. She didn't have Winifred's promise like I did.

"I'll roll up a newspaper and smack him on the nose for you."

She grinned at me. A knock at the door made us both jump. The door opened a moment later. Winifred strode in, her irritation still very evident.

"Mary, there is someone out there who'd like to meet you."

Mary glanced at the floor for a moment, and Winifred gave a long-suffering sigh.

"You know I can't promise that, Mary. Charlene is unique. If

I tried preventing him from Claiming you, the tenuous trust they have in me would be lost."

I knew what Mary had silently asked and felt sorry for her.

"Can I meet him first?" I asked. Both of them looked at me in surprise. If Winifred couldn't ask him to wait, I was willing to try.

"That would be up to Mary," Winifred said slowly.

"It's okay with me," Mary said.

"I'd prefer he come in here, though," I said, thinking of all the men who still waited for me outside. "Alone."

Winifred gave me a long look then nodded. As soon as she left, I waved Mary back toward the bathroom door. It placed me between whomever would step through the door and her.

It only took a moment for the outer door to open again. A tall man, who looked in his late teens, walked in. He wasn't the lead man I'd noticed from the window but still one of the three. His eyes skimmed over me as he searched the room for Mary. His gaze warmed when it landed on her.

I took a step to the side to block his view and smiled at him. "Hi. I'm Charlene."

He stalked toward us, sparing me a brief glance before his eyes drifted back to Mary. I quickly stepped into his path. He didn't seem to notice and almost barreled over me. I slapped both hands on his very bare chest and gave him a slight push.

"Stop for a moment, please," I said. His skin heated my hands, and I hoped Mary wouldn't think me too forward with him.

He stopped moving, tore his gaze from Mary, and gave me a puzzled glance. I nervously removed my hands.

"Here's the thing; she saw my neck and is worried."

He tilted his head and studied me, not just my neck but all of me.

"So you're the human," he said with a slight smile. "Winifred was right." He leaned in and sniffed me. "You are different."

Before I could become nervous or uncomfortable, Mary cleared her throat behind us. The man straightened away from me and smiled at her.

"She's nowhere near as interesting as you are," he said to her.

"So, what's your name?" I said, trying to reclaim his attention. He didn't look away from Mary as he answered.

"Gregory." He had a pleasant, easygoing voice.

"Gregory, this is Mary," I said, turning slightly to indicate her. "She's hoping you two could talk first."

"I'm not ready to be Claimed," she said softly.

His brows rose. He considered her for a moment and scratched his jaw. He didn't seem upset when he finally spoke.

"Why not?"

She looked around the room for a moment as if trying to decide what to say to him. Her gaze briefly met mine before it settled back on him.

"I *am* nervous about the bite, but I really just want to stay here with Charlene for a while."

He nodded slowly and looked around the room. His stare lingered on the table and the cookware on the fireplace mantel. Then he looked at me. "You're making changes."

I nodded warily. Their kind didn't seem too keen on change based on Winifred's speech.

"He's going to want to meet you," he said.

For some reason his words made my stomach clench, and not in a good way.

"Could I speak with Mary alone for a minute?" he asked.

I glanced at Mary. She gave me a small smile and nodded.

Outside, the yard was much too quiet.

"I'll just go upstairs, then," I said, and with a last look at both of them, I headed for the double doors.

CHAPTER SIX

In the yard below, the men, who'd only minutes ago fought each other, now gathered in small groups. Most cast subtle glances at the newcomers Winifred had rejoined near the front of the truck. She was speaking to the man who made my stomach flip, but I couldn't hear anything she said.

The man stood with crossed arms as he listened to Winifred. I hoped they weren't still discussing me. My presence didn't warrant that much debate. If they wanted me to leave, I'd move on as simple as that. Well, not that simple. I still didn't know where to go. But, this place was only ideal if they wanted me here, and except for Mary, I really wouldn't mind leaving.

A tap on the bedroom door distracted me.

"Charlene?" Mary said, peeking in.

"How did it go?" I asked, turning away from the window. She opened the door further, and I saw Gregory standing behind her. I glanced at her neck. It was unblemished.

"Gregory wants me to go outside with him to speak to Winifred. I didn't want to leave you in here alone. Will you come?"

"Of course," I said. I didn't really want to be inside alone, either.

I stepped into the hallway, and Gregory nodded in greeting. He stood aside so Mary and I could precede him down the stairs. Mary remained quiet as we made our way through the main room to the outer door. There, she hesitated and glanced back at Gregory.

His gaze met hers, and he gave her a reassuring smile.

"I'll go first," he said.

He pulled open the door and stepped outside. Most of the men stood with their backs to the door so Gregory had to nudge his way through. When those he nudged turned and saw me standing behind him, they made room.

"If she's so important," a raised male voice said, "take her back with you and keep our sanctuary safe."

The men around me growled in response. Whoever was speaking wasn't making friends. I wondered if the rest would challenge the speaker as they had Anton.

"As you can hear, they don't want her to leave," Winifred said.

Gregory took a few more steps forward, with Mary and me closely behind him, then stopped. The men quieted as I passed. Gregory reached back to offer a hand to Mary. She shyly wrapped her hand in his and stepped forward, leaving me alone in Gregory's shadow.

"I acknowledge Gregory as my Mate," Mary said.

She stood facing Winifred. At least, I thought she did. I wasn't ready to peer around Gregory to find out. Instead, I glanced at the men around me. A few gave me small smiles. Given the current conversation about Mates, a topic I wanted nothing to do with, I nervously returned my gaze to Gregory's bare back.

"But I've asked him to wait to Claim me," Mary continued.

"And I agreed for as long as Charlene is here," Gregory said.

He stepped aside, exposing me. Automatically, my gaze lifted to the leader, the one who so obviously didn't want me to be here. The man's sullen expression changed to one of disbelief. His arms fell loosely to his sides as his gaze swept from my dirty shoes to the top of my blonde head. As he studied me, I studied him.

His eyes were a deep blue, blanketed by thick brows that matched his dark brown hair. His nose was strong and proud with a slight bump on the bridge. A hint of a shadow covered his jaw and upper lip. He was dangerously handsome; and when I found my attention settling on his lips, I averted my gaze and glanced at his other friend. The one beside him grinned widely and winked a startling light grey eye at me. I blushed and glanced away.

I wished I'd stayed inside. My heart picked up its beat.

Mary withdrew her hand from Gregory's and moved to hold mine. The new men continued to watch me, and a few of the ones behind me grew restless. No doubt, they didn't like me receiving additional attention.

"If it's all right, we'd like to go back inside," Mary said.

Winifred nodded, her watchful gaze never leaving the dark haired man. I didn't think he was the one she needed to worry about, though. Under the scrutiny of over forty pairs of eyes, I walked the path to the door.

Mary closed the door behind us, spun, and briefly hugged me.

"I didn't think he'd say yes. And I half-expected Wini to object. I'm so glad I get to stay with you."

And I was, too. Now that I knew I couldn't control any of the men out there, the idea of staying without someone who didn't want to bite me, bothered me. I walked to the table and sat down. My cookie and Coke still waited for me.

Mary tilted her head as she studied me, and I knew she was speaking with Winifred.

"Wini wants to know how you're doing."

Every time I thought I was okay with things, something new came my way. If I were honest with myself, I was tired of the men out there and more afraid now than I was before I walked out the door this morning. I couldn't control their wills; and while Winifred could, she wouldn't use her control to force them to leave me alone. Doing so would be an abuse of power, and I understood too well how dangerous that could be. Yet, if I could figure out how Winifred split her will and try to duplicate it, I wouldn't feel so powerless here...if I stayed.

Though a small group wanted me to leave, I didn't think the majority would allow that. I wondered if that meant I was stuck here whether I wanted to be or not.

But I couldn't say all of that to Mary. So I settled for part of the truth.

"I'm tired. And on edge. Would it be possible to put off the rest of the meetings until tomorrow?"

Mary nodded.

"She's telling them, and then she's going to bring in the rest of the groceries and supplies."

Other than waking us, she'd stayed outside since she had gotten here, trying to keep the men in line. She probably wanted a break, too.

There was a brief tap on the door; then, Winifred walked in followed by Gregory and the broody dark haired one. My stomach did an odd somersault again, and I couldn't help the quick glance at his very bare chest. I struggled to keep my expression neutral though I was annoyed with myself.

"These are the other groceries I brought up," Winifred said, motioning to the bags the men carried. "Where should they set them?"

"By the pump, please," I said quietly when Mary said nothing. The table would have made more sense, but I was sitting at the table and didn't want the men that close. I tried to keep my focus on my half-eaten cookie but couldn't, so I discreetly watched them walk to the pump and set the bags down.

Outside the door, another fight started. I looked up at Winifred. Her shoulders lifted and fell in a silent sigh. Weariness radiated from her, and I didn't think it was because of actual exhaustion. I wondered if she wished she was back teaching her kids.

"I will be right back. Mary, perhaps you could make me something for dinner?" Winifred asked as she walked toward the door.

"Sure, Wini," Mary said. But Mary wasn't looking at Winifred. She was staring at Gregory. Gregory was returning her regard with a confident grin.

"I can help you," he said.

Mary nodded shyly, oblivious to me and the other man in the room.

"Since you have help, I think I'll go lie down for a bit," I said, standing.

Mary tore her gaze from Gregory and eyed me with concern. "Don't you want to see what Wini brought?"

I glanced at the bags near the pump. They rested at the feet of the one who didn't like me. He stood there with his arms folded across his chest, watching me with an undecipherable expression.

"There's no hurry," I said. I'd had my cookies and Coke and paid the price. I wasn't ready to pay anything more for whatever treats Winifred had brought.

I turned and left.

When I opened the door to my room, I sighed. The bed, marooned in the center of the room, called to me like the oasis it was. I sat on top of the quilt, kicked off my shoes, and pulled the spare blanket over my shoulders as I lay down.

After so little sleep the night before, it didn't take me long to drift off, away from the troubles of this place.

"ARE YOU HUNGRY?"

Mary's voice penetrated the fog still clouding my mind, and I blinked awake.

"What?" It was less of a word and more of a yawn. I lifted myself up on an elbow and tried to focus on her.

Squatted down beside the bed, she grinned at me.

"You must have been very tired. You have sleep lines on your face."

"It's not easy to get a good night's sleep here." I sat up, rubbed a hand over my face, and glanced at the window. Sunset painted the frame. Since there were no clocks, I didn't ask what time it was. However, based on the sky, I guessed that I'd slept for several hours.

"Did I miss dinner?"

"No, I saved you some. Everyone's outside again."

"Did Winifred get anything to eat?" I asked as I threw back the blanket and stood with a stretch.

"She did. And she thanks you for your concern." Mary moved with me as I went to put on my shoes.

"How did it go after I left?"

"The fighting quieted down once they knew you weren't coming back out."

"I meant with Gregory," I said with a laugh. I didn't care much about the rest, though I was grateful they'd let me sleep.

Mary blushed a pretty shade of pink. "He seems sweet."

"Oh? How so?" I asked as we left the room. Shadows obscured the corridor. I kept one hand on the wall and wished I'd grabbed Anton's candle.

"Careful, stairs ahead," Mary said.

I immediately slowed. Once I was on the first step, I counted until I stepped onto the lower level. From there, it was easy to set my hand against the wall and find my way to the main room. A fire burned low in the fireplace, and a lantern lit the table.

"A lantern," I said with excitement. "That's perfect."

"It was in the bags of supplies. Wini thought we might need it."

I sat at the table to inspect it. I recalled my grandmother having a hurricane lamp in her living room. This lantern was similar in that it had a wick, but the glass globe completely protected the flames. The handle and hood made it safe to hang from a hook and not burn down the building.

Mary set a plate before me and sat across from me.

"Thank you." My stomach growled when I saw a quarter of some type of fowl, a baked potato, and peas. I picked up my fork.

"You never answered," I said before I took my first bite. "How is he sweet?"

"He doesn't know how to cook. But he cleaned the pheasant while I opened the can of peas and washed the potatoes. We didn't talk. We worked together without needing to."

I stopped chewing and studied her hopelessly infatuated expression. I didn't understand their race. There was no courtship or time to get to know each other from what Mary said. The man decided whom he wanted, then bit her. Sure, she might fight back or decide to let someone else bite her, but that decision was based on what? Strength? We weren't living in the prehistoric age where only the strongest survive. The world had changed. Why didn't they see that? Winifred did. But she was trying to convince the men to change. In my opinion, she needed to start with the women.

I swallowed, took a sip of my Coke, and snapped my fingers before Mary's eyes to get her attention.

"He didn't do anything more for you than he would have done for himself. I'm not saying he isn't sweet. I'm saying you're labeling him sweet for doing ordinary things. Give him a real reason to be sweet."

"What do you mean?"

"Ask him to do something for you that your men normally wouldn't do."

She frowned and studied the table. I knew she was trying to think of something so I went back to eating.

"What would you ask for?" Mary asked after several minutes of silence.

I grinned at her. "You've slept in my bed. Which do you like better, floor or bed?"

She laughed.

"Bed."

She stood and walked to the door. Gregory must have been close because he filled the frame within seconds. She motioned him in. I turned back toward my plate and pretended I couldn't hear them.

"Hi, Gregory," she said softly.

"You want a bed," he said flatly.

I cringed. Just how well could they hear?

"Yep. I do. Charlene's bed is clean and comfortable, but too small for the two of us. I won't take hers. She needs it more than I do. But it sure is nice."

There were several long moments of silence. I kept eating and stifled the urge to turn around.

"Fine," he said finally. The door opened and closed again soon after.

Mary came back to the table and sat down with a grin. She didn't seem at all put off by his less than accommodating attitude.

Before she could say anything, there was another knock on the door. She popped up again to answer it.

"Your father and Gregory are waiting for you outside."

I turned at the sound of the voice. Him again. The dark haired leader who made my stomach go crazy. He watched me, not Mary.

"Waiting? For what?"

"You said you wanted a bed. Gregory's not foolish enough

to pick one without you along. He knows how this game is played."

Did his eyes just narrow slightly?

"Game?" I said, since he seemed to be talking to me.

"She won't like the one he brings back, right?" he said with a hint of anger.

I shook my head slowly, unable to believe he was so clueless. Trying to do something nice for a girl was a game? I turned away. Maybe she wouldn't like the one Gregory brought back, but that would be because of the quality of the item. After all, I had sent back the mattress that appeared gnawed on. Wait, did those men think I was playing games with them because I rejected some of what they'd brought? I mentally sighed at the thought.

"Charlene? Do you mind if I go?" Mary asked.

"Why are you asking her? Is she your leader?" he asked.

I couldn't help it. I turned around to stare at him. Even Mary's mouth hung open for a moment.

"I'm asking because Wini wanted to be sure she's okay staying here alone." Mary sounded like she was ready to smack him.

"She won't be alone. I'll stay with her."

Mary and I shared a look. Alone would be better. But I didn't say that.

"I'll be fine." At least, I hoped I would be. Winifred was right outside the door; and, apparently, they could hear everything. "Thanks for your concern, Mary. And have fun."

She gave me a last apologetic glance then left. The guy closed the door, and I turned back to my plate. When he suddenly spoke from behind me, I barely refrained from jumping.

"I'm Thomas."

Good for you. Now, buzz off. "Hello," I said, instead.

I took a bite of potato. A full mouth couldn't speak rude things. Though my parents had taught me to respect everyone, I was having a hard time with him. His complete and obvious resolve to be rid of me probably had something to do with it.

He sat across from me and watched me eat. My stomach did a weird flip again, which I ignored. I kept my eyes on my plate and not his naked chest.

Although he was pale, he wasn't sickly. I couldn't recall seeing many men without their shirts, but he seemed unusually muscled. Several defined cords decorated his shoulders and his crossed forearms. I totally wanted to stare.

Several minutes of silence passed. When I finished eating, I threw the slightly charred potato skin in the flames along with the bones then went to the sink to wash.

He didn't move, but I felt his eyes on me. I pumped enough water into the tin washbowl to wash my hands and face and plate. When I set the plate aside to dry, he stood.

"Winifred said you've made some changes. Show me."

I turned and studied him. He looked mildly annoyed, and I couldn't decide if his tone was a command or a question.

He watched me in return, his arms once again crossing his chest. He didn't seem like he would accept a polite refusal. Hoping that he'd leave once he got what he wanted, I agreed.

"Of course," I said, moving away from the pump.

I snagged the lantern from the table and led him out of the main room and toward the first of the small rooms that lined that hall. I pushed open the door and stepped aside so he could see in. He stopped beside me but did not enter. I studied the space as I spoke.

"We've gone through the windows, collected the whole panes of glass to create several solid windows, and removed broken glass and debris from the rooms. I plan to board up the windows still missing glass." I turned to see what he thought and found him watching me. "If I stay," I added.

His face betrayed nothing regarding how he felt about me staying.

"Which rooms have the whole windows?" he asked.

"The main room and several on the second floor. It will be easier to board up windows on the main floor."

"Show me."

We stood facing each other; he impatiently waited for me to lead, and I hesitated.

Take him upstairs? I brought my fingers up to my collarbone, as close to touching the bites as I dared, to remind myself I wasn't with people who knew how to behave politely. Going upstairs with him didn't feel like a good idea.

"Have you lost your way already?" he said with a smirk.

Irritation melted my budding worry. What an annoying man. I turned around and led him up the closest flight of stairs. Along the way, I started motioning to the rooms Mary and I had finished. Those doors stood open. Doors without windows remained closed. He barely spared each a glance.

When I stopped at the last one, my room, he looked down at me. Unlike the other repaired rooms, the door was closed. He waited expectantly.

"Does your room have a repaired window?"

"Yes." I didn't move to open the door, though. I could just imagine how he'd react to a bed and dresser.

"Show me."

I briefly narrowed my eyes at him, reached out, and opened

the room I shared with Mary. Was he just looking for signs I'd settled in so he could complain? I stepped inside. He followed me, moving further into the room. He took a deep breath as he studied everything. He looked at the bed longest.

His expression changed slightly. Some of the arrogance left.

"Are you comfortable at night?" he asked quietly. He turned toward me, letting his arms once again fall loosely to his sides.

I didn't like the sudden change.

CHAPTER SEVEN

THOMAS' GAZE HELD MINE IN THE LAMPLIGHT, AND I REALIZED THE purpose behind this tour and why he still stood there. He didn't care about the bed or the dresser or the changes I'd made.

"You want to bite me, too, don't you?"

He didn't flinch in guilt or look away as a spark of need lit in his eyes.

"Yes."

His softly spoken word made me shiver.

"Biting hurts, you know. A lot. So, I'll pass." I turned and started to walk away from him.

"I saw you, and I couldn't breathe." His quiet admission slowed my steps. "The world and all of the responsibilities it's given me fell away. There was only you, and I wanted nothing else."

I stopped walking but didn't turn. "And now?"

"Now..."

I looked over my shoulder and caught him running a hand through his hair. His gaze was on the floor, and he frowned.

"Responsibilities never go away. My people depend on me. I want you. But I can't walk away from my responsibilities to chase you."

"Chase me? I don't want to be chased." I'd been chased twice already and had hated it.

"Then give me your permission to Claim you."

I snorted. He'd almost been sweet for a minute there. But I doubted any of his kind really knew what it meant to be sweet. It just didn't seem to be in their nature. They were too wild, too disconnected with their human sides.

"You don't know the first thing about what it takes to be human," I said.

"What does that have to do with Claiming you?"

"I'm human," I said in exasperation. "Just what are you going to do with me when you Claim me?" I ignored the glint that flared in his eyes and pressed my point. "Do you think I'd survive a winter in these woods? Are you ready to live in this place permanently? How will you feed me? I've noticed your kind doesn't seem to think vegetables are a requirement in their daily menu. For me, they are. I can get sick from lack of the right foods, from exposure, from...well, a lot. And I don't heal like you." I tilted my head so he could see the bite marks still there.

"You need to learn what it means to be human before you can care for one." I didn't just mean physically, either.

He stood there for several breaths just watching me, frustration plain on his face. When he spoke, there was a hint of it in his voice, too.

"While you're in here hiding, they're out there fighting. This needs to end. I know you're the right one." He eyed me for a moment as if he expected some reaction to that statement. I gave none, and he let out a half-growl. "With your permission, we could end this chaos."

I didn't like the way he said permission, as if he thought it completely unreasonable that I had a say in my own future.

"What if you bite me, and it doesn't work again?" I said.

"It will work."

"I understand you're certain, but I'm not. What if it doesn't work?"

"I'm certain enough for both of us. I smell you, and I know."

I snorted again. I could see it becoming a habit with him around.

"The other two that bit me thought they knew, too. So, since you're not inclined to think ahead and plan for more than one possibility, allow me. If you bite me and it doesn't work, those men out there will become more aggressive. They won't content themselves with just meeting me because they'll know I've given my permission to someone, and each one will want his chance at a little nip. The fighting will escalate. And—here's the important part—I'll have another wound to try to keep clean.

"My answer remains a very firm no. If you don't like it, tell me to leave. I'm not sure this is the right place for me, anyway."

A collective howl rose outside my window. I realized too late that I'd grown a bit loud.

Thomas studied me, his expression once again closed. Then, he turned and left.

I sat on the bed. I wasn't ready to return to the main room, just in case he hadn't actually left. So I stared at the dresser that now served as shelves for the few clothes Mary and I owned. As I stared at the items, I realized that without a source of heat I would freeze in this bedroom when winter arrived. I'd need to move my bed back into the main room near the fire. Picturing the big and drafty room, I knew I'd need better clothes regardless. How many weeks did I have left before the weather started to turn cold?

When I estimated enough time had passed, I went back downstairs. The main room was empty and the fire almost out. I set the lantern on the table, put another piece of wood on the small flames, and moved to inspect the paper bags.

Winifred was smart about the supplies. There were cans of vegetables, fruit, and tuna fish, and bags of pasta, rice, and dried beans. Enough for a variety of meals. Flat sheets filled the last bag along with three spools of thread and four needles.

"I scoured rummage sales," Winifred said, making me jump.

I turned and saw her closing the door.

"Mary told me you were fixing the windows. I thought you might want curtains. Especially, for this one."

"Thank you." I fingered the fabric of the top sheet. It was plain white, well used and soft. "I might be able to find other ways to use these, too." Like for more bandages. I might need them soon.

"I thought you might," she said, and for a moment, it seemed as if she was answering my last thought. "How are you doing?"

"Just fine," I said as she walked toward me. "This won't stop, will it?"

She shook her head.

"I never meant to cause any of you trouble. I was just looking for a place to sleep."

She patted my hand. "Despite how it looks, we are glad you found us."

"We?" I laughed. "I don't think everyone's happy."

"Don't worry. Those who aren't will come around." She sat

across from me and picked up a cookie from the plate. Only six remained. But I still had some squeeze cheese and bread and jam left. I was pretty sure Mary and Gregory had sampled everything while I napped.

"When are you leaving?"

"Tomorrow night. But I'll return Friday evening again."

That meant today was Saturday since she'd arrived late last night. The idea of spending another tense week here bothered me. I frowned and reached for another cookie.

"Don't give up on us," she said, watching me. "We're rough around the edges, but we can learn."

I nodded, took a bite, and sighed. Even if I wanted to, I couldn't give up on them. Those men wouldn't let me leave, and I had nowhere else to go. We sat together in silence. Once I finished the cookie, I quietly excused myself and went to bed.

In my room, I listened to the muffled night sounds until my lids grew heavy.

As soon as I opened my eyes, I knew something was different. I was staring at a wall—a close up view. Since my bed had been in the middle of the room, the view didn't make sense.

I lifted my head and looked around. My bed was now against the right interior wall. Against the other wall, Mary lay in a bed similar to mine. She was awake and grinning at me.

"I don't have your morals about stealing," she said as I eyed the clean sheets and nice blanket. "And if you would have seen what was crawling around in that junkyard, you wouldn't either."

Sitting up, I didn't say anything about the stealing. I was

happy she had a bed, but I wondered who was now sleeping on the floor because of it. Come to think of it, how could they steal a bed at night? I hoped it hadn't been in use at the time.

"While you were gone, I looked through the extra bags Winifred brought. We can make curtains," I said.

Mary shrugged, and I guessed having curtains made little difference to her.

"Or maybe a plain sundress for each of us."

"That might be nice," she said with a small smile.

"How was your time with Gregory?" I asked.

She sighed and closed her eyes for a moment. "He was angry at first. Like Thomas said, Gregory thought I was playing a game with him. But when he saw what was in the junkyard, he was the one that suggested going somewhere else." She opened her eyes and looked at me. "He really is sweet."

"Good. It gives me hope that it's possible for others to be sweet."

She sat up with a stretch. "Winifred says they're already lining up. She's wondering if you're up for meeting some more today." Mary got out of her bed and began to remake it neatly.

I wanted to groan and hide under my covers at the thought of going through yesterday all over again. But I didn't. The sooner I met them, officially, the sooner they might leave me alone.

"Sure," I said, sitting up. "I just need a few minutes and something to eat."

She nodded. "I'll see if anything is cooking. Meet you downstairs."

She left me in the room; and though I was tempted to take my time, I slipped from the bed. Like Mary, I neatly remade it. Then, I stripped from the clothes I'd slept in. They weren't pajamas, but it kept the bed clean if I slept in a clean set of clothes. I set them on the top shelf in the dresser and looked at what was left. One clean pair of pants. I'd need to do some laundry or start rewearing things from the small pile of dirty clothes beside the dresser.

I reached for the pants and tugged them on. As I did up the button, my door creaked open. I turned, expecting to see Mary.

A man stood in the doorway. He was shaggy, a little dirty, unfamiliar, and staring at me as I stood there in my bra. My eyes bugged, and I quickly folded my arms across my chest. I opened my mouth to tell him to leave but didn't get anything out.

He moved in a blur, knocking me backward. My breath whooshed out of me as I landed on my bed. He fell with me, pinning my crossed arms between us.

Before I could register what was happening, he reached up, fisted his hand in my hair, and pulled my head to the side. The move exposed my neck. Fear gripped me. A desperate cry ripped from me, and I bucked under him. He darted forward, his mouth open.

"No!" I wailed as his teeth pierced me. Distantly, I wondered what had happened to Winifred's promise.

He bit hard. It was as if he thought his Claim would have a better chance of sticking the deeper his teeth sank. I couldn't breathe. I couldn't move. I did the only thing I had left.

Instead of trying to grab his will, *my* will surged from me, a thick unyielding cane comprised of a single thought: get off me. I hit him right between the eyes with it. To my shock and pain, he flew backward, his teeth ripping from my skin. I gasped and whimpered as he hit the dresser with a crash.

My shaking hand automatically went to my neck, trying to

ease the pain there. I was making weird noises that I couldn't seem to stop. The man stirred.

My door crashed open, and Winifred flew in. Her eyes widened at the sight of me on the bed.

She didn't pause to address the man but came to me and gently lifted my hand. I focused on her, desperate for someone to help make the pain stop.

"Mary, your sheets," she said.

There was a slight rustle, and Mary appeared at Winifred's shoulder with the sheet from her bed. Winifred grabbed it and pressed the material against my neck. Something crunched sickeningly.

God, he broke me. I struggled to think past the pain.

It took a moment to realize the sound hadn't come from me. My eyes wandered a bit, and I saw Thomas, his face twisted in anger. He had a hand wrapped around the throat of the man who'd bitten me. He opened his grasp and dropped him. The man's head lolled on his shoulders, his eyes open and vacant.

"Thomas, we need to get her to a hospital," Winifred said.

I shifted my attention back to her worried face. She didn't meet my eyes but focused on the sheet she held to my neck. That scared me.

Thomas moved closer and stared down at me.

"They will ask questions," he said softly.

"I know."

They shared a look. I sobbed a little. They were going to let me die to keep their secret. I wanted to tell them they didn't need to worry, but I couldn't talk. My throat didn't want to work.

"I'll carry her," he said. Surprise and relief made me sob again.

Winifred nodded.

"Mary, hold the cloth. Keep moderate pressure on it. I'll get the truck."

"Truck?" Mary said, bending to take over.

"We can't run with her. It would hurt her more. The truck is the best option we have."

Thomas picked me up, holding me gently. Mary walked with him, keeping pressure on my neck.

"Stay with me, Charlene," he whispered as we moved.

If they would just stop biting me...

VOICES PULLED me from the dark place. My neck hurt so much my eyes watered; the sensation of those tears trickling down my cheeks woke me further. I was lying flat but felt like I was moving.

"...animal attack..."

"...form of ID..."

The conversation danced around me, and I couldn't focus fully enough to understand it.

"Help me," I rasped.

A hand gently touched my shoulder.

"We're going to fix you up, honey," a strange voice said. "Can you open your eyes?"

I tried and couldn't quite manage. Was I dying? I thought of my mom and her request to call her when I could. Would she have to live the rest of her life never knowing what became of me?

"Help me." Tears and my torn throat made it hard to speak.

"We are, honey. Can you tell us your name?"

The moving stopped. I heard counting, a quick moment where I felt like I was floating, then I settled on a solid surface again. I didn't know what was happening, and it terrified me.

Behind my eyelids, I focused and found three strands of will near me. I gently reached out and touched each one. I wasn't imposing my will, rather feeling their wills. One of the wills was a doctor. He remained focused on examining me. He wanted to stop the bleeding. The two nurses were there to help the doctor and comfort me.

Someone put something cool on my neck. It stung and tears started streaming in earnest.

"This will hurt for just a moment, and then you shouldn't feel a thing," the doctor said.

I breathed through the pain until it, and the stinging, eventually faded. A relieved sigh escaped me.

"All right. I need you to hold still for a bit."

I held still and drifted.

In that odd place between sleep and awake, I was only vaguely aware of the next few hours. After the doctor stitched me up, they brought me to another room. I wasn't sure why and was a bit too tired to care.

They gave me a pill to swallow, and it was a hard task to complete. Though my throat didn't hurt, it didn't quite want to work the way I thought it should. After I sputtered and choked a bit, the pill went down, and the nurse let me be.

I dozed awhile, happy with the quiet. Then the doctor was back with a man in a uniform. What were police called in Canada? I liked his hat and smiled at him.

"Miss. Can you tell me your name?"

My name. I almost answered but then remembered why I couldn't. Penny. I had to stay hidden. I touched his will. Suspicion, worry, and impatience lay there. I soothed them away and replaced them. The girl looks tired. Poor thing. She should be resting, not trying to speak.

I barely shook my head to answer his spoken question. The man sighed and patted my hand.

"I understand. Your throat must hurt. I'll try back later."

I nodded ever so slightly and watched him turn to leave.

"Are you able to speak, miss?" the doctor asked, eyeing me with concern. "The bites weren't too deep, and missed your—"

"I can speak," I said slowly. "But everything is spinning."

He nodded. "You lost quite a bit of blood. Nothing that should require a transfusion, but your blood pressure is low, and we're keeping an eye on it. I made the stitches as small as possible. Between that and your age, the scars will hopefully fade into nothing with time."

I didn't care about scars. "Can I leave?"

"We'd like to see your blood pressure improve before we send you home."

He left, and I dozed again. When the nurse came to check on me, I woke and asked for another drink. She returned with a full cup of water then took my blood pressure.

"Your blood pressure is holding steady. I'll let the doctor know you're awake again. I'm sure there are a few people who need to speak with you if you're up for it."

Her will was too cloudy to read. So I grabbed it. "Tell me what you mean."

"Administration will want to talk to you. We'll need your

social insurance number to submit your stay for reimbursement. And the Mountie is waiting."

I knew what the Mountie wanted. I also knew I couldn't afford to stay any longer.

"I need a few things so I can leave," I said. "Medicine if this becomes infected, bandages, creams, salves, or whatever else you think might help. Please get everything and bring it back here as fast as you can." I could feel her resistance as she nodded slowly. "After you give them to me, you will forget me entirely. If anyone questions why you can't remember, you work a lot and need a break."

I held firm until she gave in.

WITH A SMALL PAPER bag filled with supplies, I slowly made my way out of the room I'd occupied. Lightheaded, I had to keep a hand on the wall so it didn't feel like the room was spinning so much. Any staff member who moved to question me, I turned away. The effort and the constant struggle of wills exhausted me more than walking.

When I made it down the hallway, I came to a set of double doors and peered through the small windows into the waiting area. Winifred and Mary tensely sat on the couches near the entrance. Across the room, the Mountie was having a friendly chat with one of the staff. I lightly touched everyone's wills to gauge the situation.

The Mountie wanted to speak with me again. A woman behind the reception desk wanted to question Winifred about who I was. I delved deeper and understood that Winifred had claimed to find me on the road and had given everyone a false name. I influenced the woman to forget Winifred and Mary's association with me and did the same with the Mountie. No one else in the room really cared about us.

Winifred spotted me and stood as I pushed open the door. My knees wobbled unsteadily with each step, and I felt cold and dizzy. I kept my focus on the exit and the people around us. Winifred hovered beside me. Mary wrapped her arm through mine and let me lean on her. It helped. But I hoped they would catch me and run if I passed out.

No one paid us any attention as we crossed the room. They wouldn't remember us leaving.

Outside, the sun hung low in the sky. I'd lost another day to another bite. I was as mad as I was annoyed.

Mary led me to the truck, and I carefully climbed in. The numbing medicine the doctor had put on my neck was starting to wear off, or maybe it was the pill the nurse had me swallow. Either way, the pain crept in; and the ride back home was rough.

Home. What a funny word with so many meanings. Home wasn't a place I liked. It wasn't where the people who loved me lived. Home was the place I slept. Nothing more. Should I really call it home then? What would I call it if not home? It was so much closer to a prison with wardens who liked to bite me.

My thoughts drifted as the truck bumped its way along the road. Mary had her arm around me, and I rested my head against her shoulder to help against the jarring.

The driveway to the buildings was the worst, even with Winifred going so slow.

"Stop," I finally said. "I need to walk." If I stayed in the truck, I would throw up.

Winifred eased the truck to a stop. Mary and I got out. The

waist high grass was no longer untouched. Two paths, from Winifred's visits, marked the way. I thought it might make walking easier, but my feet tangled in the matted grass and I tripped often.

"I can carry you," Mary said as she walked along beside me. I didn't doubt she could.

"Thank you, but I think it would be better if I walked. Maybe I could hold your arm, though," I said when I almost fell again. I wrapped my fingers around her upper arm and moved forward. Having her as an anchor did help steady the spinning. The fresh air and slow pace settled my stomach, too.

Winifred followed us with the truck. My shuffling pace forced her to stop frequently, but neither she nor Mary said anything about our progress. I kept my eyes on the ground until I noted a patch of grass ahead where the shade gave way to sun. We'd almost reached the clearing.

I looked up. The men must have heard the approach of the truck because they all stood silently waiting. For what, I didn't know. But as long as I had their attention, I would use it.

I stopped walking and turned to Mary. Behind us, the truck's engine quieted.

"Can you help me take the bandages off?"

She glanced at the truck then back at me before she reached forward and gently peeled the tape back from my skin. I held myself still through each tender tug and watched her face. Worry pinched her brow when she saw the stitched wounds for the first time. I hadn't yet seen them for myself and doubted I would here, not unless I used one of the mirrors on the truck. Based on her reaction, I might be better off if I didn't look. However, I wanted everyone else to see.

Once she had the bandages in her hand, I started forward

again. This time without her support. I slowly wove my way through the men, more concerned with my pain than their intense attention. When I stood in the center, I carefully turned and let my gaze sweep them.

"Biting hurts," I said, enunciating each word as if I spoke to toddlers. "Stop biting." When I found Thomas and Gregory in the crowd, I stopped moving. "Kindness and consideration are not games."

Thomas gave a barely perceivable nod. Satisfied, my gaze passed over the men surrounding me. Their expressions no longer held aggression or eagerness. Each held a mixture of guilt and concern.

"I need a week. Please, leave me alone. I just want to sleep."

Most of the men around me had the grace to look away. I should have felt triumphant, but the pain in my neck robbed me of my victory.

I trudged to the door, and everyone parted to make way for me. It was odd to see the group so still and silent. Even the ones on four legs.

Mary moved ahead and opened the door for me, but Winifred remained behind. Inside, the table was set, and a rabbit was on the fire.

I ignored the food, went to the pump, and dug in the bag for the pills the nurse had given me. I shook out a painkiller, ignored the antibiotics, and reached for the pump handle.

"Let me do that for you," Mary said.

She pumped a cup of water then followed me as I slowly made my way upstairs. I stood in the doorway and blinked at the room. The man was gone, but there was blood on my pillow. Quite a bit of it. Some even sprinkled the fitted sheet.

"Here," Mary said, quickly grabbing the pillow from her bed and exchanging the two.

I willingly lay down, and Mary covered me with an extra blanket.

Maybe sleeping on bloody sheets was just one of those things I needed to get used to while living here.

A GENTLE TOUCH pulled me from sleep, and the soft glow of the lantern greeted me when I opened my eyes. Everything around me was silent and dark, except Winifred. She watched me from a chair beside the bed.

"How are you feeling?"

"Like someone bit my neck," I said softly. Actually, I felt thirsty, but the idea of walking all the way downstairs for a drink made my mouth seem a little less parched.

"Weren't you supposed to leave already?" I asked.

"Yes. I should really leave within the hour. I didn't want to go without speaking to you first."

"About what?"

"What happened. I promised you'd be safe here..." Regret and sorrow pulled her face into a slight frown.

She had promised, yet I didn't blame her for what had happened. Promises are dangerous things. They were thin and frail and much too easy to break. My life had taught me that.

"Winifred, no one is ever really safe. I don't hold you responsible for what happened."

"You should. I spoke the command to everyone here, and as new ones came, I spoke it to them as well. He somehow slipped by me." She sighed. "I wish I knew how."

Thomas' sudden appearance and the abrupt end of my attacker ensured she would never know. But at least, I knew that creature wouldn't bother me again.

None of them would.

Chills danced along my skin as I recalled how I'd hardened my will and physically pushed him away with it. In my desperation, I'd tried to wield it as Winifred had done and succeeded, in a way. However, the implications of what I might be able to do now frightened me.

"If it's all right with you, I'd like to sleep some more," I said quietly.

She nodded. "Mary's in here with you. Her father and a few other older, Mated men are here to help keep the order as well as report any newcomers to me. I will do everything I can to keep you safe, Charlene." She tenderly touched the top of my head. "And I am so sorry for what has happened."

"I know."

"I'll see you again in five days."

I closed my eyes. Five days. If I could sleep through them all, I'd be fine. Yet, I knew it wouldn't work that way. Even though I'd asked for rest, I had a feeling the men would still want to see me.

For the next three days, I skulked about inside. Mary didn't comment on my pensive quiet or complain when I drifted off without helping clean up the dishes. I wanted to help, but I knew if I stayed in the common room too long after eating, one of the men would knock on the door for some reason or another.

So I slept, ate, and stared at my bedroom walls until I wanted to scream with boredom and maybe just a little resentment. My neck, though still sore, felt the tiniest bit better each day. The swelling went down, and the stitches started to itch, but I knew better than to scratch them. The scabs from the original bites were flaking away.

While I stared at my wall Wednesday morning, wishing for something to do, the door opened. A man with light hair and an inquisitive expression stood there.

Panic surged, robbing me of breath, but not thought. My will solidified, not a cane, but rather a branch, thick and heavy and hard to wield. Regardless, I pulled it back ready to swing it forward. Sweat beaded my upper lip, and I began to tremble, not with fear but from the effort.

"Mary is worried about you," he said, not moving into the room. "Her father and I have cleared the yard if you'd like to come out for some sun and a walk."

I hesitated a moment then released my breath and my panicked defense.

"You cleared the yard?"

He nodded.

I stood and edged to the window while keeping an eye on the man. I wasn't about to turn my back on him. His brow furrowed in concern as he watched me. I spared the yard a quick glance and found it empty like he'd said. How had he managed that? Satisfied he at least told the truth about the empty yard, I motioned for him to lead the way.

Mary sat at the table in the common room when we pushed through the door. She perked up at the sight of me. The man nodded to her, and she smiled at him in return.

"Given my recent bite," I said, watching her, "maybe it's better if you don't send strange men to come get me."

She cringed. "I'm sorry. I didn't think of that. This is Paul, my father's brother."

I glanced at the man again, noted little resemblance, and said a quick hello.

"So how did you manage to clear the yard?"

"We told them you weren't going to step out until they gave you space," Paul said.

Space wasn't what I needed. But I would take it, anyway.

"How much time do I have?" I asked.

Mary shrugged and glanced at Paul. He scratched his jawline and thought for a moment. "I'd say an hour or two before they get too impatient and start trickling back in."

Walk outside or take a bath? It was a hard choice. Fresh air and sunshine tempted me. Maybe I could have both if I hurried.

I walked to the pump and started filling the pot. Mary seemed to read my mind because she went to the fire and added wood. Once I had the pot hung over the flames, I went to the door and opened it.

A cool breeze swept through the room. Outside, birds sang. I stepped into the light, closed my eyes, and sighed. The clearing was empty, but the woods beyond was not. Their wills tickled my senses. The men waited and probably watched. It didn't dim my enjoyment of the moment. I soaked up the sun, tilting my head only slightly, just enough to show my stitches. After a few moments, I walked back inside, determined to make use of my time.

Two hours saw Mary and I both bathed in tepid water and our

dirty clothes washed. As we stood outside, hanging our clothes on the line someone had setup for us, I sensed the restless wills of those near. I excused myself, and Mary was quick to follow me.

I'd barely made it to the other end of the common room when someone knocked on the door. Before I could take another step, the door swung open and Thomas strode in.

"Enough," he said, his gaze immediately falling on me.

"Excuse me?"

"You made a big speech about showing you kindness and consideration, then you run off and hide. Where's your consideration for us?"

My mouth dropped open. I barely registered that he stalked across the room. What I'd said was that it wasn't a game. How did he get a speech from that? Why did he think I needed to show them consideration? After everything they'd put me through?

"By hiding in here, you're denying us a chance to show you any kindness."

"By leaving me alone to heal, you *are* showing me kindness."

He stopped in front of me and slowly shook his head. His nearness worried me, and I shuffled back half a step. He scowled and followed.

"You are not allowed to hide in here like a frightened rabbit."

I stopped and stared at him, too angry to speak for a moment. A rabbit?

I had every right to cower in here. Despite my stitches and still sore neck, almost every man out there had the same thought: try again. They couldn't even give me the week I'd asked for to let me rest. It wouldn't have been a surprise if they all started stomping their way into the room insisting.

"Wait. Why are you in here?" I asked.

"To talk some sense into you."

"No. I mean, why you? Why not Paul or Henry or one of the other men out there waiting to meet me? You've already met me, talked to me, and told me you're interested in me. Why did they let you through the door without a fight?"

He cocked a humorless grin at me and leaned close. A finger of fear trailed down my spine, and I struggled to hold myself still. He hadn't attacked me. He'd killed the man who had. But I knew he still wanted to bite me.

"Who says they didn't fight me?" His exhale brushed my ear on the side that was still stitched up. I wanted to step back but didn't want to prove his words about hiding in fear correct.

I'm not defenseless, I reminded myself.

He didn't immediately pull away. Instead, he stepped closer, set his hands on my shoulders, and breathed deeply. I trembled.

"Charlene," he said softly, "let me protect you."

I turned my head slightly to meet his gaze, our faces inches apart. The twist pulled at my healing skin.

"How? By letting you bite me? That's not protection. If you wanted to protect me, you'd promise never to bite me or let anyone else try."

He scowled, and I could feel his frustration and anger. His fingers on my shoulders twitched, and I held my breath. Without meaning for it to happen, my will solidified again. I held it ready.

After another moment, he straightened away and let his hands drop. With relief, I dropped the hold on my will as he gave his attention to Mary, who hesitated by the exterior door.

"Gregory misses you," he said to her. "He didn't realize he wouldn't be able to spend time with you when he agreed to postpone the Claiming."

Mary flushed, and I grew angry. He was only trying to manipulate the situation to get me to return to my old routine...if you could call it a routine. But how dare he make Mary feel guilty.

"Gregory is welcomed in here any time," I said, staring at the back of Thomas' head. "Just as Paul and Henry are. In fact, any of you who are not interested in biting me are welcome."

He turned to eye me.

"And I'll know when someone's lying," I said, crossing my arms stubbornly as I'd seen him do so many times.

He slowly bent his head in acknowledgement. Then, he turned and left.

A moment after Mary closed the door behind him, someone else knocked on the door. She arched a brow at me, and I nodded.

She pulled open the door. A smile lit her face at the sight of Gregory. Guilt jabbed me a bit. I turned and made my way back to my room. There, I went to the window and seriously considered my circumstance.

I was so convinced there was nowhere else for me. But, how did I really know for sure? Was I willing to continue to risk my wellbeing by staying here? I watched men stride from the trees. They looked at the laundry, the closed door, then up at my window. I didn't flinch away from their stares. I'd known they weren't ready to give up. More came until the yard filled. I saw Thomas, Paul, Henry, and Anton in their ranks.

This wasn't how I pictured my life when I'd left. I'd known it would be hard, that there would be struggles. But to this degree? No. I'd imagined I would eventually find a place to settle down where I could start over, and people wouldn't care where I'd come from. I'd thought I would find a place where the Pennys of the world wouldn't find me. Though I doubted Penny would find me here, I also began to doubt I could live any kind of life here.

With what I'd learned about my power during my attack, I was no longer a prisoner. I could defend myself against these creatures. I looked down at the number of men in the yard and wondered if I was crazy enough to try leaving. Did I actually think I could fight them all? Yet if I stayed, didn't I face that same potential fate? Just a few minutes ago I'd wondered what was keeping them all from storming into the room.

With a sigh, I turned away from the window. The bag I'd brought from home leaned against the dresser. Could I leave? Would they let me? I wouldn't know if I didn't try.

I packed what few clothes I had into the bag. The zipper sounded like thunder in the room, loud and ominous.

CHAPTER EIGHT

Mary and Gregory broke apart when I walked into the common room. Her cheeks were flushed and her eyes glassy from his kiss. I grinned at her. She returned the grin until she saw the bag over my shoulders.

I didn't say anything as my smile faded as well. Gregory turned from Mary and moved toward the door.

"Gregory," I said. Just his name. The warning in my tone was clear.

He stopped and watched me move to the pump. I listened to the metallic screech as I filled my water container. When I finished, I turned toward the pair. They still watched me, Mary with concern and Gregory with a carefully blank expression.

"Charlene—"

"Mary, please," I said with a shake of my head. I didn't want those outside to have an idea that I meant to leave until I was out there. I made my way across the room, hugged her, then went to the door.

Standing tall, I pulled it open. Bright light blinded me as I stepped out and turned toward the drive. Men moved out of the way, their actions slow and expressions puzzled. It wasn't until I walked halfway down the drive that one of them stepped in front of me.

"Where are you going?"

He was a face in a sea of faces. A man I might have met, but didn't remember.

"I'm not sure yet," I said.

"But you're leaving?" he asked. Everyone watched me.

"Yes, I am."

Growls arose.

"Don't go," another said. "I know I can Claim you."

The man next to him pushed into him, and they both fell to the ground, fighting. Others started pushing at their neighbors.

"That's why I'm leaving," I said loudly. I stepped around the fighting men, intending to walk away, but a hand on my shoulder stopped me.

"I suggest you let go immediately," I said without turning. My voice was low and steady despite my shaking. I'd hoped they'd just let me leave. Now, I saw they wouldn't.

My determination to stop being a victim hardened and that piece of my will became my weapon. When the hand didn't drop away, I swung it out in an arc. The men standing within four feet flew backward, as if pushed. They landed hard; and, too stunned by what had happened, they just lay there.

"You are not children, and I am not a toy to fight over."

"We wouldn't fight if you would allow one of us to Claim you," a familiar voice said.

The men slowly got to their feet as I turned toward Thomas with a scowl.

"It is not my willingness that is preventing you from

Claiming me. It's your kind's inability to Claim me, the human, that is preventing it from happening."

"Perhaps it was your unwillingness that prevented the Claim from taking hold."

I'd never before wanted to hurt someone as much as I did that man. His thickheaded persistence was beyond infuriating. I took a slow breath and made up my mind.

"Anton," I said. The crowd parted until Anton moved forward. Thomas growled low. "You promised, if I allowed you to Claim me, you would be gentle."

His eyes lit with understanding. "Not just in the bite, but for the rest of our lives."

"Then, I willingly give you permission to Claim me." He made to move forward, but Thomas spoke up.

"I challenge you for the right," Thomas said. He would have stepped forward, but his friend with the merry grey eyes placed a restraining hand on his shoulder.

"Uh-uh," I said, shaking my head. "You said it was my willingness preventing it, so your challenge is pointless...unless you're saying you're wrong. Because I'm only willing to let Anton try. No one else."

Thomas snarled, his anger plain. He wasn't the only one. I ignored them all and motioned Anton forward. He towered over me.

"Is it possible to bite the other side of my neck?" My hands shook with fear as I gripped the strap of my pack. I hadn't forgotten the pain of the last bite. And the stitches still had a few more days before they could be removed.

"It is," he said. He tilted his head and studied me. "We could wait, like Mary and Gregory."

His compassion helped ease a little of my fear.

"No. The others beat you once, already. I don't trust what they will do if we don't follow through with this now."

He nodded slowly and stepped closer. He wrapped his arms around me, supporting me as he leaned in. I let go of the straps, curled my hands into fists, and pressed them against his bare sides.

His breath tickled my neck, and I scrunched my eyes closed. For a moment, there was just his breath. Then, his sharp teeth broke the skin. A small noise escaped me, more shock than pain. As Anton had promised, he was gentle. His teeth had barely broken the skin. Before he pulled away, he placed a soft kiss on the spot. I let my hands drop.

We looked at each other for a moment.

"Well?" I said nervously.

His face fell slightly, and he shook his head.

"He barely bit you," someone said.

I rolled my eyes. "And the one who gave me stitches didn't bite deep enough?"

"You weren't willing," Thomas said again.

"Make up your minds," I said, venting my frustration in a half-scream, half-yell. "Is it the depth of the bite or the willingness?"

No one answered. Neither did they move out of my way to let me leave. My head thumped with the beginning of a headache. I didn't know if it was due to using my ability, the stress of the situation, or the fact that I was still recovering. But I did know I wasn't ready to fight them all today.

"Fine. I'll give you two hours to figure out what went wrong. Then, I'll pick someone else. I think I still have an unmarked spot on my neck somewhere. That will be the last chance any of you will have. After that, I'm done; not because

I'm not willing but because it won't work. Ever." I started walking to the door but stopped on the threshold.

"Don't waste time fighting. Work together. I won't accept the excuse that something wasn't done correctly, again." I turned and closed the door.

Mary stood in the common room with shocked, wide eyes. Gregory stood beside her, appearing equally surprised.

"What part of all of that upset you?" I asked as I let the bag fall from my shoulders.

Mary glanced at Gregory and then stepped away from him to move closer to me.

"Winifred wants to know how you knocked them down."

"Ah." I went to the table and sat down. "Does Winifred want me to stay?"

Mary came to sit with me and nodded.

"If this next bite fails, and they agree to leave me alone, it's better if I keep my secrets."

"And if it doesn't fail?" Gregory asked.

I twisted in my chair to look at him. "It will. No one understands why this ritual of yours isn't working because no one is acknowledging the obvious. I'm different. Winifred said it. They know it. Yet, everyone keeps trying to treat me like I'm one of you." I shook my head. "If I'm not one of you, why would you think the same ritual would work?"

Gregory studied me in silence. Then he dropped his gaze to the floor. He stood still, and I wondered if he was talking to Winifred. Finally, he met my gaze.

"I'd like to join the others outside," he said. "I have no desire to try to Claim you, but I'd like to help them come up with better ideas than what's been tried already."

"I promise I won't choose you. Or anyone else who doesn't want to be chosen."

He nodded and left. I turned to Mary.

"Do you think any of them have a chance?" she asked.

I shrugged. "I have no idea. All I know is that I've been bitten four times, and one way or another, the fifth will be the last."

"Want me to help clean that?" she asked, pointedly looking at my new bite.

"Sure." She stood and fetched the supplies I'd brought back. When she started dabbing at my neck, I caught her worried frown.

"He really was gentle," I said. "I'm sure Gregory will be gentle, too."

"I'm not worried about that. I'm not as breakable as you are. I'm worried what will happen next time."

I nodded.

"Me too. Has Winifred said anything else?"

Mary gave me a slight smile. "Yes. She's upset with Thomas for pushing you like he did. She's worried you really do mean to leave. Not that she wants to keep you here against your will, but she knows she won't be able to protect you as well out there."

I knew Mary didn't mean outside these walls but out in the real world. I appreciated Winifred's concern and that she hadn't pushed for more of an answer about what I'd done out there.

Mary and I ate jam sandwiches as the sun climbed in the sky then sat in silence for the remainder of the time. When Mary let me know two hours had passed, I moved across the room and opened the door.

The majority of the men stood in an arc facing the door; yet many, including Gregory and Anton, waited back by the trees. The definite separation of groups made it clear that I should select from those closest to me.

I studied the faces before me. "Was two hours enough time?"

They all nodded confidently. I glanced back at Gregory. He nodded once as well, and I sighed. Such confidence begged to be shaken. The universe was fickle like that.

"Okay. One chance," I said again, to make sure they all understood. Then I met Thomas' gaze. "Prove your theory."

He didn't walk toward me but moved to the back of the crowd. He bent and picked something up. The men parted to make room for him as he walked toward me. In his hand, he held a small bouquet of wild flowers. My heart skipped a beat at the gesture, and I quickly looked up. He uncomfortably met my gaze. His grip on the flowers tightened as if he was ready to throw them or shred them, and I realized the flowers weren't his idea.

At least someone in the group had some sense of what human women liked.

I stayed by the door, trying to quell my nervousness as he stepped from the men and stood before me. He held out the flowers. I took them and managed a whispered word of thanks. The discomfort left his gaze and something else crept in. Tenderness.

"Don't be nervous," he said softly. He reached up and gently brushed a thumb along my cheek. My heart skipped a beat—the traitorous thing—and his look of longing stole my breath. He didn't move toward my neck, just continued to touch me.

"I will work every day of my life to deserve the gift you've given me."

My heart beat faster, and my stomach twisted happily.

He leaned forward, not toward my neck, but toward my mouth. His lips brushed mine, surprising me. His touch was light and soft. A whisper of his skin, and a promise of more to come. My lids fluttered shut as I lost myself in the sensation. He kissed the corner of my mouth, my cheek, my jaw, then my neck. The light scrape of his teeth pulled me from my trance.

I stiffened, and his hands curled around my upper arms. Whether in comfort or to keep me still, I couldn't be sure.

"Everything will be fine," he whispered against my skin.

He kissed me several more times. I would be a liar if I said it didn't affect me. It did. But my fear of what he meant to do next kept me from drifting into blissful ignorance like he probably wanted.

His tongue stroked my skin, startling me from my thoughts. Tingles spread over my arms as embarrassment crashed over me. We were standing in front of a crowd of people. A light kiss, I could take, but not that.

Before I could protest, his mouth opened. I inhaled through my nose as his teeth pierced me. He went deeper than Anton but not by much. I grunted and pushed against his chest when he lingered there. He didn't budge. He slowly withdrew his teeth and kissed the skin. As if that would make it better. He'd just bitten me slowly. At least the others had the decency to get it over with. Angry, I shoved at him again.

He pulled back and studied me while I glared at him. I could feel a trickle of blood run down my neck.

"Well?" I said.

His expression changed to one of complete devastation, and I knew it hadn't worked.

"At least, now you don't have to worry about forgetting your responsibilities to chase me," I said, still bitter about the bite. I faced the crowd. "Will you let me stay here in peace or should I move on?"

"Stay," Thomas said through clenched teeth. No one else said anything. He appeared to be their spokesperson.

"To be clear, this means no more fighting to meet me. No more looking for ways to win my favor in hopes for a little nip. None of it. Because that was the last bite."

"We heard you before. We understand," he said.

"Then, thank you for letting me stay." With a minute nod, I turned and went back inside. Mary was by the table, ready with the alcohol and gauze. I sat and let her clean my neck, grinding my teeth against the sting.

I'd done it. Won my freedom without trying to fight them all. Although it didn't make the prior bites worthwhile, it gave them meaning. They weren't for nothing. I could stay here safely now.

"There's blood on your shirt," Mary said. "I'll go get the clothes from the line."

I stood and moved to the double doors as she walked outside. Though the men had given their word that they wouldn't pursue me, I didn't want to linger in the room. The building was quiet as I climbed the stairs and closed myself into our bedroom. I dropped my bag beside the dresser and started to unpack.

In the hall, I heard the creak of another door and froze. Mary wouldn't need to go into any of the other rooms. I strained to hear more and almost screamed when someone knocked on my door.

"Who is it?"

"Thomas." His familiar voice held a note of impatience.

I crossed the room and opened the door. With crossed arms, he stood in the hall.

"I wanted to let you know that Gregory and I will be staying in the room next to yours. Henry and Paul will be in the room to your right. Several other men will be staying in the rooms downstairs. We wanted to know what we should work on next."

My mouth fell open. They were moving into the building?

"Why?"

"I thought telling you would be considerate. And we have no idea what your plans are."

"No. I mean, why are you staying here? I thought..."

"You thought we'd leave?" He gave a dry laugh. "Not after your pretty little speech about being different."

"I didn't give a speech. I said that to Gregory in the—"

"Main room where we could still hear. You said no more biting, and we agreed. That doesn't mean we've given up. It means we need to figure out how to Claim you without using our teeth."

I stared at him, and for a moment, I wasn't sure how I felt about their intent. Knowing the biting would actually stop was a relief, yet I didn't like that I had no say in their decision to continue pursuing me. However, their presence could be an advantage.

"How many are willing to help?"

"Seven, so far," he said.

I glanced at the window. We had several hours of daylight left.

"Let's meet in the main room after I change my shirt."

He nodded and walked down the hall to his room. I closed the door, still slightly shocked by this new turn.

When Mary and I entered the common room, there were three rabbits roasting on the fire. My mouth watered at the smell. But I ignored my need for food to address the men who waited.

I knew Gregory and Thomas, and Henry and Paul, but not the other three. One I recognized as the man who'd arrived with Thomas. The other two I was certain I'd never seen.

"I'm Charlene," I said, extending my hand to Thomas' friend first.

He looked down at my hand, grinned, then wrapped his fingers around mine. It was less of a handshake and more of a handholding.

"I'm Grey, Thomas' brother." He released me. "These two are Bine and Zerek."

"It's nice to meet you," I said politely. "Thomas said you wanted to know what I planned to do next." They all watched me, even Mary. "Honestly, I don't know what to do next. For me to live here through the winter...well, it's a long list. And I don't know what your plans are. Will all of you be staying too? It could change what we should do first."

"What do you mean?" Thomas asked.

"If it's the eight of us, we need to consider how we'll feed ourselves. I'm guessing as hunters, you follow the food. If you're staying in one place and the game leaves, then what? Also, if you're living indoors without your fur, how will you stay warm? You're going to need shirts, shoes, socks, and other things. We'll need more bedding, a large supply of wood, and jackets, mittens, and hats. And we can't steal what we need. If we mean to stay here permanently, robbing the surrounding homes and communities would put us at risk. We need to find a way to earn money. Money will buy us the food and clothes we need."

"Bine, head out to find an ax," Thomas said. "Zerek, pull any deadfall from the woods into the clearing. Enlist whoever is willing to help." The two nodded and left, shutting the outside door.

That took care of the wood.

"Do you have suggestions for how we can earn money?" Thomas asked, turning to look at me. My neck ached as our gazes met. I tried to ignore the sensation and promised myself I'd take a pain pill before bed.

"There's always the route Winifred took. Go out and get jobs." He didn't appear to consider that option, so I moved on. "There were some useful things at the junkyard. Perhaps more could be found there and sold in town. If we can spare any wood, we could also sell that."

Thomas glanced at Gregory and Grey. As if Thomas had spoken an order, they both nodded. Gregory held out his hand to Mary, and she went to him with a grin.

"We'll find something good," she said to me, and Gregory led her out the door.

Thomas waited until the door closed behind them before speaking again. "I heard you had one of the buildings dismantled for the boards. How do you plan to use those?"

"To board up the windows with no glass. It should help keep the cold out."

Henry and Paul nodded and walked out the door, leaving Thomas and I alone.

"What else?"

The way Thomas took charge and told everyone what to do bothered me. No. It wasn't that. It was his arrogance while he did it that irritated me.

I crossed my arms to match his stance and arched a brow at him.

"Why the sudden willingness to help? I thought you didn't want me making changes here."

"Without some changes, you won't be able to stay. Like you said, you're different. More fragile." He stepped closer, looking down at me with an expression that somehow crossed tender and domineering.

"I want you to stay."

My heart skipped a beat, and I struggled not to blush.

"Why? The bite didn't work."

"No, it didn't. But it doesn't change what I know. You belong to me."

I continued to stare up at him while I wondered what he had planned. He closed his eyes, breathed deeply, but didn't move. We stood like that for several minutes until I finally uncrossed my arms and turned away from him.

The bags from Winifred still waited by the pump. I pulled out the top sheet and considered its length. A dress would be nice but given the thin material, probably impractical. Curtains would provide privacy; however, with the loose drafty panes, a thicker material would be better. What could I do with the material, then? Nothing inspiring came to mind.

"What is that for?" Thomas asked. He'd moved to stand just behind me.

"Whatever we need, I suppose." Maybe I should just leave the sheets as sheets. If Mary and Gregory happened to find more beds they might be needed.

I unpacked the bags, setting all the items on the table. The pasta, dried beans, and rice lay in a small mountain.

"Can you ask Winifred to let Mary know that we could use a cabinet or shelf to store the food?" I asked, turning my head to look at him. Our faces were inches apart as he, too, studied what lay on the table.

"Do you always have to stand so close?"

His lips twitched. "If I wasn't worried about being knocked on my back, I'd stand even closer." He didn't meet my gaze but reached out and picked up one of the items on the table. "And no, I don't need to ask Winifred. I let Gregory know."

"How?"

"Just like Winifred can communicate with all of us, I can communicate with the members of my pack."

"Members of your pack. You're Gregory's...what? Leader?"

"Yes."

"That explains a lot," I mumbled as I turned away from him. Like why he was so domineering and why he seemed to expect that people would listen to him.

LONG AFTER THE sun had gone down, I still sat on my bed, bored. I'd taken the pain pill, but with several of the men in the building, I couldn't bring myself to turn off the lamp and sleep.

Not until Mary returned, anyway. Then, as if my thoughts had conjured her, I heard her yell my name.

"Up here!" I called.

Her steps were light and barely audible on the stairs. The door opened a moment later.

"Come see everything we've found." Her eyes were bright, her cheeks flushed, and I was sure it wasn't because of what they'd brought back. There was a dark spot on her neck, a kissing mark.

I grabbed the lamp and followed her.

"It's an odd collection of things, but I think we found some amazing pieces." She paused at the bottom of the steps to wait for me.

From above, I heard Thomas' door open and fought not to roll my eyes.

I'd returned to the bedroom after a very long, very uncomfortable afternoon shadowed by him. Even in my room, I hadn't been free of his presence because seconds after I'd closed the door, I heard his door close, too.

"I'm glad it wasn't a wasted trip," I said, hurrying to get to the common room. I didn't want to linger in the gloomy hall with him not far behind me. I pushed through the doors, then stopped.

Mary hadn't exaggerated about what they'd found. An odd assortment of items littered the area. I set the lamp on the table and walked further into the room. Some of the taller objects cast shadows on other objects. It was definitely too much to go through with the poor light of night.

"Wow, Mary. How did you get this all back?"

"Winifred asked a few others to help us." She moved further into the room and patted a large looking metal upright chest.

"This is an old refrigerator. We can use it for storing food. Nothing will be able to get to it."

What did she think would try to get to our food?

"And this," she said, tapping something else big and metal and partially hidden in the refrigerator's shadow, "will come in handy for cooking."

I moved closer and grinned when I saw the old-fashioned stove. I vaguely remembered my grandparents having one like it. The metal beast had two doors and two removable plates on the cook surface. The smaller door, I knew, was for wood. When lit, it would heat the oven that was behind the second door and the cook surface above. It would also help heat the room. Mary had just made life much easier.

"That is totally amazing," I said. Most older people, like my grandparents, replaced these things years ago with gas stoves.

"And check this out," she said, waving me over to a small, potbellied stove. "This is for your room. In winter."

I didn't miss her use of the word your, however, I pretended to.

"I can't wait to look at the rest of it tomorrow when we have better light."

Mary nodded excitedly, said goodnight to Gregory, grabbed my hand, and practically dragged me from the room. I managed to take hold of the lantern on our way past.

As soon as we closed the door to our room, she grinned at me.

"That was the best evening of my life. We talked about everything. Did you know that he's Thomas' cousin? He's only four years older than me—that's a relief—and said he wouldn't mind living here if that's what I wanted to do."

"He does seem pretty sweet," I said, returning her smile.

"I'm very excited for you. How much longer are you going to make him wait?" I just wanted to know when I'd be sleeping in this room alone.

"He asked the same thing today. I don't have a set time. When it feels like it's time, I'll tell him."

I nodded, kicked off my shoes, and crawled into bed with a yawn. Now that she was back, the need to sleep kicked in with full force.

"Good night, Mary," I said softly.

She turned down the lamp. Mary saw better in the dark than I did, and there was less of a chance of her bruising her shin on her way back to the bed.

I closed my eyes and listened to her settle under her covers.

"Did you have a nice day with Thomas?" she whispered.

I didn't answer. It wasn't because I didn't trust Mary with the truth. I did. But I didn't want her to feel bad that she'd had such a great day when my day had been so awful. Plus, I had a suspicion that Thomas was in his room already. I didn't want him to hear what I had to say.

"Good night, Charlene," she whispered after a moment. "I hope you have a better day tomorrow."

A smile curled my lips. Mary was smart.

THE AMAZING MOUNDS of goods that crowded the common room looked even bigger in daylight. There were small and large tables, chairs, dressers, cabinets, toys, lamps—not the gas kind—pieces of metal I couldn't identify, bags filled with things—it looked like clothes—a pile of random tools, and many other odd items. None of it was in good condition. After Mary's excitement last night, I'd expected a bit better than what I saw. Though, the stove totally was a find.

Paul, Henry, Gregory, Grey, and Mary watched me study everything. Through the open door, I listened to the thwack of the ax and the crackle and crunch of breaking wood.

"Okay. Let's store the tools in the other building." Mary and I hadn't yet explored it, but it looked like it was in as good of repair as the main building. "Maybe take a table out there, too, so we can take stock of what tools we have."

Thomas opened the door and asked for volunteers. A rush of men fought to crowd into the room. Thomas didn't appoint someone to move the tools but looked at me. His deference puzzled me.

"Can you two start carrying the tools to the other building?" I said, pointing to two men toward the front of the group. "And you two carry a table over? Then maybe the four of you can organize them and tell us what we have?" I said everything as a question because I didn't want to sound bossy. The four I pointed to nodded and got to work.

"Can everyone else grab the furniture and move it out to the yard? The stove and the old refrigerator can stay in here."

Within minutes, the room was cleared of everything but the odd items and the bags. I sorted through some of the oddities and found several old window frames still with whole glass.

"If they don't fit, I thought we could cut the glass to work in some of the windows here," Mary said.

"Perfect," I said with a smile. "Anton could probably do that since he helped us before."

She shook her head. "He left yesterday."

I gave Mary a puzzled glance.

"There was no point in staying. He already had his chance."

"Then why is...never mind," I said. I didn't want to know why Thomas was being exceptionally persistent.

She gave me a knowing grin. "I'll see if someone else is willing to come in and help with that."

"Before you do that, what's in the bags?"

"Clothes," she said, confirming my suspicion.

"From the junkyard?"

"Yeah. Just as we were coming in, some church group was leaving. They had a sale and brought what didn't sell along with some of the stuff they didn't think was good enough to put out. We took the bags before they hit the gross stuff. Wini said that even if some of the items are stained, spare clothes are better than no clothes at all."

I agreed.

"Let's carry these outside before we check out the furniture. Maybe someone will be willing to help us sort the clothes."

Four hours later, everyone seemed to have something to do. Two work groups divided the yard. On one side, men chopped or just broke the deadwood into smaller pieces and stacked it where the old shed used to stand. The other side of the yard, cleared of everything but the tables, functioned as a general work area.

The men surrounding two of the tables sorted clothes into gender and size, adult vs. child. When a folded stack grew too tall, the man would carry it to the front entry where another table was setup to hold everything. Only a few very tattered pieces were on the ground beside the table. Most was salvageable; I'd even found myself a pair of cotton shorts and a soft top to sleep in.

On several other tables, men worked to fix some of the odd items the group had brought back. The intent was to take those things to town and sell them the next day. The tools and the paint that were brought back from the dump came in handy at those tables.

As Mary and I moved around the yard to answer questions or help as needed, Thomas, Gregory, and Grey shadowed us. They never spoke a word. Gregory's presence, I understood. He rarely took his eyes from Mary and growled at any man who looked at her for too long. Thomas and Grey puzzled me, though. I couldn't be sure if they were watching me or just listening to what I was telling the men to do.

Seeing everything well in hand, Mary and I went inside to start a late lunch. Our shadows came with us. Three cleaned rabbits waited on the table.

"Dad and Paul went hunting," Mary said, eyeing them with me.

"The rabbits are perfect. We should be able to make a stew for the group outside," I said, moving to the pump. While we started to fill a pot with water, the three men moved around the new cook stove. Their quiet conversation was lost over the noise of the pump.

"Excuse me," a voice called. I looked up from the pot to see a man and woman standing in the doorway. Though they were clothed, they were filthy, and the woman was very pregnant. The man wasn't looking at me, but at Thomas.

"We heard about the changes here. My Mate wants to stay until the cub is born, if that's all right."

I didn't give Thomas a chance to answer.

"Of course," I said, dropping the handle and moving toward the couple. "My name is Charlene, and this is Mary."

The man glanced at Thomas once more before his gaze settled on me.

"This is Ann, and I am Leif."

"Mary, would you be willing to show Ann and Leif to one of the fixed rooms, and maybe Ann would like to pick a few things out from the stuff you brought back."

Mary nodded and happily chatted with Ann as the three left the room. I turned toward Thomas. He watched me with an odd expression, not angry...more like confused.

"How long will it take to hook up that stove?" I asked. "Ann will probably want a hot bath and that stove will make the job a lot easier."

"We need some kind of pipe to vent the smoke," Thomas said, stating what I'd already guessed.

"Gregory, did you see any pipe at the junkyard?" I asked.

"We brought some back," Grey said. "It should be around here somewhere."

"See if you can find it and get the stove working. I'll keep fixing lunch."

I didn't wait for them to answer but turned toward the rabbits. We needed to make the food stretch. It wasn't something I was used to doing. I lugged the heavy pot to the fire and set it on the hook there. Then, I went back to the table and started cutting every bit of meat off the rabbits. After covering the meat with a cloth, I tied the carcasses into another piece of cloth. I tossed that bundle into the water.

"What are you doing?" Thomas asked from across the room.

"Making a broth for a stew base. My mom never used a shirt, but it should work the same and keep the little bones out of the stew while adding flavor."

He didn't ask anything else, so I turned back to our supplies. We had pasta, dried beans, rice, and canned vegetables. The beans would need to be soaked. And, even if I used the canned vegetables, I needed the carcasses to boil for a while before adding the meat.

"This won't be ready until closer to dinner," I said with a sigh. "I don't know what to feed everyone for lunch."

"Charlene," Thomas said, turning me away from the table. I hadn't realized he'd crossed the room. "We've fed ourselves our whole lives. You only need to worry about feeding yourself."

He was back to studying me, again.

"You need to stop thinking like that," I said. "Each individual only thinking about themselves...it's not helping. Winifred and Mary said your race is dying. Stop looking at your little groups as isolated families and start seeing the big picture. You all need to work together to find a way to survive. If you want to survive."

His expression never changed while I spoke. I wanted to shake him to see if he was still alive, and maybe, because he frustrated me a bit.

"Don't you see?" I said with exasperation. "It's not you who will suffer the most, but the generations after you, if you don't change your ways." He still gave no indication he understood me. I turned back to the table. "I need to get something ready for Ann to eat."

"Whether you know it or not, you were meant to come here," Thomas said. "We won't change on our own. But maybe you will change us."

He walked away before I could glance back at him.

CHAPTER NINE

I WIPED SWEAT FROM MY FACE AND GAVE THE RICE ON THE FIRE another stir. One of the men had brought in a pheasant that now roasted beside the pot for a late lunch. Behind me, I listened to the water boil on the new stove. Thomas and Gregory had finished installing the stovepipe well before Ann and Leif had returned to the kitchen with Mary. The couple had taken one of the first floor rooms, unconcerned about the broken window.

Ann had also gratefully accepted a change of clean clothes and now waited at the table while her husband—no, Mate—worked to fill the tub for her. With the new stove, it wouldn't take as long to fill the tub. But, man, the room heated quickly.

Needing to escape the heat, and because I had little left to do inside, I went out to check on the progress of the men.

Four long rows of split wood were stacked shoulder high. Not my shoulder, but the height of the men doing the stacking. The two clothing tables were empty, and on the ground lay the heap of rejected items.

I grabbed an armful of clothing to carry back inside. Though none of it was good for wearing, it could be useful for other things. I placed my armful just inside the door, and when I turned, I almost screamed. Three men were right behind me, carrying the rest.

"Thank you," I said as they dropped their bundles.

They nodded and left, and I found the absence of their previous aggression and intensity pleasantly surprising. I went back outside and walked around, studying the rest of the progress. Several of the wooden chairs, now repaired and painted, caught my eye.

"Can we carry the two empty tables and these chairs into the main room? Maybe we should set them off to the side a bit for when you want to come in and eat or just sit for a while." Two of the men nodded and went to the tables.

I wandered over to the table that had the scrap pieces of metal. I still had no idea what we would do with it.

"Winifred said there are places by her that will pay for metal," Mary said, coming up behind me. "When she leaves again, she'll take this with her and use the money to buy more supplies."

"There's nothing like that around here?"

"There are a few places, but she said we'd look suspicious carrying all this heavy stuff there since we don't have a truck. Also, this way, she can spread out where she goes so no one wonders where she gets the metal from. We plan to go back often," Mary said.

"Then we should have a designated area for metal. Let's stack all metal for recycling by the driveway and away from the house. If anyone goes out and finds anything to add to it, they can just toss it there."

Men immediately started moving the pieces, and it occurred

to me that Winifred was right. As wolves, they were surviving in the wild. But as people, they were lacking any purpose. These small tasks gave them purpose; and based on their expressions, they liked it.

"Does anyone think we can build our own ladder? Something tall enough to reach the high windows so we can start boarding them up?"

No one answered; however, several men walked into the trees. I wondered what kind of ladder they'd make.

I turned toward Mary.

"We need more dishes. Bowls and spoons first. If we work together, we should eat together."

"We should." She grinned at me then looked out at the men. "The rabbit stew will be done in a few hours. Bring a bowl and spoon if you want to eat. And no stealing."

Several nodded. Those who were already busy kept working. Those still idling around the yard disappeared.

From the trees, a thunderous crash echoed into the clearing, and I jumped a little.

"Just the ladder," Thomas said from beside me.

I jumped again.

"Where did you come from?"

"Inside. What's next?" He grinned down at me.

Hearing him say the very question I asked when I felt lost changed the way I saw him. He was still annoying in my eyes, but he was also just as misplaced as the rest of them, as I was. I tilted my head and studied him the way I often caught him studying me. He grinned wider.

"When it's just your pack, what do you do every day? What's your routine?"

"We tend to sleep most of the day. At night, when it's safer to move around, we scout the area and hunt."

I waited for him to say more, but he didn't. My heart broke. What kind of existence was that?

"So coming here changed your sleep patterns?"

He shrugged and eyed the men still in the yard.

"Some will leave for brief periods during the day to nap in the woods. We still prefer to hunt at night."

"All right. Then, what we do next is plan." I turned and looked at the building behind me. "This is going to be a lot of work, but once your kind hear what's happening here, I think we'll see more couples like Ann and Leif. We have eight rooms slightly weatherproofed. It would be ideal to replace the glass in the upper windows first to make more rooms inhabitable. For the rooms that are finished, we should try to have them equipped for whoever might appear. Blankets are a must. We should also try to put in some type of heavy curtain or drapery to keep out the cold."

"You seem very worried about the cold that is still months away," Thomas said.

Months away? He was thinking of deep winter. That's probably when he felt the cold as a wolf. I knew I'd feel it a lot sooner. Within a month, maybe a bit more, the trees would be bare. That would be the start of the cold for me.

"Time moves quickly," I said, "and I would prefer not to be caught unprepared. If there are spare furnishings, we can put them in the rooms, too. But my biggest concern is food." And how they would occupy themselves, but I didn't say that. "We'll need a lot to keep everyone fed...if everyone is staying."

"I think that will depend on whether or not you're Claimed by then."

I ignored his comment.

"Collecting metal to add to our recycling heap will help a bit with money, but we should think bigger. There are a lot of repairs this place is going to need. Any brave souls among you should try to find summer work with builders and carpenters."

The movement in the yard slowed until even the birds fell silent. I glanced at the men who stared at me. Disbelief painted many of their expressions.

"We need to think of more than just today or tomorrow. Who knows how to make the windows airtight? Who knows how to replace the shingles when the roof starts to leak? Who knows how to create a wooden bed frame? Who knows how to add decorative carvings to furniture? None of you, I'm guessing. And why should you? Where's the value in that knowledge for people who sleep during the day and hunt at night? There is no value for those people. But there is value for those who want to spend their winter building things to sell in spring. For people who want more than a life in the woods. For people who want to do more than just exist."

Several men turned and walked away into the woods. From the stiff set of their shoulders and their angry expressions, I knew I'd upset them. It disheartened me. How could they not see how lost they were?

"You push too far," Thomas said quietly.

"I'm not pushing at all. I'm questioning your purpose and giving you ideas for possibilities. Only you decide your purpose. Not me."

I walked inside, hoping the pheasant was ready to eat.

TWELVE MEN CAME INSIDE for dinner; seven brought bowls and spoons with them. Mary and I had the hot water and soap ready for the dishes. I could only imagine where they'd gotten them. Once we had everything clean, I set the bowls and our few plates on the small table next to the stove and started serving. The portions were lean, but the pot stretched to feed us all.

When the men finished, they left their bowls by the sink and drifted outside. Mary, Ann, and I started to clean up. It was the first moment since I'd arrived that reminded me not just of home but of my mom, and I felt a pang of homesickness.

I wondered what my mom and dad thought of me. Did Mom still worry? Did she hope for a call? I wanted so badly to call them, just to hear their voices.

"Are you all right, Charlene?" Ann asked quietly.

"Yes. Fine." Thoughts of the past should stay in the past. "I'm going to step outside for a bit."

I left them to finish drying the dishes.

The tall trees muted the glow of the setting sun, casting the clearing into an early dusk. Only a few men lingered in the yard. Thomas spoke quietly to two of them. Grey, Henry, and Paul were absent, and Gregory was just walking into the building with the tools.

I moved away from the door and slowly walked toward the pile of metal. I breathed deeply in an effort to let go of my concerns for my parents. I was here, now. I needed to worry about these people and our future.

A heavy mass hit me, knocking me to the side. Instinctively, I stuck out my hands to brace myself against the fall as the weight brought me down. Time slowed as I watched the dried grass rush toward me. My right hand touched the ground first, and my wrist twanged painfully. I wasn't fully able to extend my left arm in time, so it buckled as soon as my fingers touched the grass. My elbow smacked the hard surface. I scrunched my eyes and turned my head a second before my face hit. The stitches in my neck pulled at the same time the rough turf abraded my right cheek.

Before I could wonder why I was on the ground or draw a breath, a hand fisted in my hair and pulled back. My face lifted from the ground. Snarls, yips, and growls surrounded me. Legs and paws flashed by my dazed gaze.

The backward movement of my head suddenly changed, yanking hard to the right. I involuntarily cried out in pain as the move stretched my healing neck too far. The power of the wrench forced me to roll to my side, and I finally saw why I was on the ground.

Wolves and men battled in the yard and more poured from the trees. Thomas grappled with the man right beside me. The man's hand still had strands of blonde hair between his fingers. My hair. Thomas' teeth were no longer human, but long and lethal. He strove to bite the other man who was also shifting forms.

A yip nearby distracted me. I turned in time to see one wolf with its teeth sunk into the throat of another. Blood poured to the ground. Though I couldn't tell from which, I could guess. The bitten wolf yipped again as it continued its weak thrashing. How could they do this to each other?

"Charlene!" Mary cried. I turned and saw her in the doorway. Ann stood just behind her. The fear in her eyes and the hold around her large stomach was too much.

Angry, I pulled myself to my feet. In the span of just a few days, I'd been re-bitten, hospitalized, bullied, bitten again—

twice, and now knocked to the ground. Anger didn't touch what I felt.

"Enough." My voice boomed in the clearing, as unnatural as what happened next.

They stilled. Every one of them. I blinked, confused before I sensed why. Like Winifred had done, I'd managed to split my will. Each branch reached out to every man, woman, and wolf. It didn't touch their heads, though. It struck their hearts.

Then, I saw their eyes. The fear there. The suspicion. I took a deep breath. "Forget this moment, and the need to fight as soon as I release you," I thought at them. Then, I let go.

A sudden wave of nausea knocked me to my knees. I threw up on the ground and gagged again when the smell of bile and stew hit me. I raised my head and looked at the bleeding wolf. Its shallow panting barely lifted its chest.

"Are you okay?" Mary said. She helped me to my feet, and I wiped my mouth with the back of my shaking hand.

I looked around at everyone. They all watched me but no longer fought. I found Thomas next to the man who'd attacked me.

"Why?" I asked the man.

"You have no right to come here and force us to live like humans," he said with obvious disgust.

"You're correct. I have no right to force you to do anything. You're free to choose to live as you wish. However, I will continue to change things in these buildings that no one has used for years. And if there are any who wish to change how they live, they are welcome to join me."

The man glared at me.

"You have no right to this land."

"Do you own it?" I asked, feeling a hint of worry.

"No."

"Do you know who owns it?" I asked him. When he didn't answer, I looked at Thomas.

"Technically, Winifred owns it. It's why she left and has a job. She pays the...mortgage."

The way Thomas spoke slowly told me that he was communicating with Winifred. My heart plummeted and panic set in. I hadn't thought of that when I'd manipulated their wills. Had one of them said something to Winifred in the seconds before they forgot?

"And does Winifred mind if I make changes?" I asked.

"She doesn't think you're making changes; you're making improvements." He tilted his head and studied me. "Why are you worried?"

"It's nothing to think about now," I said. I addressed the man again. "So what did you hope to accomplish by attacking me?"

"A dead woman can't change a thing."

The way he said it gave me chills. Thomas' eyes narrowed on the man, and I could see the man had just given Thomas a reason to continue the fight. I stepped forward, raised my hand to set on Thomas' arm, and cringed at the soreness in my wrist.

He wrapped my hand in his and brought my fingers to his lips. The gesture surprised me, and my pulse leapt. His lips lifted in a hint of a knowing smile.

"Winifred suggests you go inside with Ann and Mary," he said, still holding my hand.

"I'd prefer to stay out here so no one else gets hurt," I said, looking at the wolf still on the ground.

"He's not one of ours," Thomas said.

"Really? He's not a werewolf but a regular wolf? The fur in

your ears is making you deaf." He grunted in surprise, but I didn't give him a chance to speak. "Stop thinking so narrowly. You can't just protect your small pack. Think bigger."

He kissed my hand once more, then let me go with a nudge toward the door. "Your neck is bleeding again. Let Mary take a look at it. I'll look at our fallen."

"Fine. The door stays open, though."

He grinned at me and crossed his arms, the gesture conveying his patience rather than any stubbornness. I gave him a last, long look, then walked toward the wolf that was on the ground. It growled at me as I knelt near it.

I tapped it with my will to silence it at the same time I spoke. "I was bitten on the neck, too. It hurts. If you can stand and come inside, Mary and I will clean you up and get you something to eat. It's up to you, though." I gently patted its side then stood and walked in.

Mary had the alcohol ready. With a sigh, I sat in the chair.

"How are the stitches?" I asked after she studied me for a moment.

"It looks like the top stitches might have torn a little." She dabbed at the wound. "It's barely bleeding. Your face looks worse."

My face looked worse? I'd been bitten how many times now? My neck had over a dozen puncture holes and several tears. Since there weren't mirrors here, I hadn't seen it; yet, I could imagine how it looked. My wrist ached, as did my elbow. I had fading bruises from the last attack and was missing hair from this one.

And my face looked worse?

I giggled; and as soon as I did, I couldn't stop. Laughter bubbled from me. It wasn't a pretty, feminine giggle. It was brash and edged with hysteria. My empty stomach ached as I bent over in my ill-hilarity. Tears streamed down my cheeks, and my laughs started to sound more like sobs. Maybe it was the stress of my existence since Penny had tried to expose me, maybe it was being knocked to the ground—yet again—by a werewolf, maybe it was the fear that my scary abilities would cause me problems, even here. Whatever it was, I was falling apart and didn't know how to pull myself back together.

Arms wrapped around me. My world spun as someone lifted me. I buried my face against a shirtless chest and hoped whatever this was wouldn't result in another form of abuse. I'd never felt so unwanted in my life, not even when Penny had tried to rat me out at school. That thought switched the mad laughter to full out tears.

I cried until I couldn't, until my already sore throat clogged and snot filled my nose. And whoever had me, held me through it all.

As I calmed, I became aware we moved slightly, a small side-to-side motion. A chin rested on my head, and hands smoothed down my back. I reached up and wiped my eyes then turned my head a bit so I could see better.

We were in my room, sitting on my bed. The setting sun painted one of the walls bright orange. I pulled back, and the chin lifted from the top of my head.

In the fading light, I stared at Thomas, his face close to mine. I saw the brown flecks in his deep blue eyes and studied his short, thick dark lashes. I realized everything about him seemed dark despite his pale skin. But, he didn't feel menacing. His gaze held concern, and it made my eyes water again. I'd manipulated this strong man's mind, and he didn't even know it. Guilt ate at me. My breath hitched in a typical post-cry rhythm.

He leaned to the side, grabbed a scrap cloth from the pile in my dresser, and handed it to me. I settled back against his chest and blew my nose.

"I'm sorry." My words were broken and full of remorse.

"Don't be," he said gently. "Take all the time you want. I'll hold you for as long as you'll let me."

His arms didn't tighten. His hold didn't change at all. Yet, his words changed it in my mind. My breathing slowed; and leaning against his chest, I listened to the steady beat of his heart. My stomach somersaulted.

I lifted my head again. He was waiting for it. Our gazes met. Slowly, he moved forward, giving me time to pull away. I didn't. His lips brushed mine, a brief soft touch. Our second kiss. This one scared me just as much because I wanted to wrap my arms around his neck and lean into the kiss.

He withdrew and watched me.

"Tell me what you need," he said.

My heart skipped a beat as a single thought raced forward. A home. A place to belong. But I didn't say it.

"Nothing. I'm better now. Thank you." I straightened away from him and stood. He caught my hand when I would have stepped away.

"Mary wants to start sleeping closer to Gregory, but she's worried about leaving you in this room alone. And, now, I worry Mary isn't enough."

I stared down at him. His dark brown hair looked like it needed a brushing. Maybe a washing, too. I wanted to reach out and smooth it back from his forehead, just to touch it. Instead, I forced myself to consider what he said. I'd known it would only be a matter of time before Mary left me. However, it seemed so soon. But it wasn't. Not really. Not when you considered that Gregory would have happily Claimed her at their first meeting. They would have been sleeping together for a long while already.

"Will you trust me to stay in here with you? To protect you?"

His open and sincere expression stopped me from immediately saying no. The idea of sleeping alone wasn't pleasant. Since my third attack, I had trouble sleeping most nights, wondering who would next creep into my room. Though I could protect myself, I wasn't always fast enough...or aware. And the idea of using my abilities like that again felt too wrong. Somehow, I knew it was meant as a last resort, and if I chose to ignore that internal warning...I shivered and didn't let my thoughts dwell on the unknown.

Now, with this most recent attack, I wondered if I'd sleep at all even with Mary or Thomas in my room. I glanced out the window. The vibrant orange was fading into a deep red.

"How do I know I'll be any safer with you?" I asked.

"I would never hurt you," he said. His sincerity reflected in his gaze. I shook my head at him, pointed at his mark on my neck, and said nothing. He heaved a sigh. "Never again."

He steadily held my gaze and my hand. I knew he meant every word, just as I recognized the impossibility of his vow.

"There are so many ways to hurt a person, Thomas. Don't ever promise someone you'll never hurt them because you will." I withdrew my hand from his. "I don't want to be the reason Mary isn't happy. You can stay. Thank you for the offer."

Thomas looked toward the door.

"Come in, Mary."

She opened the door. The lamp she held in one hand lit her anxious expression.

"Are you all right?" she asked.

"I'm fine. I'm sorry for my outburst. I'm not sure why...well, it's done, now. I heard you're ready to share a room with Gregory. Did you want help moving your things?"

Instead of smiling as I'd expected, she frowned and glanced at Thomas.

"I don't mind staying in here with you," she said when she met my gaze again.

I stepped forward and gave her a hug. "I know you don't mind. But Gregory makes you so happy. Why wouldn't you want to spend more time with him?"

I pulled back and caught her looking at Thomas again. I glanced over my shoulder at him. He still sat on my bed, relaxed and unconcerned by our regard.

"Could you step out for a minute, please?" I said.

He nodded, stood, and left.

"Winifred is worried about him sleeping in here with you."

"I'll be fine," I said, hoping Winifred's concern was for me and not Thomas.

Mary nodded hesitantly.

"She wants me to remind you she'll be here tomorrow."

I smiled.

"I'm fine. I'm sorry for crying like that. Maybe I just need a few more cookies."

Mary finally returned my smile. It was weak, but it was something.

"She said she's baking them now. I'll stay with you until Thomas returns."

I gave her another quick hug then kicked off my shoes and

changed. Another long day gone. I crawled under my covers and closed my eyes.

Tomorrow had to be better.

SNUGGLED UNDER THE COVERS, I lingered between asleep and awake. I was comfortable and felt well-rested for a change. It took a moment to remember the prior day, the fight, and the subsequent permission I had given to Thomas.

My eyes popped open. I once again had an up-close view of the wall. I held still and listened for a sign I wasn't alone but heard nothing. But, rolling over, I found Thomas sitting with his back to the door. His eyes were open, and he watched me closely.

Neither of us spoke. Was he remembering how he'd held me last night? I had to look away before I blushed, and I noticed Mary's bed and clothes were gone. They were so quiet, sometimes.

"Good morning," I said softly. He smiled slightly, making me feel a bit more relaxed. "Did you sleep at all?"

"Yes."

I sat up and winced at all the sore spots.

"Well, what should we do today?" I asked.

He chuckled, a smooth pleasant sound.

"I was about to ask you that."

"I know. That's why I asked you first. How close is the nearest town?"

"Further than you'd walk in a day."

"Where did Mary and Gregory go to find everything?"

"Town."

I arched my brow in question.

"We're faster than you are."

"Ah. I see. When will Winifred arrive? Perhaps she could take me in the truck."

"I'll take you," he said, standing. He held out a hand. "But, first, let's feed you."

I went to him but ignored his hand. He didn't make an issue of it. Instead, he turned and led the way downstairs.

The door was open in the main room, and someone already had a pot of water on the stove. The heat from the stove battled with the cool breeze that occasionally drifted through the room. The smell of pheasant roasting on the fire made my mouth water.

"Do you think instead of killing them, we could catch a few?" I asked as I took two plates down from on top of the new cabinet.

"Pheasants? What for?"

"Eggs. It would be handy in winter." I set the plates on one of the tables.

"And tempting," he said as he removed the skewered bird from the fire.

"It would be worth a try," I said with a shrug. "They would need some sort of coop, though."

"The way you think...I can't seem to guess what you'll say or do next." Thomas set the bird on his plate and used his fork to pull off some breast meat that he then set on my plate.

"Neither can I," I said with a grin. "But I can explain the eggs. I was thinking that I miss regular breakfast food like cereal, oatmeal, and eggs. And since you seem to be able to kill a pheasant easily enough, why not just keep them alive once you catch them?" I took a bite of the pheasant.

He nodded. "There are several meadows and a marsh nearby. They like the tall grasses. Perhaps, instead of walking to the junkyard, we could go there today."

If we had eggs, we could invest in flour too; and more food options would open up to us, like pancakes. We could make enough pancakes each morning to feed everyone. If we had enough eggs and flour. When I finished my pheasant, I carried my plate to the sink.

"A trip to the meadow might be a bit premature. We should have a coop ready first and food for them. What do they eat in the wild?" I asked him. I used the water from the stove to fill the sink.

He grinned widely.

"We eat them. That's all we've needed to know."

"If we want to try to raise a few, we'll need to find out what they eat. If it's something we can gather, it could work; but if we need to purchase something, we might be out of luck."

"They eat seed," Anton's familiar voice said behind me, "from the grasses, insects, and other things. Keeping them should be no problem if we build a pen in the meadow."

I turned with a smile. Anton stood in the doorway, eyeing Thomas. Thomas, still at the table, glowered at Anton.

"Welcome back, Anton," I said, pulling his attention from Thomas. "There are clean plates over here if you'd like some pheasant."

"I didn't come to eat. I came to help. I heard what happened yesterday." His gaze lingered on my sore cheek.

I nodded, but wanting to forget yesterday, changed the subject. "I'm glad you came back. Thomas and I were just talking about the junkyard, too. I'd like to go there to see if we can find anything else useful, but it sounds like it might be too far for me to walk in a day."

"I could carry you and run it," he said. "It would take an hour."

"Run carrying me for an hour? You wouldn't get tired?"

He gave me a cocky grin. "No."

Thomas cleared his throat.

"Winifred would like you to stay here until she arrives. She's concerned about your safety after yesterday's attack and feels this is the safest place for you."

Disappointed, I nodded. I didn't want to put myself in a position where I'd need to control anyone again.

"Then I suppose I'll find something to do around here," I said, rinsing the plate and setting it aside to dry. "What is everyone else working on today?"

"Bine, Zerek, and most of the others are still working on wood. A few are fixing things in the other building."

He didn't mention anything about Grey, Henry, or Paul; and I didn't ask. I needed to focus on my own purpose for the day. There were still windows to replace and a ladder to check on. I wiped my hands on my pants and added laundry to the list.

"Anton, if you're willing, can you help me with the windows?" I asked, walking toward the door.

"Of course," he said.

"If you want, you can join us when you finish, Thomas," I said, glancing back at him. His gaze was on his plate, but he nodded.

CHAPTER TEN

ANN AND MARY HAD THE EVENING MEAL ON THE STOVE WHEN I trudged in hours later.

"Heard things aren't going well," Mary said.

"Not really. Anton broke several panes of glass while trying to cut them with his nails, which is impressive to watch, by the way. And building a coop for pheasants isn't easy work. We need some kind of wire or net to go over the top of the walls otherwise the birds just fly away. One of the guys suggested breaking their wings," I said with exasperation. Neither Mary nor Ann looked as upset by the idea as I was. "How are things going in here?"

"It's going well," Mary said. "We've been working on making the unusable clothes from those charity bags, usable. We washed everything, tore the pieces into sections, removed and saved the buttons, and now have a bunch of random cloth. Wash rags, drying cloths, bandages...I think we have it all covered now. We also started sewing some curtains from the bigger shirts." She pointed to the window behind me. It now had a heavy flannel curtain pulled back with ties.

"I'm impressed," I said. "Better progress than I've made. What's for dinner?"

"Gregory brought in several squirrels. We made a stew again, like you did yesterday. Tried to, anyway. It doesn't taste the same."

I went to the stove, gave the pot a stir, and then took a small taste. It wasn't bad. There was a hint of scorch to it, though.

"It's good. But, after you add the rice, you need to make sure to stir it more often, I think. The rice settles to the bottom and can burn easily." At least, I thought that might be what had happened.

Both Mary and Ann nodded.

"We have water heating if you want to wash," Mary said.

I heaved a grateful sigh.

"Thank you."

I shut myself into the side room and peeled off my shirt. Mary had moved one of the small tables into the room, and a bowl of hot water waited. Beside it lay several folded squares of cloth. I wet one and washed my face, arms, then hands. The water was dark when I finished. I totally wanted a bath but knew dinner was almost done. I air-dried then put my dirty shirt back on.

When I stepped back out, I saw many of the men were in the room and already eating. Winifred was there, too, having a quiet conversation with Mary. Both looked my way. Mary looked slightly guilty and Winifred a tad upset. Winifred, I could understand. Dealing with these men, there was always something to be upset about. But why Mary's guilty look?

I moved to join them.

"Hello, Charlene. Mary was just telling me about the changes—"

"Winifred," Thomas said, standing from his spot at the table. "Could I have a minute?"

I didn't miss Winifred's small, slow exhale as if she were trying to control her temper.

"Of course, Thomas."

Mary and I watched her join Thomas on the other side of the room. They didn't speak openly, just stood near each other, not saying anything.

"That's a handy trick," I said softly, wishing Mary and I could do that. The ability to have a completely private conversation in this place was impossible for me. Not for them, though.

"Did you eat already?" I asked Mary.

"Yes. I saved a bowl for you, too." She pointed toward the stove.

"Thanks." I stepped away to fetch the bowl while keeping an eye on Winifred and Thomas.

He stood before her with his arms crossed over his still bare chest. I needed to grab him a shirt from the pile of clothes in the front entry. He appeared neither upset nor happy as he stared at Winifred. She, however, was turning a bright shade of pink.

The sparse conversation that had whispered through the room when I entered, disappeared. The room quietly waited for the outcome of whatever Winifred and Thomas discussed.

I rejoined Mary, who studied the pair as well, and took my first bite. The stew was a bit too thick, and my teeth closed on a small piece of gristle. I quickly swallowed it whole.

"This is really good. Thank you," I said, keeping my voice down.

"You're too nice for this place." Mary gave me a sideways glance, and I saw the start of a humorous curve to her lips.

"Enough."

Winifred's sudden outburst startled me. I looked over and saw her throw her hands up.

Thomas uncrossed his arms, but fisted his hands, giving away how he felt.

"Winifred. You started this. Now let it go."

She waved him away as she turned toward me. Her dismissal of him seemed to unlock the others in the room. Many of them rose, following her as she crossed the room. They left their bowls by the sink, and she moved to look in the bag of medical supplies.

"As soon as you're done eating, I'd like to look at your stitches," she said. "Perhaps we can take them out."

I was ready to be done eating, but dutifully took another bite. The men slowly left the room. Thomas didn't leave, though. He sat at the table and watched me. Used to his study, I didn't pay him much mind.

Without chewing too much, I had managed to swallow down half the stew when Anton walked in. He went to the stove, saw the empty pot, and started to turn away.

"Anton, you can have the rest of mine," I said quickly.

Mary grinned but said nothing. I knew she could see through the offer of my stew, but I did feel badly that there hadn't been a full portion for him.

"Are you sure?" he asked, stepping closer.

"Totally." I held out my bowl, and he accepted it with a nod of thanks.

He didn't move to sit by Thomas but stood by the sink, ate the last few bites, set the bowl with the others, then left the room.

"Take a seat at the table," Winifred said, looking at me.

Still thinking of Anton's lack of food, I spoke to Mary as I moved to do as Winifred asked.

"Tomorrow, we'll make two pots of stew. Whoever brings the meat should double what's being brought. It doesn't have to be the same kind of meat. Two rabbits and two pheasants would work."

"All right," Mary said, sitting next to me.

Winifred set the iodine and bandages to the side, moved my hair away, and bent close to look at the stitches.

"I see the tear. And the new marks." The last bit she said with exasperation.

"I thought it best to get the remaining attempts out of the way," I said.

"I'm concerned that, though those here have agreed not to attempt another Claiming, others might still want to try. What happened a few days ago proves—"

"Winifred," Thomas said sharply.

"Pup," she growled, "I will not tolerate another interruption. You've voiced your opinions; now, let me do my duty."

"Your duty is to keep the peace. There's peace here. You can leave."

My mouth popped open, and I turned to stare at Thomas. Mary tugged my hand. I looked at her and saw she was standing.

Annoyed with Thomas, I pulled my hand from Mary's and stood.

"I think you should show Winifred a bit more respect," I said to Thomas. "You told me this place is in her name. She's the only one of you out in the real world, working to make sure you can keep it. Without her, where would you be? Have you asked yourself that?"

He held my gaze and slowly exhaled. His arms dropped to his sides, and he ran a hand through his hair.

"Winifred, I apologize," he said. Though he didn't sound condescending, he didn't sound sincere either. "Do what you think is best."

He turned and left. The common room remained quiet for several heartbeats as Winifred and Mary stared after him.

"I believe he'll grow to be a good leader," Winifred said.

At first, I thought she was talking to herself, but Mary nodded. When Mary noticed she had my attention, she blushed guiltily. I frowned, studying Mary.

"Let's see if we can take these stitches out," Winifred said, bringing the focus back to my wounds.

THE SKIN of my neck felt tight as I lay in my bed. I'd escaped from the common room after my stitches had been removed, tired from a long day.

Thomas' slow breaths kept me company in the dark as he leaned against the door again. With Winifred here, I'd thought maybe she would stay in the room with me, but when I'd said I was ready for bed, she'd remained in the main room. However, like magic, Thomas had appeared.

Mary had once again blushed guiltily, and Winifred had scowled angrily. I wondered what about Thomas had both of them acting that way, and the wondering was keeping me awake. If not for Mary's guilt, I would have easily pinned

Winifred's anger on his arrogant ways. It bothered me that my only two supporters were acting oddly around the person who'd wanted me here the least. And I didn't know what to think of Thomas. After his failed bite, I'd expected more hostility. Instead, he'd held me while I cried and had kissed me. I understood why he'd kissed me before trying to bite me. He'd thought it would help. But why kiss me again? There was no point to it. And now here he was, sitting in my room to protect me.

I yawned hugely and rolled over again. The bed was warm and comfortable, but I couldn't stop thinking.

"Can't sleep?" Thomas asked quietly.

"No. I want to, but my mind won't let me."

"Want to talk?"

"I don't know..." I had questions but wasn't sure he would answer them.

"Why are you hesitating?"

"Because I'm not sure about you." And like a broken dam, the words didn't stop there; they continued to flow. "You didn't like me. Then, you wanted to bite me. When I gave you what you wanted, instead of leaving me alone, you watch me even more. You seem annoyed most of the time. I think you still don't really like me, and I know you're keeping things from me. But it's not just you. I'm questioning whether it's smart to continue making plans to stay here through the winter. My presence here obviously isn't welcome. My neck can't take any more holes; if it does, I'll start spouting water every time I drink. Even if I'm not asked to leave, how can I possibly survive a winter here? Despite the steps we're taking, I don't think it will be enough. If the cold doesn't kill me, malnourishment most likely will. How will talking about what's on my mind change any of that? It won't. Actions will.

But I upset your kind if I talk about acting too much. So, no, I don't think I want to talk about any of it."

Silence answered the tirade I hadn't planned on venting. Yet, I felt better for having said all of it.

"You will always have a place with me, and I will always listen."

The simple words touched me, and the second kiss made more sense.

"You still think I belong with you...even after the bite failed."

"Yes. Try to go to sleep, Charlene."

I sighed and did try. But my mind continued to dwell on my concerns. Especially the one I hadn't vented. Why was Mary acting so guilty?

THE RACKET in the yard woke me at dawn. I sat up, disoriented, and looked for Thomas. But he wasn't there. Mary was. She stood in front of the window, watching the yard below.

"What's happening?" I asked with a yawn. It had taken me too long to fall asleep.

"A challenge."

Her voice hitched a bit when she spoke, worrying me. I flipped back the covers and joined her at the window.

Below, the men had formed a loose circle around two wolves. The animals fought wildly with claws and teeth, clashing and backing away only to clash again. Their moves were too fast to follow easily, but the blood on the ground around them told the tale well enough.

I glanced at Mary. She bit her bottom lip as she watched and tears glistened in her eyes.

"Do you know who it is?" I asked.

"Thomas."

My heart gave a lurch; and in transfixed horror, I again watched the pair fight. I couldn't tell which wolf was Thomas. There was too much blood on both of them.

"A challenge for what?" I asked.

"Pack leader."

In the crowd surrounding the fighters, I spotted Gregory and Grey. Then, I frowned at the fight, trying to make sense of what I knew and what she'd just told me.

"Wait. You said packs are family units. So who's Thomas fighting?"

"A Forlorn." Mary spared me a nervous glance. "Charlene, I can't talk about this."

"What do you mean? Talk about what? What a Forlorn is, or Thomas fighting?"

A tear actually slipped down Mary's cheek as she helplessly looked at me. I could tell she wanted to say more. Something was stopping her. As if she'd been commanded not to speak of it.

"Mary, don't worry about it. If it's something you can't talk about, I understand." I pulled her to me, hugging her close. I understood secrets and wouldn't condemn someone else for keeping them.

The door to our room opened, and Anton poked his head in.

"She can't talk to you, but I can. Thomas has been recruiting. He's now the first leader of a non-family pack, one large enough to ensure Thomas can claim any territory he wants. He's claimed this territory. His challenger, should he win, would be Thomas' pack's new leader. That would give him rights to this compound, you because you're unClaimed and living here, and Mary, since she's unClaimed and currently a member of Thomas' pack."

Outside, the snarling increased in volume.

"I'm sure you'll have questions for him when he's done. Would you like me to escort you to the main room? Winifred asked that I keep an eye on both of you."

Anton's calm demeanor and choice of words told me he believed Thomas would be the winner. It helped me think past the actual fighting to the reasons behind the challenge. The challenger wanted leadership of not just Thomas' pack but the compound—I liked that name—and me. It wasn't long ago that I'd asked Mary and Winifred about non-family packs. They said there weren't any. When had that changed and why? Just how big was Thomas' pack now? Anton was right, I did have questions. Why hadn't Mary told me that Thomas was now her leader? What about her father, Henry? I glanced at Mary and saw her worry.

"Yes, let's go down," I said to Anton.

Anton led us to the empty main room. The door to the outside remained shut, yet we could hear the continuing battle. Mary stood beside me, eyes wide as she listened. We needed a distraction.

No food waited near the fire. Nothing to cook.

"Mary, let's boil some water for a bath." One or both of the two fighting would need a bath or at the very least, to wash. If they chose not to bathe, the water wouldn't go to waste. I felt overdue for a bath myself.

While pumping the water, I noticed two more bags on the floor and realized I'd never looked at what Winifred had brought. Once all the kettles were heating on the stove, I emptied the contents of the bags on the table. As promised, I found cookies on a tinfoil wrapped plate. I eagerly shoved one in my mouth while looking at everything else. She'd brought more dried beans and a very large cloth bag of rice. This time, she'd also included a huge bag of oats, a jar of honey, a bag of sugar, and several jars of jams, tomatoes, and pickles. It appeared that either Winifred canned or she knew someone who did.

Mary started to put the supplies into the cabinet, and I removed one of the steaming pots from the stove. I poured half the water into the bowl in the bathroom, leaving just enough in the pot to boil oatmeal for breakfast.

After returning the pot to the stove, I went back to the tub room, washed my face, and brushed my teeth. The sounds of the fight continued to filter in from outside. I moved to the stove to check the water again.

By the time the water boiled, I had the oats ready to put in, and Mary had towels ready for whoever would take the bath.

It was only after I added the oats that I noticed the quiet.

"Well?" I asked, looking at Mary.

She met my gaze with a thankful smile. "Thomas won."

Relief flooded me. "Good. Tell him we have a bath ready if he wants it. Breakfast will be done in a few minutes."

I stirred some sugar and honey into the cooking oats.

The door opened, and a very dirty and slightly bloody Thomas walked in. For some reason, I'd expected a few more injuries than what I saw. There'd been so much blood on the ground.

His gaze met mine. My heart fluttered in response, and I quickly looked away. He needed to start wearing a shirt.

Though I wasn't watching him, I was aware of his regard as he strode toward me. My skin prickled when he stopped just behind me, and a shiver traced its way down my spine.

I continued to stir the oats so they wouldn't burn and pretended I didn't notice him or my reaction to him.

"Mary, this is just about done," I said. "I'll set it on the small table so it can finish cooking without burning."

Before I could test the handle, Thomas reached around me and lifted the pot from the stove. His bare arm brushed mine, making it harder to ignore him.

"Thank you," I said, quickly stepping away.

He grabbed my hand and held the pot out to Mary without looking at her. She quickly retrieved it, her cheeks pink and an unspoken apology in her eyes. Behind Thomas, Anton winked at me and strode out the door.

"Do you have questions for me?" Thomas asked.

"How many are in your pack now?"

His lips curled in a slight smile.

"Nine."

He sounded so proud of that number.

"And what will you do with those nine pack members?"

"Fix this place. See if we can't find ourselves a new purpose."

"How exactly did you gain each of your new pack members?"

The humor faded from his expression. He studied me, and I could tell he was trying to figure out where I was going with my questions. When he didn't answer, I asked my next question.

"If he would have won, Mary would have become one of his

pack. What if she didn't want to be one of his pack? Could she just leave?"

"She could," Winifred said, entering the room. She closed the door behind her and gave Mary a reassuring smile. "However, she would have been considered Forlorn, an outcast, until she could find another pack to take her. Mated, that would be an option. However, an unMated Forlorn female is a dangerous position. Even for a moment."

"Could she just rejoin her father's pack?"

"Once her father is proven weak in a challenge, he would find himself constantly challenged by those looking to win an unMated female," Winifred said.

I turned back to Thomas.

"Did you challenge her father?"

"No."

But if she went back to her father after defecting from his pack, he would be challenged. Why had she left in the first place? Was it because she was getting ready to say yes to Gregory? Or had Thomas interfered?

"Did you tell Gregory to ask her to join your pack since they will be Mated eventually?"

He didn't respond, answering the question with his silence.

"I'm guessing being part of your pack isn't all Mary had hoped it would be. I'm also guessing that leaving her current pack to rejoin her father's isn't as easy as one might think." I turned toward Mary. "He's telling you to keep secrets and to do things you don't like, and you're feeling guilty about it. Don't. I'm pretty smart and will know whom to blame once I figure everything out." I eyed Thomas. "And I will figure it out."

His lips curled a little, not a smile but a show of his frustration with me. I kept my face neutral and stared back.

"The water's getting cold," I said.

He took the hint, let go of my wrist, and closed himself in the bathroom.

"Mary, help yourself to breakfast. Winifred, could I talk to you outside for a moment?"

She nodded and walked outside with me. Men still wandered the yard, but I saw no sign of a wounded wolf or man. I could only guess he'd already left.

"Breakfast is ready," I said to whomever might care to listen. Several of the men went inside. Winifred and I kept walking.

"Do you have your keys with you?" I asked, moving toward her truck.

"They are in the ignition."

I couldn't have been happier. Opening the passenger door, I asked, "Would you mind taking me to the junkyard? I could use a little time away from here."

"Certainly." She got in, started the engine, and we were off.

"I believe he does mean well," she said as we bounced down the driveway.

"I'm sure he does." I stared out my window for a moment. "Mary wasn't the one who wanted to start sleeping with Gregory, was she?" I asked, finally.

"No. She didn't want to leave you, yet."

My eyes narrowed at Thomas' sneaky, underhanded move.

"What does he gain by being in the room with me at night?"

"He truly believes he is your Mate. He wants to protect you and be near you."

"And the others?" I said. "Didn't they truly believe I was their Mate?"

"They did."

"What makes him think he's different, then?" I asked, studying Winifred.

"His unwillingness to give up. Ever."

His promise never to bite me again kept me from worrying about his persistence. That didn't mean I would accept him in my room at night anymore.

"Can you ask Mary if she'd like to move back into the room with me? Let her know it's okay if she wants to stay with Gregory."

"She would rather be in with you. She worries about you. I do, too. There are too many males here and not enough control. I wish I could stay with you; but as Mary and Thomas pointed out, I'm the only reason they have a safe place to roam."

"Aren't there more of you? I mean, like you?" I couldn't recall the word Mary had used to describe her.

"Another Elder?"

That was it.

"Yes."

"My predecessor died two winters ago. There is another in Europe. We talk often about the packs and the future of our kind. He worries because there haven't been any volunteers since me. Not many are willing to accept this lonely life of responsibility."

Her life sounded so much like the life I anticipated for myself.

"Can I be one?"

She glanced at me, a smile stretching her face.

"That you would ask says so much about you, Charlene." She turned back to watch the road. "Unfortunately, I can't touch your mind as I can my own kind. Without touching your mind, I cannot make you an Elder."

"Mary said you can touch the minds of all of your kind. Have you asked them if anyone else wants to be an Elder?"

"We don't touch the minds of those we protect until they initiate it, or to protect them or those around them."

"Wouldn't the point of having another Elder, especially back there, be to protect them? I don't see how you can do this on your own and keep everyone safe. Doesn't that make it a necessity to actively search out more who would be willing to share your responsibilities?"

She was quiet a long moment.

"You prove age has no bearing on wisdom."

"Wisdom is gained from experience," I said.

"It is, and I'm wondering what's happened to you to make you so wise."

I gave Winifred a sad smile.

"A lot of heartache, secrets, and lies."

We drove in silence for several minutes.

"He agrees. Elder Jean will send out the request—he is likely to receive more responses—and will direct those interested and living on this continent to me."

"I hope you find a few who are willing."

"We shall see."

For the remainder of the ride, we talked about our plans for the buildings in the near future. The conversation helped keep me from growing too nervous about leaving the safety of their grounds. Thankfully, she turned off onto a side road before we reached town.

When we arrived at the dump, she and I walked the yard looking for lost treasures. We collected more chipped dishes, bent flatware, and plastic cups. I found a shovel with a broken wooden handle, a rake with broken tines, and a few other tools that would be useful, once repaired.

Winifred found me less than an hour later as I was checking some of the old cars for loose change. I managed to find five dollars.

"We need to head back. A few of the men want to sell some of the items they've repaired, and I promised to take them into town."

SOME REPAIRED CHAIRS, lamps, and a few other odd items waited in a pile when Winifred navigated the truck into the yard. Three men stood near the items, watching our progress as we parked. Two broke away and began to unload what we'd found while the other began to carry pieces from the pile to the back of the truck.

"Go on inside," Winifred said, opening her door. "I'm sure you want to tell Mary what we've found."

I nodded and let myself into the main room. Mary and Ann looked up from the table. They were both in the process of sewing.

"Did you find anything interesting?" Mary asked, as I held the door open for one of the men.

"Not nearly as interesting as the things you found. Some dishes, a few more tools, and," I reached into my pocket and withdrew my fisted hand. "Some change." I let it clatter to the table.

Mary picked up a coin and studied it. "Interesting."

"It'll help buy us whatever we can't scrounge. Food most likely."

"Winifred says the pile of scrap will help with that, too," Mary said.

The door to the main room opened, and I looked up to see Thomas walk in. The discolored skin around his left eye made him look sickly and annoyed. No, his expression made him look annoyed.

"Don't ever leave like that again." He stomped across the room, stopped in front of me, crossed his arms, and proceeded to scowl at me.

I studied him for a moment, suppressing my natural indignant response, and went with the unexpected.

"All right."

His arms lost some of their rigidity.

"All right?"

"Yes. All right. I understand that you were worried, and your request is only so you don't worry in the future. It's a reasonable request."

I smiled and moved to check the supplies as if to decide what to make for our midday meal.

"Oh," I said, stopping and looking back at him. "And don't ever again command Mary to do something for your own personal gain. It's beneath you. Mary, I'll help you move your stuff back into our room."

Thomas didn't react as I expected. He didn't try to say his presence was to protect me. He neither denied what he'd done nor tried to excuse it. Instead, he laughed.

"Fair enough." He glanced at Mary. "I will make sure Gregory understands."

She smiled at him and nodded gratefully.

"I'll return with some meat for the meal. Did you, by any chance, find something to help keep your birds in their coop?"

I reluctantly shook my head. He nodded and left.

As soon as the door closed, Mary got up and hugged me.

"I was so worried you'd be mad."

"About him making you leave the room? No. I understand everyone's reasons."

"Do you want help?" she asked, nodding toward the stove.

"No. I think I'll do another stew, over plain rice this time, and set some water to boil. I want a bath, and there's a pile of dirty clothes to wash."

I spent the rest of my day at the stove or washing something —myself, dishes, laundry. By the time the sun set, I wanted nothing more than my bed.

I shuffled into my room and froze. Mary's bed was there, as were her things, but so was Thomas. He leaned against the wall just under the window.

"What are you doing here?"

"Keeping you safe."

"I thought I told you..." I realized I hadn't told him I didn't want him in our room, only that I wanted Mary back and that he shouldn't command her about for no good reason.

He stood, taking up too much space in the room, and approached me slowly. His gaze never left me, not even when he had to bend his head down, because he towered over me.

"You told me what I needed to hear, the truth. Someday I will figure out how to make you mine, and I can only hope I'll be worthy of you then." He lifted his hand and gently brushed his fingers over my cheek.

Pretty words meant to please, a part of me whispered. But did he really know what they meant?

"What will it take to be worthy?" I asked.

He considered me for several long moments. "I don't know."

"If you don't know, how will you know if you're worthy?" I gave him a small smile to take the sting from my words. "Be honest, not just with others, but yourself. Be loyal, not just to those you love, but to those who need you. Work hard to improve the lives of those around you. Don't waver from your integrity. And, above all..." I leaned toward him and lowered my voice to a whisper. "Don't assume you can sleep in my room again."

His gaze dropped to my mouth.

"Kiss me and I'll leave."

"In your world, my age is acceptable for Claiming and Mating. In my world, while you helped my father clean his gun, he would tell you to wait another year then come back and speak to him again. And, that would be to take me on a date. A kiss would be months after that." I stepped back, putting space between us. "Since you've kissed me twice already, I think that's enough of a compromise, for now."

"Not nearly." He tugged me forward. Off balance, I braced my palms on his chest. He wrapped an arm around me and lifted my chin with a finger before I could blink. His lips touched mine. Soft and sweet and full of promise, his warm mouth brushed over mine twice. My eyes fluttered shut, and my heart went crazy.

Every time we stood too close, I secretly hoped for this. My heart and stomach said yes while my mind hesitated. Yet, when his lips touched mine, doubt fled. He felt right. We felt right. I could understand his persistence when we kissed.

He pulled back enough to kiss my cheek.

"I will be worthy," he said softly. Then, he let me go and left the room.

I stood there with a hammering heart. I wasn't sure if it was due to the excitement of the kiss or the fear that he would be worthy, and I'd need to face an uncertain future with these people.

CHAPTER ELEVEN

Early Sunday morning, Winifred left with her empty cookie plate and a truck bed full of metal. I leaned in the doorway, watching the taillights pass through the trees.

"What should we work on today?" Mary asked. I caught her upward glance and followed her gaze. A sky, dark with heavy clouds, promised a day of rain and storms.

That meant inside work. Ann and Mary had done a good job sewing yesterday. Ann had taken several pieces with her to her room last night to make things for the baby. Earlier, Leif had come to take breakfast back to her. She wasn't feeling well.

"Sewing, I guess." Not my favorite pastime. A rumble echoed across the clearing, and I retreated indoors. Sewing beat being soaked, though.

We'd barely made it to the table when a loud boom made us both jump. Seconds later, rain lashed at the main room's window. Mary and I looked at each other. Anton had only managed to repair a few more windows on the second floor with the salvaged glass. Casements that had once held broken shards, a partial barrier against the elements, were now completely empty thanks to our repair efforts.

Rain whipped through the air from the east, the direction of the clearing. We ran from the room to start checking windows. The intensity of the deluge brought a concerning amount of water through the moderate openings in more than a dozen rooms.

"We should have boarded them," Mary said, eyeing the growing puddles on the floor.

I looked at the water and then tilted my head to look at the boards above. Drips of water fell from the ceiling of the room in which we stood. A little rain wouldn't hurt the wood too much the first time, but I recalled the already sagging porch and wondered how many times rain had already soaked this wood. How long until it turned rotten? We couldn't take chances like this.

Winifred had left me with thirty dollars from the items they'd brought to town. That made a total of forty-three dollars in my possession. It wasn't enough to replace the boards in this place if they all went bad at once.

"It's not too late to board the windows down here," I said. "But I don't think we can do anything about the second floor."

"Winifred is listening to her radio. The storm should pass in a few hours.

The wind howled outside, and further down the hallway a door banged shut. Above the noise, I heard someone call my name.

"Here," I called back.

Anton found us staring at the wet room.

"Come on. I have something to show you."

In the main room, we found several squares of wood set on

the tables. They were all just a bit bigger than the size of the windows. A man stood near them, waiting for us.

"Hello," I said, meeting his gaze.

He nodded. "Before Henry and Paul left, we started to make these with a few of the broken boards from the shed. They fit over the windows for the most part. I have more started but ran out of nails."

"These are perfect," I said, lifting one to eye the construction. It was a frame covered by boards. The frame would fit over the casement that stuck outside. I counted six on the table.

"Totally awesome. Thank you," I said, looking at the man again. "Let's put these on. I have some money to go get more nails when it stops raining."

I'd made it a step from the table when Thomas opened the door from outside.

"Not you," he said with a frown. "We'll do it. Once we have these on, we'll do what we can to protect the rest of the windows."

The man picked up a stack, Anton plucked the one from my hands, and the three left.

"What was the point of coming to get us?" I said to Mary. She shrugged.

It took them an hour to board the exposed windows. They used old, rusted nails and whatever else they could find that was solid enough to drive through the wood. It took Mary and me even longer to clean up the water. By the time we finished, the rain was letting up.

We brought the wet cloths and the pots to the kitchen. As soon as we walked into the main room, I smelled cooking meat. Two birds already roasted on the fire, and when I checked the oven, I found two more in low pans. Carrots and potatoes crowded around the baking birds. My mouth started to water as I stared at the carrots.

While Mary dumped the excess water, I pumped some more into a pot for rice. I couldn't wait to eat.

The door opened with a bang, and a group of four men I didn't recognize strode in. Rain dripped off their naked skin. I froze; my hand, full of dried rice, posed over the water. The gaze of the first man through the door settled on me.

"What do we have here? I thought I smelled smoke."

I flicked a quick glance at Mary. She was staring at the men with wide eyes. I hoped she was mentally screaming at Winifred or Thomas. I did not want to use my will against these people any more. They were beaten enough without me adding to it.

I tilted my hand, dumped the rice into the water, and fully turned toward the men.

"Welcome. There are dry clothes in the entry. You can help yourself to what you need. Food will be ready soon."

He stared at me as a slow grin spread over his features and lit his eyes.

"We were told to come here. No one said there would be unClaimed females to tempt us away from our choice to become Elder."

Understanding why they'd suddenly appeared helped ease some of my fear.

"We're not here to tempt you, but we are the reason more Elders are needed. Winifred will return Friday. Until then, you're welcome to take one of the rooms on the first floor and some clothes." I really hoped they'd get the hint and put some pants on.

The man in front didn't lose his grin as he took a step toward me. A hand clapped down on his shoulder, stopping his advance.

"Remember why we're here," the second man said.

The third stepped forward. "We're here because there aren't enough females for all of us. Yet, here are two, and one seems a definite possibility. We haven't committed to anything. Why not explore the possibilities." As he spoke, he began to change. Most notably, his teeth.

I wasn't about to allow another bite. I struck out suddenly and violently with my will. *Wait outside.* All four men stumbled back and blinked dazedly. Then, as one, they turned and left.

Mary gave me a shaken look as I exhaled slowly.

"What did Winifred have to say about them?" I asked, hoping Mary would think Winifred had sent them out.

"I'm sorry. I didn't think of her. I just reached out to Thomas. He's on his way." She paused for a moment. "Winifred is speaking to them now and to Thomas. He's angry none of the men he left here stopped them from entering."

I turned away from Mary, not wanting her to see my worry or frustration. All of Thomas' talk about protecting, and where was he? And Winifred? I thought she reached out to everyone who came here to tell them not to bite me.

"Can you set out the bowls and plates?" I said to Mary, keeping my voice level and calm. I went to the fire, removed the two birds, then set the food on the tables.

Outside, a chorus of growls rose loud and fierce. Because I was near the window, I automatically looked up.

Thomas strode from the woods. He focused on the wolves crouched near the door. I glanced at them as well. Anton, Bine, and Gregory surrounded them. Both sides eyed each other warily, with the strangers growling and casting glances at Thomas. One of the wolves looked back at the window and caught me watching. He stared at me. He shifted his position slightly, angling himself more toward the window. His muscles bunched. Would he really try to get to me through the window?

Quickly looking away, I focused on Thomas. He saw the wolf watching me, and his face twisted in rage. Instead of walking or running the last few yards, he jumped. As he flew through the air, he shifted from man to wolf and landed right in front of the one watching me. The newcomer twisted at the sound of Thomas' landing and growled. Thomas dove for him.

Mary tugged me back. "We need to go upstairs. Now. Winifred's orders."

"No. Tell Winifred, I will keep you safe. I need to know what's happening. I thought they were here to be Elders."

"Winifred says their actions show their selfishness. None of them would have passed. Two have already challenged Thomas for leadership. The three will fight. The last one standing commands the pack."

I turned to look out the window. It seemed that the two challengers had decided to help each other. One taunted Thomas while the other tried to sneak behind him. Thomas was too smart for the move. He carefully kept himself positioned so he could see both of them while he slowly backed away from the building.

One of the wolves looked back at the two who still hovered near our door. Anton, Gregory, and Bine moved to block them from joining the fight. The two outsiders shifted back into men, crossed their arms, and widened their stance. Gregory nodded his approval, and the three turned back toward the fight.

One of the outsiders glanced at the window and grinned at

me. While still meeting my gaze, he edged closer to the door. His companion remained close, guarding the movements of the first man so they wouldn't appear obvious.

"Mary, tell Thomas not to worry about us and to stay focused on his fight, no matter what."

I stepped away from the window and waited. It didn't take long for the latch to move. As soon as the door opened, I swung out. *Leave.*

This time, the man and his companion flew backward, out into the yard. One knocked into Bine and almost brought him down.

Anton, Gregory, and Bine immediately shifted into wolves. They surrounded the men, their snarls and poised positions keeping them where they lay.

I stepped out into the rain and looked down at the fallen men.

"You are no longer welcome. Leave," I said, pointing to the trees. They rose, growled at me, then turned and ran. Anton and Bine followed them to the edge of the trees while Gregory stood in front of me.

Their retreat distracted one of the wolves fighting Thomas. Thomas used that opening to lunge forward. He clamped down over the other's muzzle. If the wolf bled, the rain washed it away before I could notice.

A wolf ran from the trees a distance from where Bine and Anton still stood. I didn't take my eyes from the fight. However, from my peripheral, I recognized Grey.

Thomas shook his head, maintaining his hold and knocking the other wolf off balance as Grey raced across the clearing. The second wolf noticed Grey, too, and hesitated. He turned sideways to watch Grey's progress and the fight.

Halfway across the clearing, Grey shifted. I, at first, thought he meant to join the fight. Instead, Grey stopped just in front of me, shielding me. Gregory tried to nudge me to the door, but I tapped him on the nose in annoyance, and he didn't try again.

Seeing that Grey and Gregory had no intention of interfering, the second wolf launched himself at Thomas, trying to clamp down on his neck. Thomas twisted, keeping himself free while continuing to subdue the first challenger.

I didn't see how two to one fighting was a valid challenge for leadership. What kind of leader would the pack have if he needed help to fight his battles? The thought stopped me. A leader shouldn't jeopardize his people when he wasn't willing to jeopardize himself. But a good leader would accept help when needed, too. Whether Thomas asked or not, he needed help.

I watched Thomas finally let loose of his hold on the first challenger. The wolf's muzzle bled profusely, but he paid it little attention. Instead, he worked with the other challenger to circle Thomas. They managed to maneuver until one stood before Thomas and the other at Thomas' hind leg. The one at Thomas' back coiled, ready to spring.

"Can't either of you take Thomas on your own?" I asked, loudly. The second wolf hesitated to attack again. "If not, what kind of leaders will you make?" A snarl arose from those in Thomas' pack. "I think you'll find yourselves challenged by others in his pack." I gently laid a hand on the backs of both Gregory and Grey. "You're both attacking him at the same time because you know he's special. He has the loyalty of his pack, and even if you defeat him, what will you have gained? Gregory will Claim Mary in an instant to protect her, and they will leave, as will the rest. You'll be the leader of nothing."

The one hesitating growled at me. I didn't stop speaking, though.

"If you want to be part of something great, then stop fighting. Concede to Thomas and join his pack. Don't try to lead it. You were never meant to."

A group of men stepped from the trees, distracting me from the fight. I recognized the man who strode ahead of the rest. He'd been the one who'd attacked me several days before...the man who'd pushed me to the ground and scraped my face.

"It is our right and our way to challenge for control," he said, anger lacing his words. "You have no right here. After Thomas finishes with these two, I challenge for pack leadership and rights to this land and these buildings."

That the group had remained close was concerning. That they'd chosen to challenge Thomas immediately after he finished his current one concerned me even more. Thomas obviously fought well, but for how long? He would tire eventually.

The two wolves attacking him seemed to think the same thing. They both launched at Thomas. Snarls and growls filled the air again as Thomas twisted to avoid teeth and claws and feinted to try to score either of the pair. One got lucky and raked Thomas' head. His ear bled.

Thomas jumped, landed on the back of the one with the torn muzzle, and used his back legs to tangle with his opponent's. The move brought the wolf down and exposed its throat. Thomas dove for the opening, and a gurgle cut off the wolf's startled yelp before I could look away. The focus cost Thomas, though.

The second wolf sprang forward just as Thomas lifted his head, exposing his own throat. I gasped. Thomas twisted, looking away from the attacker. Teeth tore the side of his neck instead of his throat.

Thomas pushed backward into his attacker. The challenger lost his footing and fell onto his back. The fight ended for him just as quickly and in the same manner as his partner.

I lifted my hand from Gregory's back and wiped the wet hair from my face. Thomas stood over the second wolf, head down, and chest heaving. The two fallen wolves were slowly reverting to their human forms.

The man who'd issued the last challenge stepped forward, obviously ready to begin.

"Stop," I said.

The man turned to me with thunder in his eyes. "Do not interfere."

"Two of your kind just died. Allow a few minutes for those who might know them to remove them and grieve. That's not interference. It's respect for your own people."

He snarled at me but nodded. A few men stepped forward and walked to the fallen pair.

"Thomas, Mary is worried about you. While they are grieving, can you speak with her?" I knew better than to say I was worried or to ask him inside to clean his wounds. His opponent would most likely not allow me, the interloper, any kindness nor Thomas any quarter. But Mary was one of his own. Plus, I knew she would be worried, too.

Thomas trotted toward me, bumped me with his nose to indicate I should go first, and followed me inside.

Once inside, he reverted to his human form. He bore a cut near his left eye and bled too much from his neck to see the exact extent of the damage there. He had a nasty bruise forming on his right shoulder and a cut high on his thigh.

I nodded toward the table, pretending he wasn't standing there naked. He silently sat and waited as I quickly retrieved a cloth then began to clean his neck. Someone had managed to bite him, if the four punctures in his skin was any indication. But, they weren't so deep that the teeth between the canines had marked him. He was lucky. I hurriedly doused his skin with alcohol. My purpose wasn't to disinfect as much as to make him taste bad and deter further biting.

While I helped Thomas, Mary emptied the cooked rice onto several plates and refilled all our pots with water. We would need it. She set as many as she could on the stovetop and the remaining two by the fire.

No one spoke as we worked. I knew too well those outside probably listened, and I didn't want them to know just how bad Thomas was. I gently touched his torn ear. It needed to be stitched, but I knew there wasn't time for that. Hopefully, the next fight wouldn't take long.

When I made a move to step back, Thomas' hands wrapped around my waist, anchoring me. Our gazes met; his reflected weariness. He exhaled heavily and leaned his forehead to my chest. My stomach somersaulted. I stayed still for a moment, staring down at his dark hair, before I set the alcohol aside and lifted a hand. I touched him gently. His hair, his undamaged ear, his bruised shoulder. I tried to give him the kindness he wouldn't find when he walked back out into the yard.

Someone pounded on the door. "It's time."

Thomas lifted his head and stood. He didn't let go of me, though. A blush heated my cheeks as his hips bumped against mine. It was an unintentional result of him standing without letting go, rather than a lustful move. Yet, we both stilled. His gaze held mine, and he lowered his head. My heart thumped heavily, and I lifted my lips to meet his. My chest felt too tight the instant before our mouths touched. The heat spread, relieving an ache I hadn't recognized until it was gone.

I lifted my hands to his chest to steady myself. He tilted his head and pressed his lips more firmly against mine. Then he was gone.

My breathing was quick and short, and my eyes strayed to his backside. He stopped before the door and shifted back into a wolf, hiding his injuries with fur. The door opened. Grey held it for Thomas. When he saw me, he winked. Thomas trotted out, leaving Mary and me alone in the main room.

"For a Claim that didn't work, you sure seem interested," Mary said in a hushed tone.

I gave her a sidelong glance but remained quiet. I'd been interested in many things throughout my life—I thought of the hair ribbons I'd outgrown—but nothing lasted forever, and part of me hoped my interest in Thomas was one of those things.

Mary and I walked to the window. We couldn't see much as too many men stood around the fight. But we could hear the snarls and growls.

"I can't stay in here," I said, moving to the door.

"We can't go out there," Mary said, grabbing my arm.

Deep down, I felt I was meant to be here, that I was meant to help these people. I was certain Winifred thought that way, too. Without Thomas or a similarly sympathetic wolf in charge of the lead pack, I'd find myself removed from their lives. I couldn't let my fate solely rest on Thomas' shoulders. But, what did I think I could accomplish by going out there? I couldn't use my powers again. It was too risky. There had to be more I could do. I had to be worth more than just my abilities. If there was a way to help Thomas, I would find it.

"Mary, please. Let go."

She shook her head but let go as I'd asked. I opened the door and stepped out. Grey and Gregory, still wolves, guarded the door and moved with me as I walked forward. A few from the crowd turned to look as I made my way toward the circle. Men moved aside for me, some with growls.

Thomas and his challenger already bled. Thomas conserved his movements, letting the other circle him between attacks. I watched silently, inwardly cringing at the injuries both received as the fight wore on.

Finally, Thomas' opponent made a mistake that exposed his throat. Thomas had the wolf on its back within a heartbeat and dove for his neck.

"Wait," I said, stepping into the circle as Thomas' teeth closed down. Thomas didn't remove his hold, but he paused.

"Winifred said your kind is dying. Since I've been here, I've witnessed three maybe four deaths. You're killing each other because you have different beliefs regarding the future of your people. But you're forgetting your common belief, that your kind does have a future. Stop killing. Show tolerance and mercy."

"Thomas wants to know what you propose," Mary said. I hadn't realized she'd followed me out. She stood beside Gregory. It made sense, I supposed. If Thomas had failed, Gregory would have Claimed her.

"Ask him to join your pack," I said. "Spare his life if he consents. Give him a chance to understand your beliefs while giving yourself a chance to understand his."

"Thomas understands the pup's beliefs well enough," Mary said. "They were the same beliefs he held until he met you. This whelp has already met you and still will not open his eyes to see what's before him."

"And what's before him, Thomas?"

Mary spoke for him again.

"Certain death. Whether by me or a future without Mates, his way leads to death."

"I can't promise there are more like me out there," I said. In fact, I felt certain there weren't. "But I want all of you to think on this: Your women are scattered and in hiding for their protection. It makes it hard for you to find and meet them. If we made this place into a true sanctuary, more women like Ann might come. If they can have their children here, and those children grow up here, the Mates you so desperately want will be more accessible. But only if you protect this place and that idea. Sanctuary for your kind."

No one moved as the challenger shifted from wolf to man. Thomas didn't shift or adjust his hold on the man's throat, and empathy welled at the sight of the blood running down his neck.

"I consent to join your pack...for now," the man rasped.

Thomas growled in response.

How foolish could the man be to throw a half-promise at Thomas like that?

"I will not leave your pack because your pack will fall apart on its own," the man said. "You and I both know you're already holding eight to you. How many more do you think you can hold? So, I accept. I'm sure there are a few others who would like to join as well."

The man sounded too smug. I wanted to ask Mary what he meant about Thomas's hold and the pack falling apart but couldn't in front of everyone. So I waited with the rest, watching Thomas.

Thomas' gaze met mine briefly. Then, he released his hold. He stood on the man's chest and looked down at him until the man turned his head aside. Satisfied, Thomas trotted away. Another man stepped into his path.

"I'll join," he said. He, too, wore a smirk.

"Excuse me," I said, quickly moving to Thomas' side. Grey was close beside me. "There will be plenty of time for joining a pack. Right now, the dinner Mary and I made is going to waste. Please, come inside and eat."

The man glanced at Thomas, who stiffly faced him.

"Later, then."

Thomas bobbed his head, and I inwardly sighed with relief. Whatever this hold was, it sounded as if it was in danger, and I needed to understand why.

CHAPTER TWELVE

No one moved to go inside, so Thomas nudged me forward. As soon as I started walking, Mary joined me. Thomas, Gregory, and Grey fell in right behind us.

Inside, Mary and I went to the stove, and Thomas trotted straight into the bathroom. She and I worked together to haul the water to the tub while Grey and Gregory stood nearby, warily eyeing the outsiders I'd just invited in to eat with us. I paid little attention to the men who were slowly seating themselves.

Thomas stayed out of our way, waiting, as we paced between the stove and the tub.

When I dumped in the last pot, he had six inches of steaming water. Enough to wash in, but I knew he'd need extra to rinse. I left the small room once more; and when I returned with a cold pot of water, Thomas wasn't where he'd been. The door shut behind me. I turned and saw him slowly shifting from his wolf form.

"I'll just go help Mary," I said, quickly averting my eyes and setting the pot near the tub.

"Help me," he said. Blood smeared his face, neck, and legs. Bruises coated his torso. He walked to the tub and stepped in with a grunt. He had my pity. I sighed and turned to grab a few cloths from the washstand. I tossed one to him.

"Cover up first," I said.

He chuckled, and I blushed; but I refused to look his direction until he complied.

"You can look now."

I peeked at him then quickly looked away again. The small square of material covered him, but it certainly didn't lend any modesty to the situation.

"I really would rather someone else help you."

"Mary put the sewing kit in here. I'd rather you help me."

His ear. Reluctantly, I faced him. He leaned back in the tub, his legs stretched out with only a slight bend in his knees. The water already had a pink tint to it, and he hadn't even washed his upper torso or head yet.

Cuts littered his skin. Most were shallow, but a few appeared as if a stitch or two wouldn't be remiss.

"Fine," I said. I fetched the bowl from the washstand and dipped it into the tub between his legs.

"Lean forward."

He leaned forward, and I slowly poured the water over his head. Blood, hidden by his dark hair, trailed down his back. Claw marks scored him, raised paths of red welts occasionally broken by a cut or scrape. Bruises colored his sides. I honestly didn't know what I could do for him.

I repeated the process, wondering what good it did to rinse with bloody water.

"Can you have Mary heat more water?"

"She already is," he said, wiping a hand across his face and leaning back once more. I set the bowl aside and reached for his right arm. I lifted it to the edge of the tub. He did the same with the other arm. It gave me a better view of his ribs and chest and everything that needed some type of aid.

"I can't stitch you," I said, sitting back on my heels. "I'm horrible at regular sewing, and the thought of poking a needle through skin..." I shuddered. "Please let Mary help you."

He sighed, sunk lower in the tub, and laid his head back. "Not Mary."

Someone knocked on the door a moment before it opened.

"Hello, Charlene," Grey said, stepping in.

"Hi, Grey." I stood, moved away from the tub, and considered the door for a moment.

"Stay, Charlene," Thomas said as if sensing my thoughts. "I don't trust you out there alone."

"All right." I knew it was the men he didn't trust, not me.

Grey grabbed the sewing kit from the washstand and came to join me by the tub. He looked his brother over and chuckled at the square of cloth in Thomas' lap.

"Just the ear, I think," Grey said.

"Are you sure? He has a large cut on his thigh, and his neck has several holes."

"Those will knit together quickly. Barely a scar. The ear is different. The cartilage makes healing more difficult." He threaded the needle and used alcohol on everything.

Thomas made a small noise between his teeth when the needle pierced his skin. My stomach roiled, and I looked away.

The knuckles of Thomas' hand were bloody. I took one of the cloths, dipped it in the cold rinse water, and gently started to clean away the red. His hand turned, catching mine. His thumb brushed over the top of my fingers. I couldn't look up and meet his gaze, not with Grey sewing his ear.

I watched Thomas' thumb until Grey stood.

"I'll leave you to finish," he said. The door closed behind him.

"I can finish on my own," Thomas said, his thumb never stilling. "The room is clear of everyone but Mary and Grey. Go eat."

I still couldn't look at him. I nodded and stood, and he let my hand go.

"Save me some food if there's enough," he said as I walked toward the door. I looked over my shoulder and saw him gently touching his ear.

"I will." Then I left him, too.

Mary stood at the pump, washing dishes. Grey leaned against the wall near the door, no doubt our guard.

"There's a plate on the table for you," Mary said.

"Thank you. Did Ann get a plate?"

"Yes, Leif came for hers." Leif and Ann mostly kept to their room whenever there were more than a few men around. Leif protected Ann well.

I sat and ate a cold carrot from one of the two plates waiting on the small table. It was heaven, and my food disappeared too soon. As I brought the plate to the sink, the bathroom door opened.

Thomas stepped out wearing a clean pair of pants. His hair was still damp, but the rest of him looked dry. He followed me to the pump and reached under the trough for the bucket Mary and I used to empty the tub. We usually just emptied all the water through the trough, which ran out clay pipes into a low spot behind the building. It was a lot quicker and safer than walking around the buildings.

"It's all right. Leave it for now," I said. "When Mary and I finish with the dishes, we'll empty it. We don't want to mix bath water with dish water."

He straightened, nodded, and went to eat his own plate of food. As soon as he finished, he brought the plate to the sink then left with Grey.

Finally alone with Mary, I asked what I'd been wondering since the fight ended.

"Mary, what did that man mean about Thomas only being able to hold so many?" I asked, trying to speak softly.

Mary grinned and shook her head. "Don't worry. It's no secret. Every leader has a limit on the number of members he can hold in his pack. Winifred says it's like how much a person can lift. It's different for everyone. The connection I have with Thomas doesn't feel strained. Adding two more members shouldn't be a problem."

I nodded and began to dry the plates.

"Winifred has no limits, though, right?"

"No. But she doesn't really hold our kind together like a pack leader does. She says her role is a bit difficult to explain, and she'd rather do it in person."

"There's no need. Tell her I was just curious."

I put the dried plates on the mantel and pulled the pots from the stove. Mary had already filled most of them with water to make cleaning easier. Once we had the roasters washed, I started filling the pots with water for our evening meal.

"Do you know what kind of meat we're getting tonight?"

Mary was quiet for a minute.

"Thomas is sending the new pack members out to hunt something big."

"Big?"

Mary nodded slowly, a slight frown growing.

"There are quite a few new members. Thomas wonders if we can make enough to feed twenty."

We'd been feeding twelve, sometimes a few more, when he only had nine members. I looked at the pots on the stove and the supply cabinets.

"Yes," I said firmly. I put two pots on the stove. I emptied a large bag of beans into one. If they weren't ready for tonight, they could soak overnight for tomorrow. Carrying another pot to the pump to fill for wash water, I thought of the meal we'd just eaten and wished we had more fresh vegetables. "Do you know where the carrots came from or who might have gotten them?"

Mary shrugged.

"They weren't from one of the pack, so I'm not sure."

The door opened, and I turned from the pump to see Thomas and Grey stride in. Thomas seemed frustrated. His eyes didn't give him away; it was his hands. He tapped his middle finger on his leg as he walked. He made his way to the table and sat. I noted a dark slash on his pants and knew he'd bled a bit more after putting the clean pair on.

"Is everything all right?" I asked.

"Everything's fine. I sent all of the new members out to find bigger game since they feel it is now their right to eat at a table." He ran his hand through his hair. His fingers lingered at his temple.

"Headache? I'm not sure if medicine will work the same on

you, but there is some pain reliever left." I made to move toward the cabinet, but he stopped me.

"It won't help."

"What will help?" I asked.

"Cooperation."

I studied his face. He looked tired, which I would expect after the morning and afternoon he'd had. But there seemed to be something more weighing on him. His weary gaze held mine as if begging me to help.

"I don't understand," I said.

"Eight more have joined my pack...eight angry men with the single purpose of pulling my pack apart."

"Why let them join, then?" I asked, leaning back against the trough.

"Several reasons. As a member of my pack, there is little any of them can hide from me; and when I command them, they must obey. That means more protection for us from those who still want to cause trouble. But it also means resistance because the new members are doing things they don't want to do."

"Like what?"

"Leaving these buildings to hunt for food to feed the pack. They would rather stay and make nuisances of themselves, in hopes of making you leave. Their resistance to my command..." He rubbed his head again. "Imagine I'm holding one end of a rope, and the other end is held by a member of my pack. We are both pulling to keep the rope taut. When the member cooperates in holding their end steady, it requires very little effort on my part to keep the right tension in the rope. However, if the member pulls, I need to use more force to pull back to keep the member from pulling away completely."

It sounded a lot like how I controlled a human's will.

"Now imagine sixteen ropes. I hold the end of all those ropes in one hand, and each member holds their own end. If one of those members pulls hard enough to jerk their rope from my grasp, I lose hold on all the ropes. The pack will fall apart. A leader can only hold so many ropes here." He tapped his head. "And the more ropes he holds that resist him, the harder it becomes to maintain control."

"So you need their cooperation."

"Yes."

And he didn't have their cooperation because of my presence.

"Do you want me to leave?"

He gave a weary smile and shook his head.

"No. I want to know how I can Claim you. As my Mate, they are less likely to resist you. As my Mate, you could help me hold the pack together." He sighed, his expression rueful. "I want to keep trying, Charlene. I promise I won't hurt you again."

I couldn't believe he was asking.

"Does your neck hurt?" I asked.

"A bit."

"Good," I said. He exhaled a laugh, and I put my hands on my hips, annoyed with him. "It's not fun being bitten, is it?"

"If you were doing the biting, I'd think it very fun."

My stomach pitched wildly, and heat rose to my face.

"I'm tempted to bite you just to prove it wouldn't be."

He stood suddenly and crowded me until I backed up against the pump. The sound of a door closing distracted me, and I pulled my gaze away long enough to note we were now alone in the room.

"Do it," he said, reclaiming my attention.

He tilted his head to the side, daring me with his eyes to follow through with my threat.

"Perhaps when your neck doesn't look like raw meatloaf," I said.

"My neck hurts. My ribs hurt. My head hurts." He sighed, again, and leaned down until his forehead rested on mine. "May I sleep in your room tonight?"

I knew he was playing on my pity. Yet, I didn't want to say no. Why should I? He promised not to bite me. He wanted to stay in my room to protect me. And he was asking permission instead of assuming. He was respecting every condition and limit I'd put on our relationship.

I pulled back and focused on his eyes. Relationship? Mary was right. For saying no to Thomas, I did have a soft spot for him. But was it any different than Anton? I thought so. The sight of Thomas made my heart race and my stomach stir.

"What are you thinking?" Thomas asked.

"That you're too old and too wise for me."

"Too old?" He snorted. "I'm no more than four years older."

I grinned at him.

"I like how you didn't try to defend your wisdom."

"You're much wiser than me. Even if you're four years younger. May I sleep in your room tonight?"

"Yes, Thomas. You may."

He leaned forward, and for a moment, I thought he would kiss me. Instead, he rested his forehead on mine again, closed his eyes, and exhaled.

"If I'm the hand that holds this pack together, you'll be the heart."

THE GROUP BROUGHT BACK A DEER. Thomas made them skin and quarter it before Gregory brought it inside. Mary had enough experience that she could help me butcher it. We saved four larger roasts for the oven and tossed the rest of the meat, diced into cubes, into two pots. For such a large animal, there was less meat than I'd anticipated. But soon the smell of roasting meat filled the common room.

Thomas walked in, appearing more agitated and pale.

"Two more."

"I think you should start saying no."

"If I do, it will only make those already in the pack more resistant."

I stopped stirring the meat and went to join him at the table. Mary still sat there cutting up the last bit of meat. When I'd caught her nibbling on raw pieces, I'd left her to finish alone.

She grinned at me and popped another piece in her mouth. I shook my head and focused on Thomas, who sat across from me.

"I thought the leader of the pack could give any command and it would have to be obeyed. Can't you just command them to stop struggling against you and cooperate?"

"I can't command them to give up their freedom of will. I can remove certain choices, but ultimately, they have to be willing to obey and concede to my command. If they aren't, they can ask to leave the pack and become Forlorn."

"Wait. I thought you said if they didn't obey, they could shake the pack apart."

"A voluntary and agreed upon leaving doesn't hurt the whole pack. It's the willful resistance of many that can break a pack."

"Wini says it's nature's way of ensuring it's possible to mutiny against a bad leader," Mary said.

"Could Winifred ask them to obey?"

Thomas shook his head.

"Elders can make rules and laws to bind the will of all of our kind, but only when they are in our best interest."

"Who decides what's in your best interest?"

"The Elders."

"So two people decide the fate of your race?"

"Yes."

"She wants me to point out they are trying to find more," Mary said.

I nodded to acknowledge her. I hadn't meant to infer what they were doing was wrong or unjust. I only meant to try to understand it.

"You have to keep saying yes until the pack shakes apart, then."

"I'm hoping they run out of recruits before it becomes more than I can manage."

Tapping my fingers on the table, I considered what I knew of these new members. They didn't like me. They couldn't force Thomas to evict me so they meant to undermine his authority, thereby shaking the foundation of the pack, while also finding ways to drive me away. How did they plan to make me leave? Winifred wouldn't let them bite me—neither would I. As long as I had a dry roof over my head and food in my belly, I was fine.

They'd already brought back the food. I stopped tapping and met Thomas' gaze. Had he figured out what they would do next, too? Was that why he'd pushed to sleep in the room with me tonight?

"Charlene? Are you all right?"

"Yes. Fine. Dinner will be ready in a few hours." I stood and went back to the stove. Behind me a chair scraped on the floor. The hairs on the back of my neck rose as I picked up the spoon and stirred the meat. A moment later, his hands settled on my shoulders, and his jaw pressed against the side of my head.

"Did you know we can sense lies?"

"Yes, I believe that was mentioned already."

"Then why do you keep lying to me?"

His breath moved the hair by my ear, and I struggled not to shiver. What was it about Thomas that made me want to relax and trust him? Was it that he'd held me while I cried? Or maybe it was that he had a burden of responsibility like I did, and I desperately wanted someone to relate to me.

"Telling you I'm fine won't always mean I'm fine. Sometimes it might mean I'm not fine but don't want to talk to you," I said.

Mary started giggling behind us.

"Wini says you might want to take notes, Thomas. This wisdom is universal for females of all races. She also says 'It's fine' has several meanings. If you've done something for us, and we say, 'It's fine' that means you should go away so we can just do it the right way ourselves."

Thomas let out a long-suffering sigh.

"Must you share everything with Winifred?"

I tilted my head down as if I were staring into the pot so he wouldn't catch my grin.

"She likes me keeping her up to date. I get cookies," Mary said.

"I need to go back out. There's another waiting to make his

oath." Thomas' hands fell from my shoulders. The urge to turn around was there as I listened for the door.

I wished I could help him. I just didn't know how.

DURING THE NIGHT, a sound on the roof woke me. A single footstep, then silence. It saddened me that I'd been correct. They would try to destroy this place just to force me to leave.

In the moonlight, I could see Thomas. He sat with his back to the door, his head tilted back, and his eyes on the ceiling. From the set of his jaw, I was sure he was mentally scolding someone. From the sweat on his brow, I was equally certain that someone was resisting.

I sat up, drawing his attention. I slowly shook my head at him and held out my hand.

"Leave it," I said.

He stayed where he was for a moment then stood and walked to me. His hand wrapped around mine, and I gave him a light, reassuring squeeze before I released him. I scooted over on the narrow bed and patted the mattress.

He studied me for several long moments. The disbelief in his expression made me grin; and with an arched brow, I patted the mattress again. He quickly claimed the space, lying on his back beside me. My heart gave an odd triple beat as I stared down at him. His eyes reflected in the light as he watched me.

He reached out, curled an arm around my waist, and gave me a gentle nudge. I gave into what I wanted and rested my head on his shoulder. His arm wrapped around me, anchoring me to his side. I laid my hand over his heart and snuggled in with a sigh. He felt so right; so safe.

In the dark, we both listened for any clue as to what the new members of his pack meant to do. The longer I lay against Thomas, the more I became aware of the way he smelled. Like outdoors, just after a rain. I normally wouldn't have thought it a good smell but, lying on him, it made my head swim.

I adjusted my position, scooting a little higher, so my nose touched the undamaged side of his neck. Moving my hand from his heart, I gently feathered my fingers over his chest. The feel of his smooth skin teased my senses. I desperately wanted to kiss his shoulder and moved my head slightly. The arm around my waist held me tighter, an indication of how much he liked me close to his neck. Had he been serious about wanting me to bite him? Would he actually like that?

Worry made me stop what I was doing. I curled my hand into a fist on his chest.

He didn't say or do anything for several heartbeats. Then he sighed, and I felt him relax. His hold on my waist loosened a bit. He turned his head slightly and kissed my brow, a gentle reassuring touch.

His ease helped me relax, and without realizing it, I flattened my hand on his chest once more. When I started exploring his skin with my fingertips, his hold didn't retighten.

"Are they still on the roof?" I asked. I could barely hear myself and hoped I kept quiet enough that any others nearby wouldn't hear.

He nodded. He let go of my waist and brought a hand up to my hair. The feel of his fingers running through the strands lulled me. I stopped exploring and let my arm rest across his chest. The position pressed my lips against the skin over his collarbone. His fingers continued to travel the length of my hair.

He seemed completely at ease with our positions now. I kissed him like I'd wanted to and sighed. My mind started to drift, ready to let sleep pull it under.

As my breathing slowed, I wondered if this place would ever be a home.

BEFORE I OPENED MY EYES, I knew something was wrong. It wasn't that I was alone in the bed; it was a weird niggling feeling that told me I really didn't want to wake up right then.

I opened my eyes and almost screamed. Mary's face hovered inches from mine. The fright of it had me flipping backwards out of bed.

She laughed.

"That wasn't nice," I said, sitting up.

"I've been waiting over an hour for you to wake up. It was taking too long."

I glanced at the window. It was barely sunrise. A yawn cracked my jaw before I could say anything else.

"What's the hurry, today?"

She just grinned at me.

"You're behaving oddly," I said, pulling myself and my bedding off the floor.

"Not really. I'm just wondering if there's anything you wanted to tell me." She kept grinning at me, a big goofy smile that hinted she knew some big joke.

"Mary, did you take some of the medicine from the paper bag?"

She huffed.

"Of course not. It wouldn't work on me, anyway." She gave

me a pouty face. "Are you really not going to tell me about last night?"

"Last night?" I said, completely confused. What was there to tell? We'd gone to our room. Thomas had come in once we were settled into our beds and sat on the floor. At some point, members of his pack jumped up on the roof, woke me, then...I blushed.

"Finally!" she said. "I saw him hold you." The goofy grin was back.

"You were watching?"

"Absolutely. So...you seemed to like it."

I started to remake my bed and tried for innocence. "Of course I liked having him next to me. Someone was walking around on the roof. It was unsettling."

She snorted.

"And the touching?"

"Reassuring."

"You mean exciting. I could smell what being next to him did to you."

I stopped straightening the quilt to stare at her.

"So could he," she said. She walked around the bed and gripped my arms. "If you like him, even if he can't Claim you, tell him. Tell everyone. Be happy."

"Mary, I'm fifteen. I won't be sixteen for another few months. You know what will happen if I tell him, or any of them, I have a preference. I'm not ready for that."

"Stupid human rules," she said with a shake of her head.

"Stupid werewolf ways," I said back at her, using the same tone of exasperation.

She laughed and followed me from the room. I was quiet, thinking of what she'd said, as we made our way to the common room. Did I prefer Thomas? I liked him, but I'd had crushes on other boys before. Thomas wasn't a boy, though. He wasn't a man, either. He was a werewolf. I needed to remember that.

"Good morning," Gregory said when we walked into the main room. He lifted a pot from the stove and brought it to the table.

I peered down at a pot full of oatmeal.

"You cooked?" I couldn't keep the surprise from my words.

"Yes," he said with a smile at Mary.

I glanced at her. She blushed prettily as her gaze remained locked with Gregory's.

"I'll just take a bowl with me outside." I was talking to the room. Neither paid me any attention as I quickly served myself and left.

Thomas and a group of almost a dozen men faced off in the yard. I studied his back and wide stance. His crossed arms and tense jaw told me just as much as the glares from the men he faced.

I took a bite of oatmeal as I walked toward the group. When I reached Thomas' side, my stomach executed a wild flip.

"Good morning, Thomas."

"Good morning," he said softly, not looking at me. My pulse leapt as I thought of last night.

Thomas inhaled, then sighed and turned to me.

"Charlene, you should stay inside."

I scrunched up my face as if considering what he said then shook my head. He frowned at me. I lifted my spoon. "Oatmeal?"

Amusement crept into his gaze.

"What are you doing out here?"

I shrugged and made to eat the oatmeal on the spoon. Thomas grabbed my hand and fed it to himself. I blushed, cleared my throat, and got to the point.

"I had a thought last night as I was listening to the little patter of footsteps on the roof."

Thomas's gaze grew very serious.

"And that thought gave me an idea." I turned to look at his men. "Why not send them out to find others and spread the word about what's happening here."

Several of the men smirked as if they couldn't believe what they were hearing.

"When you're out there, be sure to tell everyone how you found females here and how we're trying to make this place into a home."

"Charlene..." The caution in Thomas' voice was unmistakable.

"We'll go," one of the men said, stepping forward. Eagerness poured from him.

"Of course, you will. The thought of finding enough men to break the pack apart and remove me, the terrible human, from your lives is perfect motivation."

That wiped the smiles from their faces. Finally, the one who'd challenged Thomas spoke up.

"Why would you suggest this if you know that's what we intend?"

"Why indeed," I said. I smiled, took another bite of oatmeal, and studied them. "Perhaps I believe there are more of your kind out there interested in what we're trying to build here. More than you think."

"We?" the man said.

"Yes. We," Thomas answered.

"Or maybe there's another reason," I said with an indifferent shrug. "You decide. However, if you go, you have thirty days to send back as many as you can. The day after you all return, Thomas will accept the new members. Oh, and you all go or none of you go. Make your time count."

The men looked at Thomas. I glanced at him, too. Sweat beaded his forehead. Then, he nodded and the men sprinted for the trees.

"Charlene, do you know what you've done?" Thomas said.

"I gave you a reprieve for a month."

"No, you've doomed the pack." He ran his hands through his hair.

"Do you have a headache?" I'd thought sending his men away would have helped that.

"Yes. You gave me one."

I shook my head at him and turned to walk inside.

"I don't think I've doomed the pack, by the way," I said over my shoulder.

"Oh?" He sounded close.

"I think I just gave it a real chance." I opened the door and took a step inside before I stopped.

Gregory had Mary pinned against the wall, his face buried in the crook of her neck. Her jean-clad legs wrapped around his waist and her arms around his shoulders. Her closed eyes and parted lips conveyed just how much she liked what he was doing to her.

My cheeks heated.

"Congratulations," Thomas said behind me.

I gave him a startled look, but he remained focused on the couple across the room.

Mary opened her eyes, released her hold on Gregory, and gave Thomas a bright smile.

"Thank you."

She stepped away from Gregory, who couldn't seem to let go. He kept an arm around her shoulders.

Then, I saw the bite mark on her neck. My stomach dropped. I'd just lost my friend.

CHAPTER THIRTEEN

"CONGRATULATIONS," I SAID.

Thomas' arms suddenly wrapped around me, pulling me back against his chest.

"Liar," he said softly near my ear. My skin prickled.

Mary didn't lose her happy smile.

"Don't worry, Charlene. I'm not leaving. Thomas is staying, so we're staying."

I nodded, shrugged out of Thomas' embrace, and went to sit at the table with my cold oatmeal. Physically, I knew she wasn't leaving, but I'd watched those two together enough to anticipate what would happen. She would be spending a lot more time with Gregory. I didn't begrudge her that time; it just meant I'd be spending a lot more time alone.

"I was wondering if one of you could talk to Winifred for me. I'd like to know if she'd be willing to extend an invitation to families who might like to stay here. Maybe we'll find a few Elder candidates that way or get a second pack in here that agrees with what we're doing."

"Packs typically don't share territory," Thomas said, coming to sit beside me.

"Oh." When I'd had the thought that we needed to make this place a happy home, I'd counted on the support from other families and packs, a united front against those in Thomas' pack who didn't want me here. Had I really doomed his pack?

"Aren't Leif and Ann their own pack?"

"They are. Small packs of two to three generally don't hold a territory. It's too dangerous in such a small group, not from our own kind, but humans."

What he said made sense.

"Where is Ann?" I said, realizing we hadn't yet seen her or Leif.

"She had her cub last night and is sleeping."

"What? Why didn't you tell me?" I really wanted to see it. Would it be a baby or an actual puppy? Did it matter? Both were adorable, and I couldn't wait to see.

Mary shrugged. "I didn't think you'd be interested. She is really cute, though."

"She?" Thomas said.

Mary nodded.

"They're both excited. Winifred is, too. She said it might bring more families with young boys."

I ate the last bite of my oatmeal and took the bowl to the sink.

"Thomas, can you call the rest in to eat? I'd hate to waste Gregory's cooking," I said.

Mary giggled, and Gregory leaned over to kiss her.

Over the course of the next several days, I caught Gregory and

Mary kissing often, spent time with the new baby, and slept alone in my room despite Thomas' protests.

The pack members who'd remained behind worked on window covers and wood splitting during the day. And they joined us for each meal. We seemed to have developed a pattern, a boring one. I knew it was ridiculous to feel bored—bored was better than bitten—but after the excitement of the last few weeks, the quiet was unnatural.

Friday morning I woke feeling grumpy and not alone.

Thomas lay on his side next to me, watching me as I opened my eyes.

"I warned you," I said a moment before I pushed him off the bed with my hands.

He hit the floor with a thud but immediately sat up and scowled at me.

"I didn't sleep in your room. I came to wake you up."

"You were in my bed without permission," I said, getting out of bed.

He studied me while I straightened the sheets and blanket.

"You're unusually upset. Didn't you sleep well?"

"I slept fine," I said, turning to look at the clean clothes in my dresser. I'd done laundry yesterday. The men had finished the windows and planned a junkyard run again today to see if they could find anything they could repair and send with Winifred to sell. I had absolutely nothing to do. Not only that, but as I'd anticipated, I saw very little of Mary. Thomas checked in on me often but mostly stayed outside doing whatever he did. I was lonely.

"Thomas," I turned toward him, "I'm...bored."

"You just lied."

With a sigh, I sat on the bed.

"I'm lonely."

He sat next to me, his arm barely touching mine, and looked down at his hands.

"Do you miss your family?"

"I try not to think about them," I said. Yet even saying that brought forth the image of my parents. "But when I do, I miss them so much it hurts."

"Will you go back to them?"

"No. Never. I love them too much."

"I've been trying to figure out why you stay. You have family out there and miss them. Here, you've been attacked repeatedly, are resented by many, protected by few...why stay?"

He turned and looked at me, his focused gaze unnerving me. I kept my mouth shut.

"I think you're hiding here because of what you can do," he said after several moments of silence.

My heart felt as if it were trying to escape out of my throat.

He nudged me a little.

"None of that. No one is going to make you leave because you're different. In fact, that's a strong reason to let you stay. You're not just human. You're more. Don't be afraid to show that you can move things with your mind."

Is that what he thought I'd done? My stomach chose that moment to growl.

He cleared his throat and stood.

"I have a surprise for you. But it means spending the morning with me. I'll feed you first," he said.

I followed him downstairs and excused myself for a moment alone with the washbowl and bucket. When I rejoined him, he had two bowls on the table, and I was surprised to see a carton of milk there, too.

"Milk?"

"It is. Did you know after we are weaned, we typically don't drink milk again? It's not necessary. We seem to get what we need from the animals we eat. Winifred believes it's because in our other form, we tend to eat it all."

Not a pleasant topic before breakfast. He motioned for me to sit.

"So I was a bit surprised to learn humans drink milk their entire lives. And tend to eat more vegetables than meat," he said.

I looked down at my bowl and saw a familiar and well-missed sight. Flakes with a touch of sugary coating.

"Cereal?" I asked in disbelief. He nodded and handed me the milk. I poured too quickly in my excitement and spilled a bit on the table. I didn't stop to wipe it up. Instead, I grabbed my spoon and took a large bite. The milk was tepid but it didn't take away from the delicious taste.

"Mmm." It was the only sound I made for the next minute. With an amused gleam in his eyes, Thomas sat across from me, watching as I devoured the cereal.

Even while drifting from town to town, I hadn't managed such a simple treat. It had been too long. I slowed down to savor the last half, unsure how long it would be until I could have more.

"Aren't you going to eat?" I asked when I noticed his bowl remained untouched.

He reached for the milk and neatly poured a measure into his bowl. I watched him closely as he took his first bite. His brow drew down, and his mouth puckered in distaste.

"You don't like it?" I couldn't believe he'd prefer whole rabbit over sugared flakes.

He finished chewing and swallowed.

"It's different."

I grinned at him, took another bite of my cereal, and tried to figure out a comparison to the taste before I swallowed.

"Haven't you ever had honey? You've had to come across honey bees out there."

"We're wolves, not bears."

My startled laugh almost lost me the bite of cereal in my mouth. I quickly finished chewing. "If you don't want to finish it, I will. Where did it come from? Is there more?"

He pushed his bowl toward me.

"I have made a few trips to the junkyard, collecting those coins from the seats of old cars. When I had enough, I went into town."

"Like that?" I eyed his bare chest.

He shook his head.

"Winifred warned me that I'd need a shirt and shoes. Why would anyone want to wear those on their feet?"

"Shoes protect our feet. Humans aren't as sturdy as you are."

"I'm learning," he said.

"You are," I agreed. He was learning what it meant to be human, and I knew it was because he hadn't given up hope of Claiming me. It warmed me to know that he'd taken what I'd said seriously.

He waited patiently as I finished both bowls of cereal and while I washed them. Then, he brought me outside.

"There's a lot of ground to cover. May I carry you?"

The idea of Thomas carrying me in his arms made my insides go hot and cold in alternating flashes. I nodded. He stepped close, crowding me, and then bent and picked me up with ease. I wrapped my arms around his shoulders. He looked down at me, our faces not far apart.

"Hold on," he said. And then he ran.

Wind whipped my face and stung my eyes. I didn't turn away from it, though. I let go with my left hand, trusting him to keep me steady, and pushed the hair from my eyes. Then, I watched it all.

He wove between the trees with ease, lightly leaping over shrubs and bramble. Animals quieted at his approach and scurried from his path when he neared. I'd never felt so alive than those moments in his arms, beaten by the wind.

He ran like that for at least ten minutes. When the trees started to thin, he wasn't even winded. He slowed to a walk as he stepped out into sunlight. The trees before us had died with the expansion of the marsh and stood like large, dark sticks poked into the ground. Birds flew overhead.

He'd wanted to show me the marsh?

He gently set me on my feet as I continued to look around.

"This way," he said, taking my hand.

We skirted the edge of the marsh, the spongy ground giving just slightly with each step. As we walked, making our way east, the weeds and reeds thinned and larger pools became visible. The trees to our right suddenly disappeared into a large clearing. At first, I thought it an extension of the marsh. Then, I noticed the tall grass instead of reeds.

"Anton found this while trying to catch pheasants. He was watching what they ate and checking if there was a food source we could gather and store for the winter...if we manage to cage any of them."

The reminder of our attempts made me cringe, and I felt guilty that I hadn't offered to help Anton again.

"We think this might be an old garden from the people who used to live here."

Excited, I parted the grass as I walked forward. The grass outlined a very large and very weed filled garden. Onions grew in a thick patch. Wild, their green tops were much larger than their bulbs. I found carrots growing in random areas toward the trees, away from the damp soil near the marsh. There were some chewed on melons, a few small green striped pumpkins, stalks of multi-colored corn, vine beans, and many varieties of squash.

"This is amazing," I said. I wanted to start picking things. Thomas seemed to read my mind.

"Before you pick anything, I want to show you one more thing. It's not useful like this. Just pretty."

That he'd described something as pretty piqued my interest.

We walked further east, away from the garden and back into the trees. The cool damp air of the woods seemed to grow even cooler with each step. In the break of branches, I caught a bright flash of light. Moments later, I stepped out of the trees onto the lapping shoreline of a lake. My shoes made divots in the sand as I walked to the water. I could see the sandy bottom several feet out.

It was clean, untouched by man, and beautiful. It stretched far enough that the trees on the opposite shore appeared tiny, less than a half an inch if I held up my fingers to measure. I kicked off my shoes and rolled up my pant legs.

"It'll be cold," Thomas said, and it was.

While I stood in the water, fish swam close. Small little things that made me smile. The large one that darted after the little ones made my eyes round.

"Thomas," I said in a quiet voice. The big fish stopped moving, turned, and seemed to be contemplating my toes.

I heard the water ripple behind me then a low chuckle. "It's just a fish."

"Do you eat fish?" I asked. The better question would have been if he was fast enough to defend my toes.

"Do you?" he asked.

"Not lately."

He dove forward. It wasn't a pretty, neat dive; it was a huge, clothes-soaking splash. Then, he seemed to beat the surface. I could barely see him with the amount of water flying in the air. Suddenly, it stopped.

He stood before me with the fingers of one hand hooked in the gills and the other hand holding the tail of the fish. It was more than shoulder width on Thomas. He looked very proud of himself.

We stared at each other for several heartbeats. I held myself still with my arms slightly out from my sides. I was soaked. Water dripped from my chin and ran into my eyes.

He burst out laughing.

Three large fish, onions, carrots, and rice baked in the oven while Thomas and I worked together to heat bathwater. We stunk like fish. He'd carried me home, and I had to carry the fish and onions.

In the silence, it struck me that since waking I hadn't seen anyone else.

"Where is everyone?"

"I sent everyone out. Mary and Gregory are in town, trying

to determine what jobs are available and what skills are required. The rest are at the junkyard. They wanted a break from cutting wood, and the man running the place was willing to pay them to break down some of the metal for recycling. They'll earn more than if they would have taken the metal."

"I'm impressed."

"I can't claim responsibility for any of those ideas. Winifred has been promoting jobs since you suggested it."

"And they all went along with it?"

"Mostly. There were a few grumbles at first, but they seem to be enjoying it now."

He carried one of the steaming pots to the tub, dumped it, then came back to refill it. I caught myself staring at the muscles in his back and arms as he worked the pump, and I quickly looked away. My face was warm, my mouth a little dry, and my pulse too fast.

"I'm going to run and get some clean clothes," I said, moving toward the main door.

"Hold on. I'll go too."

I stopped by the door. "There's no need."

"I need to grab some clothes." He started walking toward me. I swallowed hard, staring once again at his naked chest.

What was wrong with me? He'd carried me like that, and I hadn't had so much of an issue at the time. Granted I'd been too stunned by the experience of him running to notice him. And on the way back, I'd been carrying dead fish. There was nothing remotely romantic about dead fish.

"I can grab them for you," I said, meeting his gaze.

He tilted his head and studied me.

"My kind tends to attack you when you're alone. I'd rather not leave you."

"Okay." I turned and started to walk before my heating cheeks could give me away.

"Charlene, is something bothering you?"

"Yes, but I don't want to talk about it."

He chuckled.

"Honesty. It's refreshing."

"Not really. You're just more of a pain when I lie."

He laughed and waited in the hall as I grabbed clothes from my room. When he went to his room, he left the door open. It was the first time I looked inside. There was nothing within except another pair of pants on the floor.

I stepped in further, looking around.

"It's so...empty. Someday, it won't be like this," I said, imagining what his people could do if they worked together.

"What do you see in your someday?" he asked, coming close.

I stared into the room, no longer really seeing it.

"This building and the other buildings will be brimming with life, an ever changing community of families. Most will stay to raise their young in the protection of a safer environment. These rooms will be their homes within our home. And I see happiness. A lot of laughter and friendship. No more dying race or hiding in the woods."

"I like what you see. And someday, I know you'll help make it all happen."

"How do you know?"

"Because, without you, no one has a reason to stay."

He reached up and gently brushed his hand across my cheek.

I wrinkled my nose.

"We need our baths."

He smiled and dropped his hand. I left the room and started down the stairs, listening to him follow.

"You know," he said, "we wouldn't need to heat as much water if we shared."

"That's not going to happen," I said over my shoulder.

He chuckled.

THE FISH FINISHED COOKING before I was done with my bath. Thomas had insisted I go first since I wouldn't share. By the time I opened the door, Mary and Gregory had returned and were sitting with Ann and Leif at the table.

"Ann, I'd be happy to hold the baby while you eat," I quickly offered.

"Oh, thank you, Charlene." Ann stood and gently placed the sleeping girl in my arms. "She is so sweet, but it's nice to sit and eat."

"I've been wondering. If the babies are born as babies, how does that work in the woods? How do wolves carry babies?"

"We try to give them a week before we force the change. During that week, we typically don't leave our birthing den. It's safer that way," Ann said.

"Force the change? You mean they can change into a wolf already?"

She nodded.

"A small, fluffy, blind cub. Adorable. But it's painful for them and scary. Some don't live through the process. While I was still pregnant, I asked Winifred about it. I know she has no cubs, but as an Elder I thought she might have an answer."

"Answer to what?"

"If the forced change was the reason we have such a low population and even fewer females. Is it really that less are born or that less survive? She didn't know. But, she's let many of the expecting mothers know about this place. We're hoping to stay until the rest of the pack returns, before we try to force the change."

"How do you force the change?"

"Our wolf form is our defensive form. We naturally shift when startled badly enough."

"So you're going to scare her?" I looked down at the babe, her mouth puckered so her glistening bottom lip stuck out. Scaring this baby—any baby—just seemed wrong. "I hope you can stay longer than a month." But I knew that would depend on the mood of the pack members Thomas had sent away.

I walked the baby until Ann finished eating then took my own place. The men from the junkyard came in. Their hair was damp but their clothes were dry and dirty.

"If you want to change, I'll wash those clothes for you tomorrow," I said as they all moved to the stove.

"Thank you. We appreciate it. And dinner," Anton said. He seemed to speak for the group as the rest gave some measure of agreement.

Thomas stepped out of the bathroom, toweling his hair.

"What did you learn in town?"

Though he looked at Gregory, Mary answered.

"There are a few jobs that might work. A plumber is looking for an apprentice. It would require someone to move into town, though."

Thomas sat beside me as Mary spoke.

"The man has his own business and takes calls any time of

night. He has a room in the back of his garage he'd rent out. He'd be willing to deduct from someone's wages to cover it."

"I'll go," Bine said as he sat at the table.

"We looked at the room," Mary said. "It has a cot in it and nothing else. No electricity or stove for when the weather gets cold."

"I'll manage," Bine said.

Thomas nodded.

"Anything else?"

"Nothing we thought any one would be interested in. The library needs some part time help as does the grocery store for stacking shelves at night. The store might be too tempting."

I agreed with Mary. Thomas seemed to as well because he didn't push either of those options.

"Bine, your wages first need to house you, feed you, and clothe you. Anything you can spare should return to the pack so we may do the same for all the members," Thomas said. Bine dipped his head in agreement. "And when you need to run, come here."

With Bine's contribution and the wages from those working short-term at the yard, we might be able to build up a surplus of supplies. I finished my fish, brought my plate to the sink, and opened the supply cabinet. I inventoried everything with a frown. We'd gone through more than half of what Winifred had brought with her, and that was without the full pack here. We needed to plan ahead for meals, portions, and supplies needed. Having the lake and the old garden would help supplement us but as the pack grew, we would need more.

"Charlene?" Thomas asked from just behind me, making me jump. "What's wrong?"

"Nothing is wrong. I'm only thinking of supplies and lists

and what we'll need over the next few months." There were only a few handfuls of oats left for breakfast. I wondered if Thomas had more cereal hidden somewhere. "How much did Winifred get for the metal?"

"She was able to buy larger bags of oats, rice, beans, peas, pasta, flour, and sugar. She also has some spices, a tub of lard, yeast, books, more clothes, blankets, oil lamps, and chocolate chips."

"Chocolate chips?" I asked, glancing away from the supplies.

"She wants to bake the cookies here with you."

I wondered what bribe the cookies were for. I guessed I'd find out soon enough.

"When is she arriving?" I asked.

"She is just leaving now and doesn't expect to be here for several hours. She suggests you go to sleep as usual, and she'll see you in the morning."

I nodded and moved back to the sink. Thomas brought over some of the warm water from the stove and filled the tin pot in the trough so I could wash the dishes. Then, he moved to help dry them. Together, we worked through the dishes everyone brought to us. When we finished, I turned and found the room cleaned and empty.

Thomas' hands closed over my shoulders, and his thumbs gently rubbed the muscles that I hadn't thought sore a moment ago.

"Did you enjoy today?" he asked, hesitantly.

I glanced back at him. He wasn't the hesitating type. His gaze searched mine.

"I did. Why are you asking?"

"I don't want you to be lonely here, Charlene. If you're feeling that way again, tell me. Please."

I nodded. His hands dropped to his sides, and after a moment, he went outside.

Winifred had brought eggs. Dozens of eggs. And sausage links. The smell of them as they sizzled in one of the pots made my stomach cramp. I hovered near the stove, using a fork to turn them. A few times, I had to yank my hand back as grease popped and spattered.

"Please," Thomas said again, watching me wince. "Let me."

"No, it's okay." I didn't want to surrender the fork. As soon as I found one cooked through, it was going to be mine.

He plucked the fork from my hand. "Mary, pump some cold water for her, please." He pushed me toward the sink.

"Bully," I mumbled as I dragged my feet toward the pump.

Mary grinned and shook her head. When I got close enough, she started pumping. I stuck my right hand into the cold water. There were four red dots on the back and one large one on the knuckle. I let her pump until my hand grew numb. Mary didn't seem to grow tired or mind.

"It's done," Thomas said.

I turned and found the men lined up behind him. They all had plates. Thomas had a plate, too, already piled with eggs and sausage. He moved to the table and set the plate down as I tried to hide my disappointment and guilt. I wasn't the only one starved for something more than oatmeal, which was what I'd served for breakfast the past week.

I'd almost passed the table to stand at the back of the line when Thomas snagged my hand. He tugged me to the bench beside him and offered me a fork. I smiled as I understood he meant to share and quickly sat. The first bite of sausage made me want to groan. As I chewed, savoring the salty meat, the men sat at the tables near the main door. They dug in with enthusiasm. As usual, Thomas had yet to take a bite. He sat beside me and watched me.

I finished my sausage and quickly skewered a second. That one I waved in front of his face.

"If you don't start eating, there won't be anything left." It was a bluff. Though my eyes wanted me to eat everything on the plate, my stomach would eventually rebel if I tried.

He smiled and chomped the sausage right off the fork before I could yank it out of the way. I blinked at my empty tines. Maybe I was the one who needed to eat faster.

He picked up his fork and started to eat. He ate slow, sticking to his side of the plate while I vacuumed the food in until my stomach ached. I set down my fork with a groan. I'd eaten a bit more than my share. He pulled the plate in front of him and finished the rest in a few moments.

Then, he did something that made me stare. He licked my fork. I sat there stupidly as he stood and carried the dishes to the sink. I was glad for the space. The rest of the men stood and followed Thomas' example. Then, they all made for the door, leaving Winifred, Mary, Ann, and me.

Winifred had collected Ann's new daughter as soon as she'd arrived. The two women were still speaking quietly. Mary and I went to the pump and began washing dishes.

While I dried, I kept looking at the bags of supplies. There were so many. I couldn't wait to dig into them even though I already knew what they contained.

We had just finished with the dishes when Winifred said, "Mary, Gregory is waiting for you outside."

Ann left the room with her daughter, and I watched Mary nod and walk to the door. Winifred closed the door behind her.

"Ready to bake?"

"We can bake," I said. "But I'd feel more comfortable doing it if you would tell me why another bribe is needed."

Winifred sighed.

"It's not a bribe, dear. But I did intend it to be a relaxing activity while we discussed what happened after I left."

I cringed remembering the fight, my insistence to watch, and my general interference.

"I'm sorry," I said sincerely.

"For what?"

"For interfering. But if I'm going to live here, shouldn't I act like I'm part of your community, too? If I don't, I can't see ever being accepted."

Winifred came close and gave me a brief hug.

"You did well interfering. I'm proud of how you handled yourself and the situation. I think sending the malcontent away was the best move given the circumstance." She stepped away, picked up a bag, and set it on top of the cleared table.

"However," she said, "there is something else I'd like to understand."

She began to unpack, and with trepidation, I moved to help.

"That was the second time you knocked a few men back without lifting a finger. How is that possible?"

It felt as if my heart stopped and dropped into my stomach like a rock. I didn't let panic control me, though. After a calming breath, I answered.

"How is it possible that werewolves exist, or that you can

control them with a thought or command? Some things are just possible. The reasons behind the possibilities aren't for us to understand or explain; we're just meant to accept them." I continued to unpack bags as I spoke. "I've accepted that I'm different and can do things others can't. Now that you know what I can do, can you accept me?"

Winifred turned from placing the large bag of rice in the cabinet and studied me.

"I accept you for what you are, and hope that you will explain what, exactly, it is you can do."

With the terrible moment of truth before me, I slowly sank to a chair. Did she, like Thomas, think I only moved things with my mind? Once I told her the truth, would she then want me to leave? I folded my hands together and met Winifred's gaze.

"I ran from my home, from everything I knew and loved, because I understood my secret, my ability, would change how everyone saw me. My secret is just as dangerous as yours and can never be shared."

She sat in the chair across from me and nodded. I took another steadying breath and tried to ignore the feeling that I needed to keep my ability to myself.

"I can control people. With a thought, my will becomes their will. I've never ill-used my ability. Since the day I was born, I've known it's meant to help and protect; others before myself.

"I can't control your kind. Not like I could mine. I think I understand how you control the pack, though. You implant your thought in them. It's essentially how my ability works with humans; I hold a person's will and let my will flow into them. But with your kind, I couldn't hold your wills long enough to influence anyone. But when that man attacked me in my bedroom, I..." I shrugged and shook my head. It felt so wrong talking about what I could do. I'd kept this secret for too long.

"You found a way?" Winifred said. Worry flooded her gaze.

"Not exactly. I couldn't control him, but I knew what I wanted. I wanted him off. In my desperation, it was like my desire to have him off me hardened into something physical. I hit him with it, and he flew off me. That's when you came in."

She nodded.

"And those times in the yard?"

Guiltily, I looked at my hands. In the yard, I did more than just beat back men. I controlled them. But something cautioned me against revealing that detail, a detail of which she was hopefully unaware.

"Every time I moved one of them, it was the same thing," I said, carefully wording my answer to avoid a lie.

She exhaled and considered me for a moment.

"As an Elder, I need to do what is best for the whole of our race. It relieves me that you can't control us. That would represent a dangerous potential. Yet, as a human, you are at a disadvantage here, and hearing you have the ability to defend yourself is a relief. Mates are important. Without them, we have no future. As a potential Mate, *you* are important to our kind. Yes, your ability is unique, but I see no reason it should concern us." She patted my hand and stood. "Now, let's finish this up and make some cookies."

I returned her smile with a weak one of my own and moved to help. She accepted me because she sensed little threat in me. What would she do if she knew the truth, that I could control them, too?

CHAPTER FOURTEEN

It was a relief when Winifred left with another truck bed full of metal. Throughout the weekend, she'd continued to be nothing but kind. It just made keeping something from her harder. I wanted to tell her. Yet every time I set my mind to do so, something stopped me. It was as if a little voice in my head whispered caution.

"I wish she would have brought more eggs," Mary said as I closed the outer door.

Winifred had brought six dozen. We ate three Saturday and three again that morning. It wasn't just the men who liked to eat well. Mary did too. I grinned at her.

"She said she'd bring more next weekend. Until then, you'll have to make due with oatmeal," I said. Mary made a face and turned back to the dishes. I went to join her.

I was mentally preparing for another week of monotony when Thomas and Gregory walked in from outside.

"Ready, Charlene?"

"For what?" I asked, setting aside a plate.

"I thought we'd start with a walk along the north border."

"Is that far?" I finished drying the last plate and wiped my hands.

"Far enough that I'd need to carry you there and back if we don't want to sleep out there."

There wasn't much to do here. The laundry from the weekend could wait until tomorrow, and Mary was already making eyes at Gregory.

"Did you need me here for anything?" I asked her anyway.

"No. Go on and enjoy your day. Gregory and I will find something here to occupy ourselves."

A slow grin spread on Gregory's face.

I blushed and focused on Thomas.

"All right."

He chuckled and motioned for me to lead the way out the door. As soon as we were in the yard, he scooped me up in his arms again. The feel of his skin under the palm of my hand made me blush further.

He ran with ease, covering the distance to the lake and then past it. Bramble filled in between the trees, but Thomas always managed to find narrow trails around or through them. When my face grew a little cold from the cool forest air, I turned into his heat and laid my cheek against his shoulder. It amazed me that his breathing remained even. I laid my hand over his heart. It beat steadily.

Suddenly, he stopped, and I was on my feet. Trees surrounded us. How did he know where the property ended? I looked up and met his gaze. The focus I found there startled me.

He reached for my hand and lifted it up to his chest. He placed it over his heart once more. Then, he took my other hand

and placed it on his skin, as well. He held them in place as he took a deep breath and exhaled slowly.

"I never thought such a simple touch could do so much," he said. He shook his head. "I understand what Gregory means."

"About what?"

"Every little thing Mary does drives him crazy. All he wants to do is touch her, hold her close. The waiting is testing his resolve."

His insinuation that he was experiencing the same thing with me made my stomach twist happily. He kept his left hand on my right one, and with his other hand, lightly traced the curve of my jaw.

"You tempt me, Charlene. I want to kiss you every time I see you and lay beside you every night. Claimed or not, I belong to you, and the distance you want is getting harder to maintain."

His thumb skimmed the edge of my bottom lip and my breath caught.

"Thomas, please. I can't..." Couldn't what? Kiss him? I already had. And I really wanted to again. But he wasn't after a single kiss. He wanted much more. He wanted commitment, a Claim I couldn't give him. "We don't know what will happen when the rest of your pack returns."

Frustration crept into his gaze.

"Right."

He picked me up again and continued running. I was careful to keep my hands hooked around his neck.

We didn't run much longer before he slowed to his version of a jog, then finally stopped. He bent as he released my legs, straightening once my feet touched ground. He didn't release his hold around my shoulders but used it to hug me close to his chest. I tipped my head back, wondering at his mood. But he quickly dropped a kiss on my forehead and released me.

"This is the edge. Winifred posted it when she officially purchased it." He pointed to a sign that prohibited the hunting of *any* animal on this land. "Beyond this, there are a few parcels of open land and then protected land. It's perfectly placed for us to roam. But only here are we truly safe."

We started walking to the left. Ahead I saw another sign nailed to a tree.

"My mother and father ran on a stretch of land much further north. I grew up with snow three of the four seasons. When they died, Grey and I decided to head south. We'd heard about this place and were curious why an Elder would waste time with it. It lived up to our low expectations. Still we stayed in the area."

"How long ago was that?"

"Grey was twelve, and I was nine."

Nine. I was stunned.

"That's a long time to be on your own."

"Not on my own. I've had Grey."

"If Grey's older, why are you the pack's leader?"

He gave a single, short laugh.

"If you asked Grey that question, he'd tell you he spent enough time leading me that he didn't want to do it anymore. And maybe some of that is the truth. He's always watched out for me. I think pushing me to lead the pack was another way of leading me. If that makes sense."

Not really, but I didn't say so. For a long while, we walked in silence. Eventually my stomach started to rumble. He grinned at me and took my hand in his.

"There's a creek ahead."

I didn't see what a creek had to do with my growling stomach. When we found it, he dropped to his knees and studied the moving water. Then, his hand darted forward, splashing into the water and immediately retreating. He held up an ugly looking brown thing with beady eyes and two pinchers.

"What is that?"

"Lunch," he said with a grin. He broke off the tail, put it to his mouth, and sucked. When he pulled it away, the shell was empty. I barely noticed that. I stared at the thrashing top half. He noticed, and his expression changed from amusement to mild shame.

"Sorry," he said. He quickly tossed the top half into the water. The little creature sunk to the bottom. I watched others like it scurry forward. Soon it was buried under several of its own kind.

Thomas stood, looking uncomfortable.

"You were fine with the fish," he said.

I understood what he meant. Before, while he'd caught the second fish, the first had flopped around on shore until it stilled. That hadn't bothered me. I was realistic. I knew I needed to eat. I just couldn't eat something while its top half was alive to watch.

"It's fine, Thomas. Just a bit shocking. I'm not that hungry anymore."

He nodded and led me away from the creek. My stomach continued to growl as we walked, though. He remained silently thoughtful beside me, his eyes on the ground rather than the trees ahead. Then with a sniff, his mood shifted. His gaze searched the bramble around us, and he increased his pace.

A few more feet and we found a small patch of picked over blackberries.

"Better?" he asked.

"Much," I said with a smile. We worked together to find a few with enough juice left in them to eat. I licked my stained fingers when I couldn't find any more.

"Here," Thomas said, holding out a handful of berries.

"It's all right. You eat them."

He picked one out of his palm, popped it in his mouth, then extended his hand again. "Your turn."

My stomach wanted more, so I gave in. When we finished, we returned to walking the property line.

"So what exactly are we doing out here?" I asked.

"Keeping you from loneliness."

I stopped walking and turned toward him.

"Thomas, I didn't mean to take you away from your responsibilities."

"I can do what's needed from here," he said and tapped his temple to remind me of his connection to his pack. "I thought you wanted space before. That was the only reason I stayed away."

I didn't know what to say to that. First, he'd resented my presence. Then, he'd met me and resented that he wanted to Claim me. Now, he wasn't even that man. He'd admitted to wanting to kiss me, spent time with me, was very considerate of my feelings, and listened to what I thought. My chest felt uncomfortably tight.

I wanted to escape him for a while to regroup and reconsider all the reasons I needed to avoid him because, at the moment, I couldn't think of any.

"Maybe we should head back." As soon as I said it, I

realized my mistake. He would have to carry me. There was no escape.

He scooped me up in his arms and settled me next to his chest. Before he started running, he met my gaze.

"Haven't you figured it out yet? You don't need to run from me. I'm willing to be whatever you need. Even patient."

He ran, and I held on.

We stopped by the lake on the way back and picked some vegetables for a stew to go with the four rabbits Thomas said Gregory and Mary had waiting. I was ready to run the rest of the way, but he insisted on carrying me again. All the constant, little brushes of skin here and there caused a long lasting blush.

When we finally entered the yard, I sighed with relief.

"I only meant to keep you company," Thomas said softly as he set me on my feet.

"You did. I'll just bring these in," I said about the carrots, onions, and parsnips held in the bottom of my shirt. I turned and fled inside.

I felt guilty over my agitation. I wasn't annoyed with him. I was annoyed with myself. I didn't like being bitten, yet I couldn't help feeling attracted to Thomas. What kind of mixed signals was I sending him? Plus, Claiming wouldn't even work on me. What would happen when families started showing up with young girls like me? One was bound to pique Thomas' interest. And where would I be? Standing in a corner with a broken heart.

I needed to keep myself busy. If Mary couldn't spend time with me, I needed to seek out Ann. Hopefully, the families would start coming soon.

SOMETHING HEAVY PRESSED me down into the mattress. It wasn't a sudden weight that woke me, but one of which I slowly became aware as I struggled to breathe. It pinned my torso and legs. I opened my eyes and blinked, trying to see in the dim light. A familiar ear and dark wavy hair swam into focus. His slow and steady breath warmed my neck.

What did he think he was doing? Sleeping in my room with permission to protect me was one thing, but in my bed—no, not even in my bed but on me—that was something else. I frowned and tried to wiggle free. He didn't budge, didn't twitch. His breathing remained uninterrupted.

His chest pinned my left arm but not my right. I grabbed his shoulder and pushed. No reaction.

"Thomas," I whispered. "Wake up." His breathing didn't change in the slightest.

What was his deal? I'd never seen him sleep this hard before. I paused and realized I'd never seen him sleep. The times he was with me, he was always awake before I woke. That just meant he slept less, didn't it?

I pulled in another breath.

"Thomas," I said right in his ear. Nothing.

I hesitated calling out for help. Mary and Gregory were in the room right next to us, the room her dad and uncle had used. They would hear. But did I really want them coming in here? Thomas was heavy but not really hurting me. Yet. I didn't know how much longer I'd be able to stand his weight, though. Since he wasn't doing more than sleeping, it didn't feel right using my will either.

"Now what?" I whispered into the dark.

I turned my head slightly. My mouth was right next to his ear. He'd once told me he'd like it if I bit him. I grinned in the dark a moment before I nipped the firm shell of his undamaged ear.

His breathing stopped. He didn't move. I held my own breath, waiting for his reaction. What I felt pressed against my side was enough to send me into a panic.

"Please tell me you're awake and in control of yourself," I said lightly in his ear. The warble in my words gave away my worry.

"Barely." The one rough word made me shiver.

"Barely awake or barely in control?"

"Both."

He turned his head, and his lips skimmed my ear. My heart hammered against my squished ribs. My right hand still gripped his shoulder.

"Thomas, I can't breathe."

"I have the same problem when I'm this close to you." His tongue traced my ear.

I wanted him to stop and to keep going. I wanted to wrap my arms around him and pull him closer as much as I wanted to push him away and drag in a deep, cleansing breath.

My need for air won.

"No, Thomas. You're too heavy. I can't breathe right."

His weight immediately lifted, but he didn't leave me. His tongue continued to explore the outer shell of my ear as his arms braced his weight.

I pulled in a much needed lungful of air, and he shifted his attention to my jaw. Little kisses scorched a path to my chin, then he claimed my lips.

I sighed and gave into the urge to wrap my arms around him. His tongue traced my lips. My skin felt hot and tight, and I didn't know what to do other than to surrender to the sensations. He tilted his head and nipped at my lower lip. I opened my mouth slightly. He growled and traced my lips with his tongue again before dipping it into my mouth. I trembled and tightened my hold. I touched my tongue to his. He shuddered, and his hips settled onto mine, breaking the spell with another surge of panic.

Turning my head, I gasped and pushed at his shoulders.

"Stop." It was begging, but I didn't care.

He groaned and immediately pulled back. He didn't leave me, just gave me room to breathe once more.

"Please, Thomas. I need you to go."

"I can't." His words tickled my ear.

"You can, but don't want to. Please," I said again.

"One more bite," he said. I wasn't the only one begging tonight.

"You promised. Never again."

"Not me. You. Bite me one more time."

I turned my head to look up at him. In the dark, I couldn't see much. Just the shadows of his face and the slight glow of his eyes.

"You were starting to hurt me," I said. "I'm sorry I bit you, but you wouldn't wake up."

"I didn't mean to sleep on you or scare you. I'll go back to my spot by the door. Just one more bite, Charlene."

My remaining naivety was precious to me. Life's hard choices had opened my eyes to much many girls my age didn't yet have to deal with. I was afraid giving into his request would open my eyes to one of the few remaining mysteries in my life.

"No. I'm not ready for that."

He growled in frustration and dropped his head to my shoulder.

"Thomas...you should go."

"I should," he agreed. "But I can't get past this feeling...this rejection. When I'm not with you, it feels as if there's a hole in my chest, and when you're close enough to touch, my hand tingles until it hurts. I've been waiting for you to show any sign you feel a tenth of what I do, but you don't. Your disregard just makes the hole in my chest grow larger, emptier. I'm lost, drowning on feelings I don't understand and losing to instincts that don't work with you. I can't sleep. I don't taste what I eat. And every time I breathe in, your scent torments me. Everything I want is right here, yet I have nothing."

His words stunned me.

"Charlene, please, give me something."

How could I not after that?

"Do you promise not to take more than I'm willing to give?"

His weight shifted. His hands clasped my arms, and suddenly, he was under me, and I was sitting on his stomach.

"I swear, nothing more than you give."

His hands fell to my knees, the open palms warming my skin as he looked up at me. My pulse thrummed rapidly as I blinked down at him. My stomach twisted. Could I? Should I?

I laid my hands flat and leaned over him. His heart beat swiftly under my palm. I hesitated.

"I don't understand why you want me to bite you."

"I don't either. It's not what you think. Well, it is in a way, but it's more. I feel like we'll be closer then."

I couldn't see how biting brought us any closer than we were. I was sitting on him for Pete's sake. Regardless, I leaned down, until my chest touched his. His fingers, still resting lightly on my knees, twitched.

He turned his head, exposing his throat. I wanted to kiss the shadowy column, not bite it.

"I can't, Thomas. I'm sorry," I quickly slid from him and stood beside the bed.

He lay there for several moments, breathing deeply and staring up at the ceiling. Then he sat up, ran a hand through his hair, stood, and moved to the door. There, he sat, staring at me, the glow of his eyes interrupted by infrequent blinks.

Without a word, I curled back under the covers. I couldn't guess how long I lay there, but eventually I drifted off to sleep.

When the same weight woke me again, my temper flared. It was still dark out, and I couldn't see much.

"Thomas, get off me." I didn't bother with whispered subtlety.

He didn't move.

"Thomas, I'm serious. You're too heavy." I shoved at him, but he didn't respond.

"Fine. Have it your way." I turned my head and bit his neck hard. The coppery tang of blood tickled my tongue as he exhaled loudly.

Knowing I had his attention, I stopped biting.

"I'm certain, I made myself clear before. Out. Of. My. Bed."

I moved to wipe my mouth on the back of my hand. He lifted his head before I finished and gently kissed my palm.

My anger didn't fade exactly, yet another emotion blanketed it. Awe, a complete sense of wonder and elation.

I frowned. I wasn't elated. I was still mad. And he was still on top of me.

"Move, Thomas. Now, or so help me, you won't like what happens next."

He chuckled, kissed my forehead, and rolled off me. He

didn't get out of bed but pulled me to his chest, cuddling against me. He kissed my temple.

"Whether you like it or not," he said, "you're my world now. Sleep. I promise I won't wake you again."

He sighed and relaxed behind me. I lay there stunned. What had just happened? Was his head damaged? I still hadn't given him permission to sleep in my bed. Despite my angry thoughts, I couldn't seem to hold onto my agitation. Contentment and something softer continued to defuse my hostile emotions, which just made me angrier.

I drew back and elbowed him. He grunted and quickly caught my arm.

"Sweetheart, why are you so angry?"

Sitting up, I glared down at him.

"Sweetheart? Since when am I your sweetheart? And I'm angry because you're ignoring me."

"I am most definitely not ignoring you."

"Then why are you still in my bed?"

"Because I'm not ignoring you."

"You are making absolutely no sense."

"Charlene, what do you feel?"

"Annoyed."

His eyes glowed brighter for a moment and a tendril of desire washed over me. I was thankful the dark hid my blush.

"What now?"

I stared down at him.

"How did you know...?"

"Because what you felt wasn't your emotion; it was mine." He lifted a hand and gently tugged the end of a section of my hair. "Did you know the moonlight is highlighting your already beautifully pale hair? It almost glows to me. It's softly curling around your face. You've never looked prettier. And when you're angry, your lips and cheeks take on a darker shade of pink. I can't see anything else but your lips when you're upset. It's as if nature's daring me to kiss you just then. 'See if you can make her happy again.' And I want to try now more than ever before. But I won't." He wrapped his hands around my face. "Because you were right. You are different. I won't forget again."

He was talking in circles, and I had no idea what to make of it.

"What are you talking about?" I said.

"I couldn't Claim you, because you had to Claim me."

My annoyance disappeared in a poof.

"Past tense? 'You had to Claim me.' Why are you talking like I've already—" Panic set in. "No." I pulled away from his touch. He remained on his back, watching me.

"Winifred extends her congratulations."

"I don't want her congratulations or her cookies." There wasn't any anger behind the words, just panic. I'd just attached myself to these people. Part of me was happy. Though it wasn't my plan, and I truly wasn't ready for the relationship these werewolves had described, Claiming Thomas did secure my place here. Plus, Thomas was amazing. I scowled, realizing his contentment and happiness was influencing my thoughts.

What if Winifred found out about what I could do? She wouldn't if I stopped using my ability. Claimed, I should have a certain level of protection—I hoped.

I recalled Mary's words about Claiming and what usually comes next. I swallowed hard.

"Will you still keep your promise?" I asked.

"Which promise is that?"

"You won't take more than I'm ready to give?"

"I swear."

Unless I knew how to undo a Claim—information I doubted Thomas would share—I was stuck here. I considered him for a moment. Was this such a bad place to be? I sighed heavily then curled against his side and laid my head on his shoulder.

"What will your pack say?" I asked as he wrapped an arm around me.

"Should I tell them now and see?"

"No," I said quickly. "I think we can still use the reprieve of their absence."

He kissed my temple again.

"No more talking. You need sleep."

I kept quiet and listened to his breathing slow. He seemed to need the sleep more than I did. As I lay there in the dark, my thoughts circled around several facts. Thomas had taken my request to learn about me, about being human, seriously. He'd never wavered from his conviction that I was the right one for him. And he freely admitted just how much he cared about me. If I were honest with myself, I cared about him, too.

I'd initially decided to stay here because I felt they could keep a secret about what I could do. Though I'd continued to believe they could keep secrets, I hadn't been willing to part with mine. Claiming Thomas changed things. I didn't want to build a relationship with him on misconceptions or lies. Yet, I wasn't sure if I could trust Thomas with the truth.

THERE WAS A WOVEN basket on the table when we entered the main room the next morning. The room was otherwise empty.

Curious, I stepped up to the table, peered into the basket, and saw Ann's sleeping daughter.

"Where are Ann and Leif?" I asked, turning to look at Thomas.

The washroom door opened, and Leif stepped out. His hair was damp, and he held a towel.

"We are here," he said, moving close to check his daughter.

"The basket is wonderful. Who made it?"

"I did." He gently touched the babe's cheek.

"Leif, that's totally amazing. Could you show me how to make one?"

He glanced up from the baby and nodded.

"I would be happy to. I'm not sure what you'd use it for, but you should know the cattail leaves will shrink as they dry, and the basket will grow holes. Typically the leaves should be dried before they are used."

A slow grin spread as I stared at Leif. We'd just found our winter occupation.

"I've never felt that much excitement before. What are you thinking?" Thomas asked.

Leif tilted his head at me and sniffed.

"Claimed?"

I blushed and focused on the baby.

"Yes," Thomas said. "Last night."

The urge to hide myself somewhere grew stronger as they continued to speak of the event as if it wasn't private. Thomas stepped close to me and laid a comforting hand on my back.

"Ann thought she heard you two arguing," Leif said with a laugh.

The main door flew open, and Mary rushed in.

"What? Claimed?" She threw her arms around me and

hugged me tight, squealing. "I'm so happy for you." The baby started to squall, and Mary pulled away from me. "I'm so sorry, Leif."

"I understand your enthusiasm. Ann feels it, too. She will be out in a moment to share her congratulations," Leif said, lifting his daughter from the basket.

Mary continued to grin at me, but the grin faded as she eyed my neck.

"Where's the bite?"

"She bit me, Mary," Thomas said, his thumb rubbing a soothing circle on my lower back.

Mary's eyes rounded, and a snort escaped her. She bit her bottom lip to keep from laughing outright. Gregory walked into the room, eyed Mary, and came to stand behind her. I didn't fail to notice he positioned himself just as Thomas had with me.

"Congratulations," he said, meeting my eyes.

"Thank you," I said quietly. The heat refused to leave my face. "Mary, let's make breakfast."

I walked away from everyone and immediately missed Thomas' touch. A gentle wave of reassurance washed over me. Feeling these emotions that weren't my own was disorienting and scary. What was he feeling from me? He already knew when I lied and that I kept secrets. Would he feel when I used my ability? Would he know, then?

Would he tell Winifred? And would Winifred then see me as a threat as she'd hinted?

CHAPTER FIFTEEN

When the rest of Thomas' pack returned for dinner that evening, a few gave me long looks and nods of acknowledgement but no one acted any differently. Except Anton. As I scooped a portion of the food onto his plate, his nostrils flared.

"Claimed?"

"So I've been told," I said, handing him his plate.

He glanced around and saw Thomas watching us. "Normally, I'd say congratulations. But I think you'll need luck instead."

A trickle of annoyance reached me, and I knew it was Thomas. Anton stepped away and took his seat as Thomas started toward me. When he reached me, he moved to stand behind me and rested his hands lightly on my shoulders. It was comforting. He stayed with me until everyone was fed. Then he left the main room with the rest.

After cleaning up, I went to play with Ann's baby for a while before going upstairs. I was nervous. What would he expect now that I'd Claimed him? Yes, he'd said he wouldn't take more than I was ready to give, but could I trust that? Not only did the physical expectations concern me, but our apparent mental connection did, too.

I opened the door and found him standing in front of the window. The last light was fading, and he'd already lit the lamp I kept in the bedroom.

"Excitement was the best thing I felt from you today," Thomas said without turning. "Your fear and constant worry..." He sighed and turned to look at me. "I will do everything in my power to turn this place into a safe home for you."

He moved toward me, wrapped me in his arms, and kissed the top of my head. I set my cheek against his chest and listened to his heart. For a moment, I let all my fear and worry go. Underneath, I found what he felt for me. Adoration and respect flowed from him.

I wrapped my arms around him in turn. A wisp of desire brushed against me, and my fear returned. I dropped my arms to my side, and he exhaled his frustration.

"Your fear is torture." His hand smoothed down my back. "Will you tell me, is it me? The thought of losing this place? I can't fix what I don't know," he said, pulling back to study me.

"All of it and more," I said honestly. "If you think my fear is torture, the things you feel when you look at me...I'm struggling with my own feelings, I can't deal with yours, too. Everything is more confusing now than it was before. I don't know what to do. What's safe? Will you keep your word and leave me be? When the other's return, will they agree with the Claim I unintentionally made?"

Will you discover my secrets?

"I can't help what I feel for you, and I won't apologize for it," he said softly. "My hope is that someday you'll feel the same for me. Until that happens, I'll wait. I'd like to continue sleeping in your room beside you, but nothing more. Will you allow me that much?"

I wanted to say no. I wanted to tell him to leave. But since he'd pulled away from me, I felt empty and abandoned. I didn't understand why or if those were even my own emotions. All I knew was that having him near made me feel safer and not so alone.

"Yes, you can sleep by me."

He smiled, reached out to touch my cheek, then flooded me with comfort. Before I could react, he left the room. I wasn't sure how, but I knew he waited right out in the hallway. He wasn't being impatient or aggressive. Just protective.

I changed into the light shirt and cotton shorts I'd been using for sleeping and then climbed into bed. I lay there tensely for a moment before I called him in.

My stomach churned nervously as he entered. He didn't look at me as he walked to the dresser and blew out the lamp. I blinked in the sudden darkness, unable to see him. The mattress dipped as he sat, and my heart stuttered. His fingers touched my hair.

"So much fear because of so little trust."

I stared in the direction of his voice and saw his vague shape.

"Trust has to be earned," I said softly. "If you recall, you bit me."

"Only because you allowed it."

I snorted. "As if I had a choice. I knew you wouldn't leave it alone."

"I'm sorry I hurt you, but I'm glad I didn't leave it alone." He eased down next to me. Lying on his side, he rested an arm over my middle. The weight felt comforting rather than confining.

"Go to sleep, Charlene."

Despite my racing heart, I somehow managed.

I WOKE with a weight on my chest, and for a disoriented moment, I panicked. I pushed at the weight at the same time I struggled to kick off the covers.

"Shh. It's all right," Thomas said as the weight disappeared. I saw the vague outline of his head.

"What were you doing?" I asked, no longer trying to escape the covers.

He touched my hair and the weight settled back onto my chest.

"Listening to your heart."

For a moment, I said nothing. Would I ever understand Thomas?

"Why?"

"Sometimes, when you dream, your pulse races; and it sounds so fragile. I don't like it. I whisper to you until it calms."

His admission caught me off guard. How often had he listened to my heart like this? "Don't you sleep?"

"I do. Not very much, though."

The idea that he stayed awake next to me should have been troubling. So why wasn't I troubled? His fingers drifted from my hair to trace the curve of my jaw. I closed my eyes and tried to relax.

"Am I allowed to kiss you?"

"No."

I could picture him grinning at my abrupt answer.

"Sleep well, Charlene."

"Stop staring at me, and I will."

His chest vibrated with his laughter. I couldn't help grinning in return.

For the remainder of the night, I slept comfortably. When I woke, I had the vague recollection of wanting to roll over at some point but being unable to do so because of a weight on me. However, Thomas was already gone, so I couldn't ask him about it.

I dressed and went downstairs. Before I entered the main room, I smelled breakfast, and my stomach rumbled. Thomas stood before the stove, stirring something. Mary and Gregory were at the table, glumly eyeing their bowls of oatmeal.

As I walked past the table to see what was left on the stove, I heard Mary's comment to Gregory.

"Tomorrow, you wake up first."

"Good morning," Thomas said, drawing my attention. I peeked over his shoulder and saw a pan with eggs and onions. It wasn't much. Enough for two humans.

"Where did you find eggs?"

"I went to the marsh this morning," he said, scooping some egg onto a plate. "For you." He handed me the plate.

I accepted it and turned away before I blushed. He'd gone to the marsh just for me. I couldn't prevent my small smile as I sat next to Mary.

"What does everyone have planned for today?" I asked, taking my first bite. I didn't miss how Mary's gaze tracked my food.

Gregory looked at Thomas for an answer as Thomas sat across from me.

"Bine took his things and walked into town after Winifred left. That leaves Zerek in the workroom, creating more window coverings, and the rest went to see if the man at the yard needed more help. What needs to be done around here?"

"Well..." I thought about it for a moment. The pile of wood outside was impressive. They had long rows stacked high with logs driven into the ground to hold everything up. And with Zerek working on the windows, I was less concerned about freezing this winter. I was still worried about going hungry though.

"If Leif has time, maybe he can show us what to collect to make baskets. While we're out there, we could weed the garden and get a really good look at what we have."

"I'll talk to Leif while you finish eating," Gregory said, standing.

"We'll leave for the marsh when you return," Thomas said with a nod.

I was excited to get out and do something active. I quickly ate my eggs and pretended not to notice when Mary stole a small bite.

Hours later, I sat down in the chair with a groan. My lower back didn't just ache; it burned from the strain of the hours I'd spent pulling weeds and picking reeds. Pain radiated from my hips to mid-back. I just wanted to lie in my bed, but it seemed too far to walk.

Mary sat next to me with a grunt and set her armful of cattail leaves on the table. Gregory and Thomas were making another trip back to the marsh for the rest of the cattail leaves we'd harvested.

"You need better ideas," Mary said, leaning back.

"I thought werewolves were all tough and strong." I couldn't even lean back. My spine was set to forward only. I rested my face on the table.

"Weeds will kill us," Mary said. I snickered.

The main doors opened, but I didn't look up. I couldn't.

"How did the gathering go?" Leif asked.

I reached out a hand and lifted a frond.

He chuckled.

"Does this mean you won't want to start working on baskets today?"

"Nope. No basket weaving," Mary said for me. I heard her stand. "Will you help me pump water?"

At first, I thought she was talking to me but then Leif answered, "Yes." With relief, I stayed at the table a few more minutes before I struggled to my feet.

"I'm going to lie down," I said.

"You sure? They're bringing back fish for dinner, and I have water heating for a bath."

I smelled like marsh and sweat but didn't care.

"I'm sure. Tell Thomas to let me sleep. Even if it's through dinner," I said, shuffling to the door. "And if he lays his head on me tonight, he'll lose it."

She snorted a surprised laugh just before the door closed behind me.

I trudged my way upstairs, stripped from my smelly clothes, and feebly dressed myself in my shorts and shirt. With a groan, I sank onto my mattress. Typically, I slept on my back. However, when I tried to lie that way, it hurt too much. Lying on my stomach hurt even more. So I curled on my side and tried to relax.

HEAT PRESSED against my lower back in rhythmic sweeping moves. It ached, but in a good way. I let out a sigh that was a half groan and snuggled deeper into my pillow. The pressure increased on my back, easing some of the soreness. I curled up more, bringing my knees level with my hips. The warm sweeping pressure continued, undisturbed by my movement.

I sighed and drifted back to sleep.

I WOKE WITH A CONFINED STRETCH. Something wrapped around me. A blanket. I untangled myself and slowly sat up, not opening my eyes. My back cracked in several places. It was still sore, but nothing like it had been when I'd gone to bed.

I stayed there, sitting on the mattress for several seconds as I debated if I wanted to open my eyes and officially wake up, or if I wanted to lay down and try to go back to sleep. My head hit the pillow. However, lying on my back wasn't comfortable. I rolled to my side. My shoulder hurt a little, and I guessed I'd spent a lot of time on my side last night.

Fingers gently dug into the muscles of my lower back and startled my eyes open. I twisted in bed and saw Thomas sitting on the edge of the mattress.

"You slept a long time," he said, keeping his eyes on my exposed back.

I glanced at the window and noted early morning light. I

felt his concern. This time it was my turn to send out some reassurance. If only I could figure out how. I settled for words.

"I'm thinking about sleeping longer," I said, relaxing my head against the pillow. "Especially if you keep doing that."

With my face pressed against the pillow, I smelled marsh and wrinkled my nose. On top of an already sore back, I would need to do laundry.

"Hmm. Does that mean I should tell the new family what room to pick?"

I sat up quickly, dislodging his attentive fingers. "New family?"

"Yes. A Mated pair and their cub. A little boy about two."

I was up, out of bed, and frantically searching for clothes. A family. It was a start to what I saw this place could be. Hope and excitement filled me, along with Thomas' amusement.

"They're eating oatmeal in the main room. Come down when you're ready," he said, standing.

I nodded and with clean clothes in my arms, shooed him out the door.

Mary and I showed Rilla the rooms on the first floor and the clothes in the entry. Her adorable son ran around us in his fur. It was really hard not to play with him like he was a frisky puppy, which was totally how he acted.

They picked a room near the back of the house that Mary and I hadn't yet swept. It also had no glass in the window. But Rilla didn't seem to mind at all. She set the clothes they'd taken just inside the door, then she and the cub went off to find her husband. Thomas had offered to show the man the rest of the buildings.

As Mary and I walked to the common room, I thought of what we had to offer new families.

"It just doesn't seem like clothes are enough," I said, thinking aloud. "The men only wear pants because I asked. Would you be wearing clothes if Winifred hadn't said something?"

"It's getting cooler out at night, so probably."

"Funny," I said, knowing she was just being smart. "How can we make this place more comfortable for those who aren't sure if they want to be a part of it or not? I know you were willing to sleep on the floor, but that's going to be hard and cold in the winter." But no worse than snow and frozen ground, I supposed.

"I like my bed. But if I had to choose what I like best about it, it would be the pillow. I could go back to sleeping on the floor if I had a pillow."

"Then, we have our project for the day," I said with a smile. "We'll see if we can come up with a way to make some pillows."

"Just so we don't have to weed."

When we pushed our way through the main room doors, the room was empty and the breakfast dishes waited. It had been a hectic morning. I didn't know who to thank for getting up early to make the oatmeal. It wasn't Mary. I'd pulled her from her bed so she could come with me to greet the new family.

I went to the stove and saw someone had been kind enough to put a pot of water there. It was already boiling. Mary and I got to work. Before we had half the dishes clean, Rilla and Ann joined us with their children. Together, we finished the dishes quickly.

Leif walked in from outside as we stacked the dried plates and bowls. In his arms, he carried a bunch of the reeds.

"If you're finished with the trough, can I use it? Weaving works better if we keep this soft," he said.

I nodded and watched him set them in the trough. He pumped some water and poured it over them.

"Ready?" he said with a smile.

"What are you doing?" Rilla asked, curiously eyeing the leaves.

"Leif is going to teach us how to make baskets so we can store things," Mary said.

"I would love to learn that, too," she said. Leif handed her several of the leaves and took a few more himself. They brought them over to the table.

"We'll need to spread out to have enough space to work, but let me show you how to start."

Before I could join the rest at the table and watch Leif, Gregory came in from outside.

"Not you two," he said, looking at Mary and me. "We're going back to the marsh."

Mary and I both groaned.

"What you brought back was a good start," Leif said. "But we'll need more to make enough baskets to store what's in that garden. If you pick enough, we can make mats for the floor, too. And bring back whatever tops you can. It makes a soft stuffing."

Gregory held the door, waiting while Mary and I shared a look. We'd both slept deeply because of the day before. I hadn't asked her how her back felt, but the idea of spending another day doing the same thing made me want to run for my room. I was willing to bet she felt the same way.

Yet, going back to the marsh meant mats for people to sleep on and possibly stuffing for the pillows she and I had just talked about—Leif had probably overheard us. Making this place into a home would take some work, backbreaking, sweat-inducing work.

"Come on," I said with a sigh.

Together, we walked out the door.

On the ground just outside, I saw two finished baskets. One was the baby's and the other Leif must have made the night before. Mary picked up both and started following Gregory across the clearing.

I took two steps, then I found myself swept up from behind. I squealed and automatically wrapped my arms around Thomas' neck. My pulse jumped as he grinned down at me.

His boyish smile and the amusement pouring from him warmed me.

"Ready?" he asked.

In his arms, I felt like I was ready for anything. I nodded, and he ran.

WHEN I WOULD HAVE KICKED off my shoes and stepped into the cattails, Thomas stopped me.

"It's getting too cold for you to do that. You stay here and stack what we pick."

Stacking the fronds the three of them pitched onto dry ground wasn't very hard; but within an hour, my back wanted to quit. I stretched, twisting this way and that, in an effort to relieve the ache.

"Ready to stop?" Thomas asked. Mud smeared his arms up to his elbows as he stood calf-deep in cold water. His pants were rolled up to his knees.

"We were never ready to start," Mary grumbled. She and Gregory were similarly dirty and standing in the water. Gregory moved over to her and gently rubbed her shoulders. I watched her sag against him.

"Yes, I think we have enough for today," I said.

Cattail tops filled both baskets, and a very large stack of leaves waited beside them. If Thomas carried me, it would leave more for Gregory and Mary to carry.

"I know I'm slow, but I think I'd like to walk back," I said. Hopefully the walk would loosen up my back muscles.

No one argued with me, and we worked together to tie the leaves into bundles. Gregory and Thomas carried the majority. I managed the last two bundles while Mary carried the baskets. When we had everything in our arms, Mary and Gregory took off, running ahead. Thomas and I walked through the trees.

Again, I wondered if I was doing enough to make the buildings into a place where people would want to live. Were pillows, mats, and clothes enough? Would it sway the rest of the pack when they returned?

"Have you heard from them?" I asked. He didn't ask who I meant.

"They don't contact me. But I did let them know about Ann and Leif's daughter. I think they sent the new family, too, by sharing that news."

"How's your head? It hasn't seemed to bother you since they left."

His gaze softened as he glanced at me.

"It's been better since they left. One or two of them tests my hold daily but the rest of the time it's tolerable."

"Do they know about me?"

He shook his head.

"You asked me not to say anything. I won't. But others might. It's only a matter of time."

I frowned, worried. What would happen when they found out?

"I can feel your concern, Charlene. It will be all right. Even if they do find out, they've separated into smaller groups to spread out and cover more territory. They won't be able to cause trouble until they're back together, here."

That worried me more. With Bine living in town and most of Thomas' pack leaving daily to look for work, it left very few to help Thomas if the need arose. At least he kept Gregory close. Then I realized there was one person I hadn't seen at all since Claiming Thomas.

"Where's Grey?" I asked.

Thomas sighed and looked off into the trees. "He worries as much as you do. He's left the pack so there's one less rope to hold."

"What?" I couldn't believe what I was hearing.

"It's not as bad as it sounds. He's with Winifred. They're preparing him to be an Elder."

"Elder Grey?"

He nodded. Though his expression was blank, I felt the wave of sorrow that consumed him.

"What's wrong?"

"Nothing's wrong. Grey is doing what he has always done, sacrificing his future for the future of someone else. Only this time, his sacrifice will benefit all of us, not just me." He caught my confused look. "Being an Elder means you serve the people, never yourself. He can never have a Mate once he becomes an Elder. If he even thinks about it, he'll die. He'll never have cubs..."

I'd lived with them long enough to know a Mate and cubs were at the top of every man's mind. To give that up to protect not only his brother but me and the future of his people was humbling.

I shifted the bundles in my arms and reached out, gently touching Thomas' shoulder. "Tell Winifred to thank him for me."

Thomas nodded. We walked together in silence for several meters before I heard a rustling ahead. Gregory and Mary ran toward us. Mary wore an amused smile. Gregory ran just a few steps back and to her side, keeping an eye on her.

They stopped in front of us, and without a word, Gregory took Thomas' load. Mary held out her arms for mine.

"You don't have to," I said.

"Tub's half full," she said, "and there's more water hot on the stove. If you hurry, you can have the tub first. Take too long, and it's mine."

I surrendered what I carried and looked up at Thomas as they took off running. There was only one way to hurry back.

Thomas opened his arms.

I LEANED back in the hot water, sighing yet again. It was heaven. My sore back didn't feel sore anymore, and my hair no longer smelled like marsh.

Voices carried through the door. Rilla, Ann, and Leif were still working on baskets. Mary, Gregory, and Thomas had been watching what they did, trying to learn, when I'd closed the door. When we'd returned, all of the leaves gathered from the day before had almost been used. Rilla was working on mats for sleeping since it was an easier weave, and Ann and Leif were making the baskets.

I knew I should get out of the water, dress, and join them, but I couldn't quite make myself move. My fingers weren't pruned enough. I closed my eyes and relaxed further.

Someone tapped on the door.

"Charlene," Thomas said. "If you fall asleep in there, I will come in."

"Chill," I said, opening my eyes. "I'm almost done."

I sat forward and reached for the towel I had waiting on the chair. Standing, I wrapped it around me and squeezed the excess water from my hair. Minutes later, I was dressed and opening the door.

Thomas looked up from his spot at the table and smiled at me. My stomach did its funny dance it liked to do. I turned away from him. His amusement filtered in through our link as I went to the stove and checked on lunch.

Someone had started a soup. Vegetables, fowl, and pasta floated in the broth.

Hands settled on my shoulders as I gave it a stir. Thomas' amusement faded and something that felt like hunger replaced it. I turned my head to look at him. His hands skimmed down my shoulders, feathered over my upper arms, then transferred to my sides. I was fully clothed. His hands didn't stray from my sides. Yet, it felt completely indecent. His hunger wasn't for food; it was for me.

My lips parted, and his gaze shifted down to them. I wanted to tell him to give me some space but I couldn't speak. His hunger consumed me and became my hunger. I set the spoon aside and turned, slowly. His head lowered. My pulse leapt, and I licked my lips.

"How's the soup?" Mary asked. Barely contained laughter laced her words. But hearing her voice was enough to break the spell. Thomas' hunger turned to mild annoyance.

I exhaled slowly and ducked around Thomas. Heat marked my cheeks as I headed for the common room's doors.

"Mary, finish your basket," Thomas said from behind me.

His irritation filtered through the connection we had. I wasn't sure if it was at Mary or me because I was trying to put some distance between us.

One of the men chuckled as I left the room. Seconds later, I heard the door behind me and knew Thomas was following me. I didn't look back at him, and he didn't try to catch me until I was in the upstairs hallway.

Thomas' hand curled around my upper arm before I made it to my door. He didn't try to pull me to a stop. He didn't need to. His touch was enough. Had he not touched me, I would have stepped inside my room, closed the door on him, and hid away at least until my blush faded.

Instead, when he touched me, I pivoted and took us both by surprise. I reached up, grabbed his face, and pulled him down for a kiss.

For several moments, just our lips touched. Then, his hunger returned in force. His hands settled on my sides again. He steered me back against a wall. My hands slid up into his hair. I opened my mouth to him. He growled and kissed me hard.

My head spun. I wasn't sure if it was the kiss or if maybe I wasn't breathing.

His lips left mine and trailed along my jaw to my neck. It was then that I noticed he was moving me again. Step by step, we were shuffling closer to my room.

I panicked, fisted my hand in his hair, and yanked hard.

"Ow!" He took a step back and scowled at me while he rubbed his head.

"What do you think you are doing?"

"It's called kissing," he said, dryly.

"No, you were trying to back me into my room. Why?"

He stopped rubbing his head and stared at me a moment. I felt the rush of hunger once more. But now I knew what he meant to do with it, and it didn't wash me away.

"No, Thomas. You promised. Nothing more than I'm ready to give."

"But I thought that was a yes."

"That was a kiss, remember?"

He looked mildly annoyed with me for a moment then sighed.

"I'm sorry, Charlene."

He stepped close and slowly pulled me into a hug. I resisted at first until I felt his sincerity.

"I'm sorry," he said again.

He held me in the hall for a while then pulled away.

"I'll save you some lunch. Mary will come up to sit with you."

He was giving me space while still making sure I was protected. My heart softened a little.

"Thank you," I said, then turned away and closed myself into my room.

A few minutes later, Mary came in. She had a partial mat, and extra leaves. She sat on the floor, spread out her work, and looked up at me.

"So what earned him the hair pull?" she asked. She didn't sound amused, just concerned.

"He told you?"

She nodded and started weaving another leaf into place.

"When he asked if I would come up here. He said you were upset enough with him that you pulled his hair, but he couldn't leave you alone, even if you were mad at him. So what did he do?"

I blushed but confessed everything.

"I kissed him. He assumed it was a sign for more and was trying to nudge me into the room."

"Yeah. Sleeping in Gregory's room is nice, but I have to watch what I do. They're always trying to read into things, hoping you're finally saying yes without using the word. I haven't pulled his hair yet, but I've come close." She took a new leaf from her pile and started to weave that one in. Her calm acceptance had me blurting my concerns.

"Mary, I'm really not ready. I know he's worried about what will happen when the pack returns and he thinks...mating," I swallowed hard, "will help with that, but I'm just not ready. What am I supposed to do?"

Her hands stilled as she looked up at me.

"Is it okay if I ask Winifred to join this conversation?" she asked hesitantly.

I thought about it for a moment then nodded. Mary sat quietly for a minute, then a corner of her mouth quirked in a smile.

"First, Winifred wants you to know she supports whatever

decision you make and applauds you for standing up for what you wanted and pulling Thomas' hair. She's not pushing one way or the other. She said you need to think about the reasons why you're not ready."

"I'm too young," I said automatically.

"Do you think I'm too young?" Mary asked, and I knew she was speaking for herself.

"Yes, I do."

"Why?"

I stared at her.

"How old are you?"

"I'll have been born sixteen years ago when the leaves fall."

"And don't you think that's a little young?"

Mary shrugged.

"I don't feel young. I've hunted with my family since I could walk. I've been learning about the dangers of the human world since before I could speak, and I have listened to the history of our race. Like you said, we're dying. Don't I have a responsibility to try to keep us going? And I love Gregory. It's not like I'm even sacrificing my happiness for the sake of everyone else. Once we're Mated, he'll never leave me. He'll always care for me and love me in return. This isn't something that fades or goes away. The only reason I'm waiting, is because I don't want you to be upset with me. I saw your disappointment when I let him Claim me."

"Oh, Mary," I said, moving to kneel beside her. "I'm so sorry. I never meant to make you think I'd be upset with you. I won't be." I hugged her, and she wrapped her arms around me. "If you felt my disappointment, it was because I thought you'd leave. None of your kind really seems to like being here."

"Living here is different," she said, pulling back. "But we stay because you make this place somewhere we want to be."

My eyes watered.

"I've never had a better friend than you," I said. "If Gregory makes you happy, don't hold back because of me."

"If Thomas makes you happy, don't hold back because of age or doubt. Waiting won't change how he feels for you. Once our kind finds a Mate, it's for life."

And if I were honest with myself, that worried me more than my age. She watched me for a minute then went back to weaving, letting me think things through.

If I mated with Thomas without telling him the truth, what kind of life would we have?

THOMAS WASN'T in the main room when I finally went to find him. He wasn't anywhere outside, either. I stood in the sun, closed my eyes, and concentrated on where I usually felt him. It was like concentrating on my left hand but in my head. I found the spot and felt a hint of frustration coming from it. How did you call someone with feelings? Impatience? I didn't want him to think I was mad. Not when I was about to tell him the truth about myself. My insides twisted at the thought. And I didn't want to wait for him to come back on his own.

I knew two things that would most likely have him rushing to my side. Fear and hunger. I blushed, opened my eyes, and started to think about the kiss we'd shared in the hallway. The memory of his hands on my sides made me shiver, and my pulse jumped. The frustration disappeared. I imagined his mouth on mine, not a gentle, light touch but a starved press of his lips.

My gaze swept over the trees, and my breathing changed as I kept the memory playing in my head.

"You better be ready to run," Mary said from behind me.

I jumped and spun around. Like a bucket of cold water over my head, her appearance stopped all thought.

She grinned at me.

"What were you doing?" she asked.

My already flushed face heated further.

"Trying to get him to come back."

Hands settled on my shoulders, and I let out a small "eep."

Mary laughed, shook her head at me, and walked back inside.

"You succeeded in gaining my undivided attention. Was there something you wanted?" Thomas said from behind me. What he felt flooded me, and my stomach did a nervous dip. Why hadn't I felt anything until now? I'd thought it wasn't working.

"I wanted to talk to you privately but maybe now isn't the best time."

He scooped me up in his arms and took off running into the trees.

"Now is the perfect time," he said, glancing down at me. His hungry gaze devoured me.

"Don't run into a tree," I said, nudging his chin up. He grinned and focused on our path.

As he ran, I tried to settle my nerves and my pulse by taking several deep, calming breaths.

We broke through the trees to the lake's grassy shore. I was glad he hadn't taken us to the marsh or garden. He set me on my feet and turned me.

"There's no one around to hear us. Now, what did you want to discuss?"

I felt like throwing up. The little voice that had cautioned me when I'd thought about telling Winifred was screaming at me now to keep my mouth shut. I looked out over the water, unsure what to do.

"Hey, it's okay," Thomas said. He pulled me close and wrapped his arms around me. "I hate when you worry this much. You can tell me whatever you want or keep it to yourself. I won't be upset with you either way. Just stop worrying like this."

His hands smoothed down my back, and the voice quieted. My worries tended to fade when he just held me like this.

"I can control people with just a thought," I said against his chest.

His chin settled on the top of my head. "I know. Winifred told me. She and I talked after the first time we saw what you could do. We thought it was tele-whatever, where you can move things with your head. When you told her it was something else, she told me."

I frowned, not saying anything. I said it needed to be kept secret. And when she'd nodded, I'd thought she'd agreed.

"Don't be angry," he said.

I needed to figure out a way to keep my emotions in check.

"She told me because she had to. She's responsible for all of us. Keeping information to herself about the possibility of someone in our midst who could control us could have killed her."

"What?" I said, lifting my head.

"Like I said about Grey. Elders serve us, not themselves. If she knowingly did something that could potentially jeopardize us, she would die."

I stared at him, unable to speak.

"Winifred does want to protect you. She believes that you're a key to our future. She will do what she can to keep you safe. That's why she told me what you can do and asked that I keep an eye on you. I saw what you can do. It's impressive and as far as I'm concerned, there's no reason for us to worry. The damage you can do is no worse than when we challenge each other."

I could do so much more than he imagined. I could make them do things then make them forget. And if Winifred found that out, she'd need to tell Thomas or risk her own life. What would Thomas do if I told him? Would he keep it to himself? I studied his face. He wouldn't. He loved his people too much. If he knew there was a way I could control them, he'd warn Winifred, at the very least. She'd need to tell all of the rest. I was very unwanted already. It would be my death.

I felt sick but quickly pushed it aside. I couldn't fall apart; he'd know there was something more to what I could do. Fear snaked its way into my belly, and I saw his expression begin to change.

I did the only thing I could to distract him, to distract us both. I kissed him.

THOMAS' head lay on my chest. His breathing was slow and even. I didn't move to wake him. Instead, I lay there and let out all the worry and fear I'd suppressed since our kiss at the lake.

If I mated with Thomas as he wanted, as I wanted, I

would need to lie to him for the rest of my life. I could try to run, again, but knew he wouldn't let me go. Even if I managed to leave this place, he would come and find me. He hadn't wanted to give up his Claim before it had been official. Now that it was official...I sighed and looked up at the ceiling.

"What next?" I whispered in the dark.

Thomas shifted in his sleep, relieving some of the pressure.

I ran my fingers through his hair. I'd made it this long without deciding. Maybe I just needed to be patient and wait for the universe to actually answer.

Thomas and I stood outside, working together to hang laundry on the line. Everyone else was still inside working on weaving. I'd tried to start a mat but discovered I didn't have the patience or skill for it. The leaves didn't cooperate and, instead of a rectangle, I ended up with a weird shape with too many gaps. So, I'd opted to do laundry instead.

"Weaving's not for everyone," Thomas said.

How had he known what I was thinking about?

"What gave me away?" I asked.

"Your frustration. It felt the same now as it did in there."

I wrinkled my nose at him. Thomas' mat had been perfect.

While I was making my face, his expression went from amused to alert. He turned to look at the trail. A light blue and white truck rolled into the yard. Not Winifred's truck. I stopped straightening a shirt and squinted against the glare of the sun reflecting off the windshield. I caught sight of a man behind the wheel as the truck stopped and the engine died. I turned back around to keep my face averted. Thomas moved toward the truck.

The man opened the door, and a metal on metal screech filled the air.

"Afternoon," Thomas said as the man stepped from the truck. Thomas' voice seemed pleasant enough, but I felt his tension.

"Afternoon," the man echoed. "Sorry to come in here without warning. Am I interrupting something?"

I reached for the man's will but didn't find anything more than friendly curiosity. Keeping a light hold on his will, I hung another shirt.

"Just laundry," Thomas said.

"Not a shirt left to wear, huh?"

I blushed as I realized how odd Thomas must look standing there in nothing but his pants. I'd grown so used to it, I never thought of getting a shirt for him anymore.

"Yeah, the Mrs. lets it pile up at my place, too," the man said when Thomas remained silent. There was a slight pause before the man continued. "I've seen your smoke for a few weeks now and wanted to stop in and warn you. We've been seeing some wolves around. They've left our livestock alone so far and don't bother the dog none, even though that thing yaps up a storm."

"Wolves?" Thomas said, sounding deeply concerned. "Which direction did you say?"

"I live a few miles to the west. It's a farm just off the road."

Had I walked a bit further all those weeks ago, I would have seen the farm. How different would my life be if I'd gone to knock on their door instead of walking an old trail at dusk?

"And you saw our smoke from your place?"

The man laughed.

"Not from my place. I've seen it when I go to town for supplies."

A thread of impatience touched me, and I smiled. Poor Thomas. I wondered when he'd last spoken to a human. Excluding me, of course.

"Thank you for letting us know about the wolves," Thomas said pleasantly. "We haven't seen any yet, but we'll keep watch and let you know if we do."

"It's no trouble," the man said. "It's nice having neighbors again. Thought the lady who bought this place from the hippies was just going to let it rot."

The man was obviously not ready to leave. I knew we should invite him in or seem friendlier, but I didn't think anyone here would welcome him if I extended any type of invitation.

"That's my aunt," Thomas said. "She was thinking about it but asked me and a few of my friends to move out here and start fixing the place up. Might still rot."

I could feel the shrug in Thomas' words. Hanging up the last shirt, I calmly walked inside and felt the man's curiosity as he glanced my way. I should have at least said hello. Instead of thinking me odd, I nudged his thoughts toward shy.

Mary closed the door behind me.

"Thomas said to stay inside until he leaves."

I didn't need her to tell me that. I went to the window and peeked around the curtain. The man stood near his truck. Thomas appeared very relaxed beside him.

"Let Thomas know he should shake the man's hand when he thanks him for the information," I said.

Mary giggled.

"Gregory didn't know about that when we went into town.

You should have seen his face when the plumber offered his hand."

Thomas stuck out his hand as he thanked the man again. The man shook Thomas' hand, and I felt the man's relief that we were normal people, unlike the last group here.

Thomas stayed outside until the taillights disappeared down the road. When he came inside, he didn't appear as troubled as he felt. He walked over to me and set his hands on my shoulders. I'd noticed when others were around, it was usually just a casual touch; but when we were alone, he tended to curl around me.

"What part bothers you?" I said. "That someone came here or that he thinks I don't do laundry?"

"That there are wolves to the west."

"I don't understand why that's troubling."

"Winifred says there are no wolves to the west."

That didn't sound good.

"Could it be some of your pack trying to cause trouble?" I asked.

"No. Most of them are to the north or the east."

"Maybe they're just real wolves," I said.

"Maybe."

CHAPTER SIXTEEN

THOMAS' PLACE BESIDE ME WAS STILL WARM WHEN MARY CAME TO wake me Saturday morning.

"You're going to like what we get to do today," she said, nudging my shoulder.

"If it's collecting more reeds, forget it." I'd never thought so many reeds would be needed for basket weaving.

"Nope. Winifred's brought apples. Rilla and Ann are already in the kitchen. We're making pies."

I opened one eye to stare at her. "Do you even know what an apple pie is?"

She grinned down at me. "Winifred brought one already made. It was good. Thomas is trying to save you a piece."

I tossed the covers off me and hurried to dress. Eating a pie was much more motivating than the idea of making one.

The five women worked together in the kitchen all day. It was a nice break from reed gathering, weaving, and laundry, and I decided we needed some diversity in our schedule. When Winifred left on Sunday, I mentioned my idea to Thomas and he agreed.

Monday and Tuesday, the women worked hard to make small pillows. I was good at stuffing them with the fluff and cutting even rectangles, but I left the sewing to Ann and Mary.

Wednesday, we tried our hand at homemade bread. The oven was a little touchy, and the loaves came out dark on the outside and still doughy in the middle. The following batch baked more evenly. It didn't seem to matter either way. Werewolves weren't picky eaters, and they devoured all the loaves.

That night, I contentedly fell asleep in Thomas' arms, and he surprised me by staying in bed until I woke again. His awe and adoration flooded me as I slowly opened my eyes. I smiled sleepily.

"That's a nice way to wake up," I said.

He kissed my temple.

"Would you like to spend the day together?"

I nodded. How could I not? I loved having his undivided attention, and whether I wanted to acknowledge the passing time or not, we had less than two weeks until the rest of his pack returned.

"I'll meet you in the kitchen." He kissed my temple once more then left me to dress.

When I found him several minutes later, he was waiting beside the outer door with a bundle in his hands.

"What's that?"

"Lunch," he said with a grin.

He was learning.

He didn't ask to carry me, but held out his hand. Together, we walked away from the buildings.

"Are we going anywhere particular?"

"Not really. I'm already where I want to be."

And I knew he meant with me.

THE NEXT MORNING, I sat at the table, eating my last bites of oatmeal. As usual, I was one of the last ones awake. This morning, though, I noticed an unusual number of men still lingering outside. Thomas walked in through the open door and smiled at me.

I waited until he sat next to me to ask about the men.

"The man at the junkyard has no more work for them. He told them to come back in spring. Anton put the cash they'd earned on top of the food storage."

What would the men do now to keep busy? Thomas seemed to read my mind.

"We'll take what baskets we have and start picking from the garden," he said.

I nodded and watched him stand to rejoin the men milling around outside. Besides the Mated men, Thomas always left someone he trusted behind whenever he left, so I wasn't surprised when Gregory walked in with a grin.

As soon as the men left, Rilla and Ann started washing the dishes while Gregory, Mary, and I fetched the reeds and other supplies we'd need for the day. Then, we worked hard to make more baskets, mats, and small pillows. I mostly ran back and forth fetching whatever supplies they needed.

Twice a man returned with a full basket of vegetables to ask if we had another one complete. Both times, we were able to say yes thanks to Rilla's amazing skill.

The men returned before dusk, with fish and two more filled baskets. Ann and Mary took the fish. The oven was hot and ready for them. Rice already steamed on the stove, along with a pot of mixed vegetables.

We were just clearing away our work from the tables when someone knocked on the door. Those men who stayed here, no longer knocked. The man closest to the door opened it. Outside I saw, three men, two woman, and two children.

"We heard families are welcome here," one of the new men said.

"Come in. Please," I said, stepping forward. "I'm Charlene. This is Thomas." As soon as the door had opened, Thomas had been at my side.

"Welcome," Thomas said. The two families stepped in.

I smiled at the older kids. "Would you like to see what we've done?"

It only took a few minutes to show them around. I did most of the talking. Thomas didn't mind in the least. When the families selected their rooms, Mary brought the mats and pillows they'd need. I was so happy we had enough so that no one slept directly on the floor.

SATURDAY, Winifred brought more than just eggs and the usual supplies. She also had books and things to help the children learn to read.

During breakfast, the kitchen was full of chatting women and laughing children. I stood back and enjoyed the moment. Thomas came up behind me and rested his hands on my shoulders, his satisfaction wrapping around me like a hug.

The next week was hectic, but in a good way. Basket's full of produce from the garden hung from the rafters in the rooms just outside of the common room—the stove kept the room too warm for them to stay good for very long.

Cooking for the large group wasn't difficult with so many helping hands. The vast quantities of food we consumed would have been concerning if not for the game that always appeared every day. The Mated men took turns going out with a few of the unMated to hunt larger game. Though we still had the occasional pheasant, we more often had deer, moose, or boar. The women worked together to butcher and cook whatever the men brought. However, when someone brought back a bear, I stepped out of the room to let Mary handle coordinating that meal. Thomas considerately brought me a jelly sandwich.

That Thursday, Grey returned to us as a new Elder. Thomas greeted him with an enthusiastic hug while I stood back. Grey didn't seem to act any differently. When he finished hugging Thomas, he turned to me.

"Welcome to the family, Charlene." Then he hugged me, too. It was much briefer than Thomas' hug. "Will you introduce me to the families?"

His ever-present smile grew just a bit brighter when he saw the children, and Thomas' words about what Grey had given up came back to me. Over the next few days, Grey mostly stayed near the families and children and left everything else to Thomas.

TUESDAY MARKED the twenty-ninth day since Thomas had sent his pack out. Leif and Ann left with their daughter before lunch, and I couldn't help the nervous worry that burrowed into my mind as I waved goodbye.

That night, it took hours before I fell asleep to the feel of Thomas's fingers slowly running through my hair.

He woke me with a kiss to my cheek.

"I'm going downstairs now. I'd feel better if you came, too. The rest of the women will be with Winifred."

"And Grey?"

"Outside, to keep an eye on things."

"He won't be able to help you, will he?"

Thomas shook his head.

"How many more do you think you can—"

He stopped my question with a kiss and shook his head again. It wasn't something he ever wanted to talk about aloud. I understood why. Yet, it didn't stop me from wanting to know. At what point tomorrow would I see him break?

He hadn't pushed for anything more than I'd been willing to give, which I'd limited to kissing. Yet, I knew I could have helped ease his pack's acceptance of me if I would have Mated him. I was still hoping there would be fewer who continued to oppose me, thus making mating unnecessary.

He kissed my forehead, stood, and held out his hand to help me stand. Then, he waited outside while I dressed and walked downstairs with me.

"Good luck," I whispered before we entered the main room. He nodded and pushed the door open.

Mary was already at the table with Winifred. They were cracking all twelve dozen eggs into two pots. Several of the older children read books at a table with their parents.

I watched Thomas walk outside then took up a knife and started slicing onions. No one minded my sniffles.

Rilla pushed through the door with her son in tow a minute later. Her husband walked with them.

"How can I help?" she said.

"Can you start the sausage links?" I asked quietly. There were several wrapped packages waiting on one of the longer tables. Rilla retrieved them and started separating the links at the stove.

I listened to the sizzle and tried not to worry. Thomas was out there acting as the official welcoming party. Last night, Thomas had talked with Winifred and Grey. They'd decided to welcome everyone by showing them that living here could offer safety and a sense of community. Hence, the big breakfast.

I focused on the wills of those around me. They were easy to feel. I also sensed several men outside. I tried to look further, stretching out into the woods, but wasn't able to detect more. So I sliced as I waited and added what I cut to a hot pot. Rilla poured the grease from the sausages into the skillet to help brown the onions. Soon, the room smelled divine and distracted me from my concentration.

Mary cleaned up the eggshells while Winifred brought over the pot of eggs and poured half the mixture in with the onions. She set the other pot on the stovetop behind the sausage then went back to the table. I carefully stirred the eggs in both pots and glanced at Rilla. Instead of moving the sausages around, she was looking over her shoulder. I did the same and saw Winifred sitting at the table. Her complete motionlessness alarmed me.

"Winifred?" As I spoke, I concentrated on the wills around me. I gasped at what I found. Over eighty people waited outside.

"Thomas," I whispered. A wave of reassurance washed over me, and I exhaled in relief.

I glanced at the food again. This would be enough to feed eighty humans but not eighty werewolves.

"Pull the sausages off," I said nudging Rilla, "and start chopping them." Rilla quickly brought the pot to the table. I opened the wood door and threw a few more pieces of wood in, bringing the bright bed of coals to flames that licked the metal stovetop. I moved the eggs to the far side.

"Mary, could you bring that water over here, please?" I said, closing the door. We'd set a pot on the hook in the fireplace in preparation of the dishes we'd need to do.

I went to the supply cabinet and pulled out a bag of rice as Mary carried the water over.

"Mary, can you chop some more onion. About two handfuls."

I added a generous portion of rice to the already steaming water on the stove. As soon as Mary had the onion chopped, I had her throw it in, too. I stirred the eggs again. They were cooking faster now. I handed the spoon to Mary and went to help Rilla finish cutting up the sausage.

We worked in silence, each of us glancing at Winifred who'd not once spoken. By the time the food was done, my stomach was twitchy with nerves. I made up plates for the kids. The parents didn't eat, just hovered close.

Having the families present for the breakfast had been a debate. Winifred had worried about their safety. Everyone had, really. But, we'd agreed their presence was part of what we wanted to show those coming to join us. So the parents stayed close and trusted Winifred to keep their children safe.

"We're ready," I said, touching Winifred's shoulder.

She reached up and patted my hand. "I hope you are."

The door opened at that moment, and Thomas walked in.

He looked tired and annoyed. When he stepped aside, the first of too many newcomers poured through the door. Many glanced at the women and children. I tried to gauge their reactions but was soon too busy.

Each man took a plate and stood by the stove. They waited patiently as I scooped a portion of eggs and rice mixed with sausage onto their plate. Those who sat down first ate quickly then brought their dishes to the sink and filed out. Mary and Rilla washed and dried everything, and brought it back to the stove.

It seemed to be a never-ending loop for a while; but, finally, I saw the last man step through the door. I stopped conserving the scoops and generously fed those remaining in line. It didn't take the room long to empty after that. After the final newcomer left, one of the Mated men closed the door and the tension eased from the room.

Looking around at the mess, I realized I'd never fed Thomas. I scraped what was left into a single pot, covered it, then went to help with the dishes. With so many hands to help, the room was quickly back in order; and the families returned to their rooms.

I went to the window and looked out. The men milled around the yard. Grey and Thomas walked among them. Many stopped Thomas to talk to him.

I glanced at Winifred and found her watching me. Mary was standing by her side.

"Can you tell us what's happening?" I asked.

"They're discussing you now."

"Me?"

"They scented the Claim."

I moved away from the window and went to Winifred.

"Is it bad?"

"Not as bad as you imagined, but worse than we'd hoped for. There are several who are willing to accept you as one of us now that they know a Claim is possible. However, the majority are still against you, saying you're too human. They need to know you're not, Charlene."

Mary gave Winifred a puzzled look.

"Not what?"

"Not too human," I said.

I wasn't stupid. After Winifred's and Thomas' talks about protecting me, about how important I was to their future, and about how they weren't concerned about my ability, I'd figured it might come to this. That she would want me to reveal my secret to everyone in an effort to win their support and keep me here.

"They will try to use me," I said.

Winifred shook her head.

"It would expose us. I would never allow that."

"Then they'll tell someone to try to get rid of me."

"I'll forbid that as well. Revealing you would reveal us."

"Please, Winifred," I begged. "Don't do this."

"I won't. You and Thomas will. Show them what you can do."

"It doesn't work like that. I can't just use my ability to show it off any more than you can use yours for personal gain."

She was quiet for a moment. Sounds exploded outside. Growls, howls, snarls, and barking.

"Save him," Winifred said, standing.

I knew what she'd done. She wasn't trying to force me; she was giving me a valid reason to use my powers. Regardless of her reasons, I was angry. I ran to the door and threw it open.

Bodies clogged the way. I screamed at them to let me through. Body by body, I pushed my way to the writhing mass.

Winifred, what have you done?

Thomas, the man, twisted and dodged attacks from the five wolves around him. They all moved incredibly fast. Each jump, each pass they made, left a mark somewhere on Thomas. There were just too many of them for him to combat or defend.

My hands curled into fists. I could so easily stop them all as I'd done before. But I wasn't sure about Winifred. Her will wasn't like the rest, and now there were two Elders. My gaze shifted to Grey. He remained focused on his brother.

Thomas grunted as one of the wolves clamped down on his arm. I felt his pain. It surged through our connection and stole my breath. A bite to the arm shouldn't feel—Thomas turned, and I saw the wolf hanging from his back.

Get off him.

I hadn't realized I'd grabbed my will until the body of the wolf jerked away from Thomas. I hit him again and again, beating him until he loosened his hold. Then, I swung out at the ones still circling Thomas. Two flew into the crowd.

The evened odds gave Thomas a chance. Lightning fast, he reached out and caught one of the two remaining wolves.

"Enough," I said as Thomas grasped the wolf's throat. Thomas hesitated a second then opened his hand. The wolf yipped and fell to the ground.

Thomas glared at the remaining wolf, almost daring it to attack, while I eyed Thomas' cuts and bruises. At least, they hadn't ripped his ear, again. I didn't want to pick out any more stitches. The wolf finally looked away. Satisfaction coursed through me, then Thomas' tired gaze met mine.

I gave him a worried frown. When I'd asked him a month

ago what he'd needed, his answer had been correct. Cooperation.

I turned to address the men around us.

"If you want to behave like animals, then society will continue to treat you like animals. You will be hunted down and killed. Maybe you can accept that but look through that door," I said, pointing toward Mary and Rilla, who'd rejoined us.

"They don't want to accept that. They are willing to change to give the next generation a chance."

"A chance for what?" one of the men said. I turned, trying to find the voice in the crowd but couldn't.

"A chance to survive."

"There aren't enough Mates. You're promising the impossible," the voice said again. I recognized it. It was the man who'd attacked me then later joined Thomas' pack.

"Aren't there?" asked Winifred, stepping out. "You sensed Charlene was a possibility when you first arrived here. Her desire to change things upset you, and you've refused to see her as what she is. A potential Mate. I've listened to your concerns. She's too human. She's too weak. Did she look too human or too weak just now? She stopped this fight, not me. Not Grey."

The men stared at me, and I struggled not to look away. Fear and shame dug into my belly. Hands settled on my shoulders, and a wave of reassurance washed over me.

"We Elders have spoken with her and have watched the changes she's made. We believe she is the future of our race. We can't force you to accept her, but we will not let you harm her or drive her away for as long as her existence continues to benefit us."

I sensed her will split at the same time I sensed Grey's. They worked together to touch every wolf. Numerous strands whipped out of the clearing, fading from what I could feel, only to return moments later with the rest. They'd spoken a command to all of their kind, not just those here.

I reached up and placed my hand on top of Thomas'. He leaned forward and kissed the back of my head.

"Your race can be something great," I said, "but it will take cooperation and hard work. The things we do today will impact tomorrow and the future of your people. What future do you want? More fighting amongst yourselves?"

"I want a future where my son has hope of a Mate," Rilla said from behind me. "I want a safe place to live until I give birth to this next one." She patted her still flat stomach.

The tension in the crowd seemed to break after that. Many of the men shifted position to study Rilla, and I wondered how many were hoping she carried a girl. Her husband stood behind her, a protective hand on her waist.

Thomas' hand dropped to my back, and he nudged me toward the door.

"Wait, what about the new members?"

At the sound of the familiar voice, I stopped moving. I wanted to reach out and grab the man by his throat. Instead, I took a calming breath.

"Recall our deal. He will accept new members the day after you return. That's tomorrow. Today, give yourselves time to get to know one another."

I kept walking forward, glad that Thomas stayed with me.

"I have warm water in there for you," Mary said to Thomas as she walked out of the tub room.

I moved to step aside since he was still behind me, but he

wouldn't let me. His hand stayed firmly on my back as he steered me toward the tub room.

I twisted to give him a look.

"I can't reach my back," he said softly. With a sigh, I willingly went with him.

A chair waited near the washbowl. He sat sideways so I had full access to his front and back. I wet the cloth and started with the marks between his shoulders. Several of the gashes worried me. These weren't small, clean cuts but jagged tears. All of them had stopped bleeding already, though. So I gently washed away the blood. When the water was dirty, I left the tub room to empty the bowl and fill it with more.

Grey and Gregory sat at the table near the door. Rilla and Mary sat at the smaller table near the stove. They were in the process of butchering a deer. I saw Rilla snitch a piece. Mary caught me gagging and grinned.

I retreated to the tub room again and closed the door behind me. Thomas was in the same spot, but his eyes were closed. I wanted to hug him.

"Save your pity," he said softly. "These scratches aren't worth it."

"It's not pity, its compassion," I said as I set the bowl down. I rewet the cloth and moved to stand between his legs. His eyes opened then.

"Can't you tell the difference between the two?" I asked as I pressed the cloth to a small gash caked with blood. I had to wipe at it several times in order to clean it. He grunted.

"Nope. Not with you."

"Baby," I said. I made to move away from him, and his arms snaked around my waist.

"Show me some compassion." His head was tilted up just

slightly so he could meet my gaze. I stepped closer, set the cloth on his shoulder, and cupped his face in my hands. His eyes closed, and he exhaled slowly.

I kissed the scratch on his chin first, then the one on his cheek. The one just above his eyebrow got two. I gently kissed the other side just because. Then the tiny split on his upper lip caught my eye. I lowered my mouth to his and kissed it gently.

My compassion ended there. The second kiss I pressed to his lips was hunger. And he understood. His arms wrapped around me, and he stole my breath as he took over.

When we finally broke apart, my chest heaved from lack of air. His lips were red and looked more abused than they had when we'd walked in here.

"I think I should finish cleaning you up," I whispered. I took the cold cloth from his shoulder and went to rinse it.

"I like when you're compassionate."

I grinned stupidly at the pink water, then cleared my throat and forced a more serious expression on my face before I turned around again.

"I'm sure you do." I handed him the cloth. "I think you can do the rest. I'm going to go help cook."

He grinned at me.

"One of these days you'll stop running."

I was afraid he might be right.

THE MEN REMAINED OUTSIDE until lunch was ready. Before Winifred let anyone in, she asked Rilla, Mary, and I to eat first and leave the room. She said the men were too tense and with two of us unMated and Rilla pregnant, it would be best if we weren't there.

After we ate, we escaped upstairs to my room with Grey standing outside our door as a guard. Rilla and Mary wove mats while I watched and handed them their next reeds. When Grey opened our door to tell us the men had cleared out, we went downstairs to clean up. Only, everything was already done. Gregory and Thomas were setting the last stack of dry dishes to the side.

The outside door opened and two men entered, carrying two wild boar.

"Thought we'd need a head start on the next meal," Thomas said when I glanced at him.

"I think I'll try to weave," I said, stepping aside.

AFTER MARY, Rilla, and I ate dinner, Rilla's husband came to take her and their son to their room. Gregory came in next, holding out his hand for Mary. With a grin and a wave at me, Mary left with him.

Grey, who'd eaten with us, winked at me.

"You get me tonight," he said with a smile.

I smiled back and followed him upstairs, and he left me at the door with a goodnight. I rarely saw him without a smile. He didn't seem the least bit upset about what he'd given up to be an Elder. I still felt for him, though. He'd entertained Rilla's little one most of the time we were together. I could see he liked children. I hoped that by staying here, he'd have a chance to raise little ones, even if they weren't his own.

Long after I'd gone to bed, my door opened. I still had the lamp lit, so I looked up and watched Thomas silently walk in.

"Why aren't you sleeping?" he said softly.

"I couldn't. I was waiting for you. What took so long?"

He smiled at me, blew out the lamp, and sat on the edge of the mattress. His fingers combed through my hair.

"A lot of the men wanted to talk to me. Some, I think, wanted to know what kind of leader I might be if they decided to join tomorrow. Some were just curious about you. Where did you come from? Are there any others like you? Things like that." He lay down next to me. "I think they were disappointed to hear you're one of a kind, so far."

I rolled on my side and laid my head on his shoulder.

"Tomorrow..." I didn't say anything else. I didn't know if it was all right to speak my questions aloud.

"Don't worry so much," he said softly. His arm wrapped around me, and he pulled me close.

How could I not worry? Tomorrow would determine my fate.

CHAPTER SEVENTEEN

AFTER BREAKFAST, I REFUSED TO BE SENT AWAY.

"It's too dangerous," Winifred said, shaking her head.

"Not for me. You saw what I can do. They saw it, too. The only reason this all started was because of me. What does it say if I'm not out there with Thomas?"

"It says you're intelligent and very aware of the danger," Winifred said.

Thomas stood behind me, very quiet. I turned to him.

"You have nothing to say on the matter?"

"I want you by me always. And I want you safe. In this case, one conflicts with the other. I'm not sure which is best."

I scowled at him.

"You should have stopped with I want you by me always."

He took a slow, deep breath. It wasn't impatience or frustration, it was a stall as he made up his mind.

"Grey will be out there to keep the peace. If the peace breaks, he can bring you in here first before trying to help calm things out there. Stay by Grey," Thomas said, looking at me.

I nodded and moved to stand by Grey. In a staged whisper, I

said, "If the peace breaks, stand at least five feet back so I don't accidently hurt you." I knew whispering did no good when in the same room with any of them.

"It's a deal," Grey said, earning a scowl from both Winifred and Thomas.

"Lead the way," I said, motioning Thomas to the door.

He walked out. I followed, with Grey right behind me.

The yard wasn't as crowded as it was the day before. The original malcontents were there at the front. Several of them looked smug. There were at least thirty more behind them.

"If there are any who would like to leave the pack, step forward now," Thomas said, surprising me. It made sense though. Wheedle down the numbers before adding to them.

"I formally request to withdraw from the pack," a man said, stepping forward. "I mean your future Mate no harm, nor do I want to break apart your pack." His gaze shifted to me. "I bear you no ill will."

I nodded. "You will always be welcome to stay here whether you are part of Thomas' pack or not."

He bobbed his head, turned, then left.

I glanced at Thomas as another man stepped forward.

"Is it true there was an unClaimed female here?"

"She was only a month old," Winifred said. "Before they left, her parents told me they liked it here. They said they wouldn't mind raising the girl here once this business settles and it returns to the peaceful place it was. We hope this place can turn into a community where all our young are safe and where any of our kind can come and stay. However, any female here will be protected by the presence of an Elder and Mated couples at all times."

The man nodded. Another stepped forward and asked to

leave. Within five minutes, three left the pack. Thomas asked again, and no one else moved.

"Any who would like to join the pack, please step forward," he said.

Fifteen stepped forward. The number worried me, and I wished I knew how many wanted to join just to break the pack. If I divided my will to touch them all, they would know, just as they'd known last time. Only this time, Grey and Winifred would know, too. And with the Elders' ability to split their wills, I was afraid they would be able to connect with others that I couldn't and tell them the truth before I could make everyone forget.

"Thomas has the largest pack we can recall, going back at least one thousand years," Grey said. "You are making history today."

While Grey spoke, I tried touching the wills of the fifteen the old way. As I expected, each will slipped from my grasp. However, since I wasn't focused on trying to control them but read them instead, I was able to find that two wanted to join for the right reason.

Grey looked to Thomas. Before Thomas could speak, I stepped forward. I met the gaze of one of the men who didn't want to join.

"Mary told me she grew up learning the history of your kind. As Grey said, you are making history. When you step forward, please state your name and why you want to join so future generations will remember you."

While I spoke, I attempted a dangerous thing. I focused my will on the leader and two others. *I don't want to be remembered this way.* I gently tapped their hearts with my will as I finished speaking then stepped back beside Grey. The three suddenly frowned and looked at the ground. I struggled to maintain a sense of calm as I prayed the subtle tap had gone unnoticed.

Thomas looked to the man furthest to the right. The man stated his name and said simply that he was here to make history. Thomas nodded, and the man stepped back. There was no noticeable change in either of them. I glanced at the line. Four to go until he reached one of the men I'd influenced.

By the third man, Thomas frowned, and I could feel a twinge of discomfort coming from him.

Thomas finally addressed the first man who I'd connected with. The man still looked troubled.

"I don't want to be remembered as one of the men who broke the largest pack in history," he said without giving his name. The man nodded to Grey and me then left.

I glanced at Grey. He gave me a slight smile before turning his attention back to the men.

The next man hesitated before he gave his name and said he wanted to make history, too. Thomas nodded. Then, it was the lead malcontent's turn. Sweat beaded the man's upper lip and for the longest time he said nothing. My pulse slowly increased and anxiety filled me. Did he suspect something? I'd hoped by only changing the hearts of a few, my influence would go unnoticed yet still sway the majority.

The man glanced up at Grey. I stopped breathing. Did he know?

"Perhaps, we can take a break," Grey said, looking at the man. The man nodded, pivoted, and strode to the trees. Several others followed him.

"Thomas, you should take Charlene inside," Grey said.

My heart felt like it would explode. I tucked my hands in my pockets to hide their shaking.

Thomas turned toward me as Grey stepped back.

"I think you should show her some compassion," Grey said.

Oh, God. They knew.

Thomas quirked a smile at me.

"I think I can manage that," he said, holding out a hand.

It took a second for Grey's innuendo to click, and a shaky relieved exhale escaped me. I pulled my hand from its pocket and reached for Thomas. His fingers closed around mine, and he led me toward the door. We didn't stop in the common room but went straight upstairs. He let go of my hand, lay on the bed, and closed his eyes.

I finally noticed how sweaty he was. I sat next to him and gently rubbed his temples. I had no idea if it helped or not because he didn't move at all.

A swell of compassion rose within me, and I leaned down to place a kiss over his heart.

"Charlene," Thomas said.

I straightened and looked down at him. He opened his eyes and met my gaze.

"Kiss me like that again, and I'll give up everything for you."

My pulse jumped, and I understood what he was trying to tell me. He was barely holding on, and I was distracting him.

I nodded.

"I'll be downstairs with Grey."

He let me go.

He came down only a few minutes after me. He looked different. Relaxed. His face was dry, and I no longer felt any discomfort from him. I wondered what had caused the change.

He must have felt my curiosity because he met my gaze and shook his head. He and I really needed to figure out a way to make one of these rooms soundproof so we could talk openly. When he reached me, he set his hands on my shoulders and kissed my forehead.

"Ready?" he asked.

I nodded, and holding his hand, followed him out the door.

Grey stood in the same spot. About half the men waited before him, the same number of men still watched.

"Can you call them back?" Thomas said to Grey.

Grey looked at his brother and laughed.

"This is the group."

"What happened to the rest?" I asked.

Grey shrugged.

"They decided they didn't want to make history."

It took Thomas less than five minutes to accept the rest into the pack. Before the crowd could break up, a man stepped forward.

"I challenge you," he said, "for her." He pointed at me.

The man wasn't as tall as Thomas, but he was solid. His dark hair hung over equally dark eyes. I reached out and touched his will. Before it slid away, hate, anger, and greed swamped me.

"She's already Claimed," Thomas said.

"Good. Then there's still a chance. A fight to the death," the man said.

The man's confidence scared me. He was completely certain that he would win.

I looked at Thomas.

"Death?"

"Death dissolves the Claim, so another can Claim you."

I stared at him and recalled how I'd wanted to undo our Claim. I'd never given death a thought. And I never would.

"No," I said. Thomas rubbed a thumb across my cheek then looked up at the man.

"I accept."

"No," I said again, this time feeling a little panicked. Thomas had fought five wolves the day before and still wore the marks from that. And something about this challenger was off. When I'd touched that man's will, it had felt so different from the rest. Maybe it was the extreme hostility. Regardless, I wasn't going to let them fight.

"I'm not one of you," I said. "Your way of Claiming doesn't work on me. I have to Claim you. And I refuse. So the challenge is pointless." I turned to Grey. "Right?"

Grey was quiet for a moment. "We agree with Charlene. The challenge is pointless if she's not willing to change her Claim."

"I'm not willing," I said firmly.

The man stared at me for several long heartbeats, and I thought he would argue. He wore his anger plainly on his face. His eyes narrowed then his gaze swept over the crowd. The men behind him shifted restlessly until his gaze once again settled on me.

"It begins," the man said softly.

"What begins?" Thomas asked.

"The hunt for the other human women," the man said. Something about the man unnerved me. And, almost as if he sensed it, he smiled genially and met Thomas' thoughtful gaze. "We have to hope there are more, right?"

Thomas nodded slowly.

"It's always been about hope."

"And courage," the man said. He gave me a last look then turned and left.

Relief flooded me. I wanted the fighting to be done. For good. I turned and looked at Thomas. I wanted to run and throw my arms around him, but I didn't need to. He came to me.

"Go ahead inside. The rest is just pack business."

My need for him to hold me vanished. Pack business? After all his talk about me being the one, he still thought of me as an outsider. I tried not to feel hurt over it. He was right. I wasn't his pack. I wasn't one of them and never would be.

I turned to go as he asked but ended up scooped in his arms instead. Despite my effort to suppress my hurt, he'd obviously felt it. He walked inside with me and up the stairs to our room.

He nudged the door closed behind us and then set me on my feet. Embarrassed, I stared at his chest. A tiny thread of annoyance tickled me, and his fingers touched under my chin with gentle upward pressure. I gave in and met his gaze.

"Tell me what I did that caused that much...unhappiness."

"Go ahead inside. The rest is just pack business," I repeated. "I'm not part of the pack."

His shoulders dropped, and he heaved a sigh.

"I told you, you're the heart of the pack. Without you, we don't exist. I wasn't excluding you; I was trying to give you an opportunity to do something you might find more interesting."

"I *am* doing what I find interesting," I said. "If I'm to be the Mate of the pack leader, I should know pack business."

A wave of hunger washed over me.

"You should," he said.

I knew I needed to retreat.

"All right. Good, then. I'll just go and make sure we have enough food for everyone. Let me know what pack business you discuss."

My attempt to leave the room failed. Before I made it a step, he caught my hand, and turned me around. His lips settled on mine before I could focus on him. The kiss was intense but thankfully brief.

"Save some food for me," he said. Then, he walked out the door.

THOMAS WATCHED me hungrily throughout the remainder of the day as his pack business seemed to follow me wherever I went.

I helped find rooms for those who were staying. I handed out mats. I helped sort through our dwindled supply of clothes to find extras for those who were considering jobs. And I cooked.

After dinner, I excused myself and headed up to my room. Thomas was two steps behind me. I thought he'd give me trouble, but our routine didn't change. He left the room so I could put on my night clothes then came in and blew out the lamp. He settled next to me and held me, just as he always did.

However, his hunger remained.

I WOKE with Thomas wrapped around me again. It was still dark out. Thomas' breathing was steady, but not as slow as it usually was when he slept.

"I doubt I need that stove installed in here," I said, wiping

the sweat from my upper lip.

He chuckled and lifted his head from my shoulder. "I'll keep you warm every night until the day we die, if you let me."

My pulse leapt. I loved this man with an intensity that scared me. Despite my doubts about our ages and my efforts to ignore how I felt, I knew my feelings wouldn't go away. I couldn't imagine a world without Thomas by my side. His calm acceptance of his responsibilities, his dedication to his people, and stubborn refusal to give up on me had won me over long ago. I surrendered to the feelings of love and commitment.

As if sensing my acceptance, Thomas growled and kissed me with a passion that stole my breath.

"Tell me you're mine," he said, pulling back to kiss my nec

"I'm yours."

His satisfaction washed over me.

"Forever." He nipped at my collarbone.

"Yes. Forever," I whispered as his hands skimmed up u my shirt.

I squeaked in surprise when my shirt disappeared with my shorts. Then, his lips met mine in the longest, sw kiss we'd ever shared. Afterwards, he pulled away and down at me. He had that combined look of tenderne intensity that stole my breath.

"I love you, Charlene," he whispered.

My heart was his.

"I love you, too," I said.

He gave me a small, satisfied smile and dipped his kiss my neck again. His teeth scraped me as he kiss there. I wasn't concerned. I trusted him not to However, my heart skipped a beat as his bare hips se mine.

"Shh. Don't be afraid."

He slowed his kisses, and his patience eventually melted me from the inside. Each sensation took me further away from the physical world.

In my passion-clouded mind, I sensed the connecting threads of his pack and his continued struggle to hold so many. It distracted me from his caress along my leg, and I barely noticed his weight settle more securely. I felt one of the threads he held slip slightly as he nipped at my collarbone again. The pressure between my legs increased, and a sudden pain pierced me, pulling me from mindless passion. As I gasped, a thread pulled free as my will tried to slip into place. I quickly grabbed for the lost thread, and before another could escape, I wrapped my will around them all. *Together. Always.*

"Charlene. I'm sorry," Thomas whispered in my ear. "Are you all right?"

It took a moment to realize he wasn't talking about the threads. I noticed the pressure between my legs and how he shook above me.

"Yes."

I held the collective will of the pack; and before I could lecide if I should tell him, he moved; and I lost myself to the noment.

WOKE FIRST, an unusual event. While I snuggled against homas, I gently explored the threads I held. Through his nnection, they felt so very human. I knew that, if I wanted, I uld easily manipulate them as I could a human.

I traced the threads to their counterparts and felt each

individual's will. Mary and Gregory were there, easy to distinguish from the rest. As I touched Mary's contentment, I noticed something more. It was as if several other threads drifted from her. I lightly touched one and felt Winifred. Through Winifred, I felt hundreds more and gasped aloud. They were all connected like a spider web.

"Charlene?" Thomas said sleepily.

"Sorry," I said. "I didn't mean to wake you." I tried to quell my panic but it didn't work.

"What's wrong?" His arms wrapped around me and gently rubbed my bare skin.

"Thomas, can you read my thoughts now?" I asked. Fear consumed me.

"In a way. I can only read the thoughts you send to me."

I have secrets, I thought at him.

"I know you do. And whatever they are scares you. Keep your secrets, Charlene. It doesn't bother me. If you ever want to tell me, I'll listen. But your secrets won't change this or how I feel about you."

What if they do?

They won't, he thought back at me, *because I love you unconditionally.*

I touched his will. It didn't slide from my grasp anymore. Through my hold, I felt my will spider out through his connections and further still through the other connections. When I touched Winifred and Grey, and the Elder in Europe, the number of connections exploded to the thousands. Near and far, I had complete control of them all.

Though Thomas's love was unconditional, I knew his acceptance would always have conditions.

I was now the potential threat he and Winifred had feared.

CHAPTER EIGHTEEN

Present...

"You've been doing that a lot since we left," Thomas said, coming to stand behind me. His hands settled on my shoulders as I continued staring out the hotel window. Bethi, Gabby, Luke, and Clay were now barely visible in the glow of the streetlights. They were on their way to find the fifth member of our little group. Bethi's excited nervousness and her desperation had been palpable.

I was relieved that only the four were going. Emmitt, Michelle, and Jim were a door down from our room. Close enough to keep safe, though Gabby had assured the Elders she would be watching for Urbat. So far, their net hadn't closed on this area.

"Doing what?" I asked, gently laying my hand on his.

"Drifting off. Do you want to talk about it?"

"No, I don't," I answered honestly. He wouldn't accept less. "Mostly I'm thinking about my past." And what I would do to keep the ones I loved safe.

"You're worried."

"I am. I'm worried that my secrets, when you hear them, will be more than your Claim can withstand."

He turned me, and I met his serious, dark gaze.

"You've always been stubborn. But I can't believe that after all these years, you still doubt me."

"It's not doubt in you or your ability to love me. I'll never doubt either. I'm worried you won't be able to forgive me everything."

He frowned. "Now, you're worrying me."

"I know. And I'm sorry. I love you, Thomas. More than ever." I sighed and looked out the window once more. "Something is pulling at me. Something dark and ominous. It's whispering to me to be strong, to wait. It's telling me the end is near. The end to what? I don't know. But I sense it's not going to be good. When Bethi started talking about Judgements and balance, it felt right."

I sighed again and said the words that had been weighing on my mind.

"The cycle is almost at its end. I feel like it's the end of our time here, of me."

Thanks for reading *(Un)bidden*, book 4 of the *Judgement of the Six* series! The series continues with *(Dis)content*, Isabelle and Carlos's story. Keep reading for a sneak peek!

AUTHOR'S NOTE

Are you worried yet? You should be! Things are in motion in the Judgement world that cannot be stopped. *giddy dance*

If you liked Bethi's sass and Charlene's firmness, you're going to love Isabelle in *(Dis)content*. Keep reading for a sneak peek.

If you've been reading the author notes in each of these books, I probably don't need to mention my newsletter again. Hopefully, you've already signed up. ;) But just in case, you can do so at melissahaag.com / subscribe.

Happy reading!

Melissa

SNEAK PEEK

(DIS)CONTENT

JUDGMENT OF THE SIX: BOOK 5

Now Available!

Jaw clenched, I shoved the key in the apartment building door. My skin felt too tight from all the crap I had to deal with at the office. *I should have quit like Ethan said,* I thought. *Who cares if I spend my whole life tending bar?* It would be easier, especially with the setup Ethan had.

Stopping to grab my mail from the entry, I gave a tight smile to my downstairs neighbor. Waves of annoyance rolled off him and soaked into me. My skin grew tighter. I quickly grabbed my mail and moved on before he could pull me into a friendly conversation.

My neighbors all liked me. They didn't even know me, but that didn't stop them from treating me like a close friend. As a rule, I didn't socialize with anyone in my building. It just didn't seem right. After all, I robbed them of any negative emotion they might have. So, how could they not like me?

As a child, I'd always wanted friends. When Ethan came along and seemed to understand me better than anyone else ever had, I gave up on having friends and settled for having a friend—singular. And Ethan was enough.

I trudged up the stairs to the second floor, opened my apartment, and stepped inside with a sigh. My eyes fell on my bag hanging from the special support the landlord had installed for me. I wanted nothing more than to start hitting it, but knew once I started, I wouldn't stop until I was drained. First mail, then change, and then dinner. After that, I could have at it.

Kicking off my flats, I sorted through the mail while walking to the kitchen. I didn't need to pay attention to where I was going. My apartment wasn't that big. The living room and kitchen flowed together with a tiny island separating them. The living room had my bag dangling from the ceiling and that was it. My bedroom had a T.V., bed, and dresser. I didn't need much.

I stopped mid-sort and stared at an envelope with a hand written address. No return address. No postage. Weird. I threw the bills to the side and set the envelope on the counter. The bills I'd write out later, the envelope I would open while I waited for food. The freezer had a nice selection of dinners waiting for me. I grabbed one at random and threw it into the microwave. While I listened to the hum of my dinner cooking, I tore open the envelope and pulled out a hand written letter.

No matter how I write this, you won't believe it. All I ask is that you don't throw this away...just consider it.

There are people looking for you. They know what you can do.

They must not find you. If they do, they will hurt us both, and so many more.

Don't trust anyone. Run. Stay hidden. Our time's almost up.

I turned it over and glanced at the blank back. There was no greeting and no closing. Just an unsigned note. My eyes fell on the one sentence that truly concerned me. "They know what you can do," I murmured.

The microwave beeped. I used a magnet to stick the letter to the refrigerator and drifted to my room to change. Dressed in Spandex shorts and a tight exercise tank top, I padded out to the living room and ignored the cooling dinner that waited for me. I slipped on my gloves to protect my knuckles and started exercising my demons.

The idea that someone might know about me didn't scare me. I found it amusing. No one really knew but Ethan. My parents had their own ideas about me—how could they not after raising me? But their suspicions weren't close. They thought I exuded positive energy. I'd like to blame their hippie thoughts on their habits in the sixties and seventies, but they weren't that old. The reality of what I did wasn't that I released positive anything. It was the exact opposite it seemed.

I mostly siphoned negative emotions. But if I wanted, I could pull the positive ones too. I felt what the people around me felt. Like sampling ice cream, their emotions had different flavors letting me know their moods. Unfortunately, the siphoning wasn't voluntary. No matter how hard I tried, I couldn't completely turn it off. But, boy, could I turn it on. If I wanted, I could drain a room in two heartbeats. Taking away all that negativity made the people around me happy, but did the opposite for me. The more I siphoned, the less I felt like myself. I grew agitated, angry even. My skin tingled the more I absorbed until it felt painfully tight. The only thing that helped relieve it was physical activity.

I hit the bag, timing the back swing and setting a grueling rhythm. Who would ever think someone could do what I could do...and why would they come after me?

Good luck to whoever thought they could take me, I thought. I'd leave them on the floor with a gap-toothed smile.

MORE BOOKS BY MELISSA HAAG

Judgement of the Six Series
(and Companion Books) in order:

Hope(less)
*Clay's Hope**
(Mis)fortune
*Emmitt's Treasure**
(Un)wise
*Luke's Dream**
(Un)bidden
*Thomas' Treasure**
(Dis)content
*Carlos' Peace**
*(Sur)real***

optional companion book

***written in dual point of view*

Of Fates and Furies Series

Fury Frayed
Fury Focused
Fury Freed

Other Titles

Touch

Moved

Warwolf

Nephilim

APPENDIX

The Judgements:

- **Hope** — Gabby, recently Claimed Clay [*Book 1: Hope(less)*]
- **Prosperity** — Michelle, Mate to Emmitt, son of Charlene [*Book 2: (Mis)fortune*]
- **Wisdom** — Bethi, Mate to Luke [*Book 3: (Un)wise*]
- **Strength** — Charlene, Emmitt's mother, Mate to the werewolf leader Thomas [*Book 4, (Un)bidden*]
- **Peace** — Isabelle [*Book 5: (Dis)content*]
- **Courage** — [*Book 6: (Sur)real*]

Additional Characters:

- **Clayton Michael Lawe:** Future Mate to Gabby.
- **Samuel Riddel:** An Elder of the werewolves.
- **Winifred Lewis:** An Elder of the werewolves.
- **Thomas Cole:** Mate to Charlene, leader of the largest pack.
- **Emmitt Alexander Cole:** Son to Thomas and Charlene; Mate to Michelle.
- **Jim Grayson Cole:** Brother to Emmitt; son to Thomas and Charlene.
- **Grayson (Grey) Cole:** Brother to Thomas and an Elder of the werewolves.
- **Carlos Cole:** Found in the woods and essentially adopted by Grey, so he uses Grey's last name.
- **Gregory Meur:** Cousin to Thomas; Mate to Mary.

- **Mary Meur:** Charlene's friend and Gregory's Mate.
- **Paul Hantus:** Mary's uncle.
- **Henry Hantus:** Mary's father.
- **Paul and Henry Meur:** Gregory and Mary's children, named after her father and uncle.
- **Blake Torrin:** Leader of the Urbat.

The lights Gabby sees:

- Werewolf — Blue center with a green halo
- Urbat — Blue center with a grey halo
- Human — Yellow center with a green halo
- Charlene — Yellow with a red halo
- Gabby — Yellow with an orange halo
- Michelle — Yellow with a blue halo
- Bethi — Yellow with a purple halo
- Isabelle — Yellow with a white halo
- Olivia — Yellow with a brown halo

CPSIA information can be obtained
at www.ICGtesting.com
Printed in the USA
FSHW012004070220
66944FS

9 781502 952141